EYE CANDY

FIGHTING FOR LOVE BOOK #3

JIFFY KATE

WWW.SMARTYPANTSROMANCE.COM

COPYRIGHT

CHAPTER 1

VALI

"*H*ear, ye! Hear, ye!" Cage bangs his fist on the breakfast table, startling everyone in the room. "The Erickson Family Meeting is now starting. Are all members present?"

Gunnar groans, rolling his eyes. "Dude, it's too early for all this formality. You can see we're all here."

I raise my coffee mug to silently announce my presence, but also in agreement with Gunnar.

Cage has always let the fact he's the second oldest go to his head. Now that three out of five of us are in Green Valley, he's assumed the role as oldest in Viggo's absence. Fortunately, Gunnar and I are used to it and we're both pretty easygoing, so we usually roll with it, except for when he calls these family meetings at absurd hours, like seven in the morning.

"Where's Frankie?" Cage asks, glancing around the table.

About that time, Frankie steps into the room and gives us all a wave. "I'm here. I just wasn't sure if I was supposed to attend or not." Even though she and Gunnar have been together for a while now, she still seems fairly reserved around us.

I get it. After learning about her backstory with her estranged father and all she's been through since learning the truth about her past, it's easy to understand where her reservations come from. However, she has started to come out of her shell a bit in the last month or so, which is good. She's going to need to learn how to hold her own if she's going to survive the Ericksons. At some point, all of us will be together and we're a lot to handle.

"Of course you're supposed to be here," Tempest says, smiling at Frankie as she serves her up one of her famous muffins she brought over from Donner Bakery. "You're family."

"Told you," Gunnar says as he pulls his girlfriend onto his lap. "You're one of us, so you have to put up with these bullshit meetings too."

Cage started having these weekly meetings last month before Christmas. And he intentionally scheduled them on Wednesdays at seven in the morning so Frankie could come before she leaves to volunteer in Maryville at the women's shelter and Tempest can be here after she finishes her shift at Donner Bakery.

Even though we're missing Ozzi and Viggo, our family here in Green Valley is growing.

"Watch it," Cage warns Gunnar, shoving his head and almost making him spill his smoothie. If that had happened, the fight would probably be on.

"Fucker," Gunnar mumbles under his breath, bringing his smoothie up to his mouth to cover his smartass remark. Frankie rolls her eyes as he pulls her closer, using her for more of a decoy.

Cage's hand goes for one of the muffins on the plate in front of him, but Tempest grabs his wrist.

"Don't even think of using my muffins as weapons, Leif Cage Erickson."

He looks at her incredulously, acting affronted by her admonishing. "Damn, woman. I was going to eat it, not throw it," he argues. Tempest doesn't look convinced and I'm calling bullshit too.

This little display is just one example of how perfect Tempest is for my big brother. I love how she's not afraid to call him out.

Looking around the table, my heart warms at seeing my brothers so happy and in love, but I can't help the sting I feel at their displays of affection. I had that once—happiness, love, someone I wanted to spend forever with.

But not anymore.

"So, what's on our agenda this morning?" I ask, clearing my throat. I'm ready to get this show on the road and I'd like to have something else to think about other than how fucked up my love life is… *was*.

"You got some hot date we don't know about or something?" Cage asks.

"The only date Vali has is checking out today's local gossip column in the paper," Gunnar says, giving me a shit-eating grin. "Any time his name is mentioned, he cuts the article out and adds it to his spank bank."

"Spank bank? You mean, like, porn?" Tempest turns to me, looking intrigued.

Pointing to Gunnar, I say, "You, shut the fuck up." When I look back at Tempest, my tone is a bit softer. "No, I don't have porn here. That's what computers are for, anyway. Now, can we move on from my masturbatory details, please? I'm bored."

When you're in a small town like Green Valley, Tennessee, you have to find unique ways to keep yourself entertained. So, excuse the fuck out of me if I've found a new interest in the local gossip column. But they're not part of my spank bank.

I have a perfectly good imagination for that, thank you very much.

Cage clears his throat, getting the attention back on him before he begins. "First, I'd like to start by congratulating Gunnar again on his victory against Mikey O'Malley, the Muscle of Memphis, last weekend!" Pointing to Gunnar, he adds, "You keep it up and we'll be headed for that title belt sooner than you think, my brother."

The entire table erupts in applause and Gunnar accepts the praise humbly. Well, as humbly as an Erickson prodigy can. At least he isn't taking a bow and blowing kisses. Instead, he dips his chin in appreciation before burying his face in the crook of Frankie's neck.

"Also," Cage continues, pride washing over his features, "it's time for the grand opening of our brand-new, state-of-the-art ring in the gym expansion downstairs. And we need to decide how we want to celebrate. Do we have an exhibition, something to raise money, or do we just want to host a party and let the public come check it out?"

"State of the art," I snigger. "It's a fucking boxing ring, bro. Does it have some special powers I'm not aware of?"

"Yeah, it has a force field around it to keep wannabe fighters, like you, out. No posers allowed." I swear, Gunnar is gonna get his mouth busted if he keeps this up.

"Listen here, asshole—"

"Enough!" Cage booms. "Both of you are on my last nerve. We're not kids back in Dallas anymore, so nut up and start acting like adults. Which leads me to the last topic on my agenda…" My older brother turns and looks directly at me before asking, "Vali, why the hell are you still in Green Valley?"

His question catches me off guard, so I just stare him down, casually bringing my coffee cup up to my mouth and taking a drink, buying me time to formulate an answer.

"Cage," Tempest mutters, rolling her eyes. "Vali, you're welcome to stay here as long as you want." Reaching across the table, she places her small hand over mine and squeezes, giving off a motherly vibe. "That goes for you too, Gunnar. And if Ozzi and Viggo want to join in, I'm sure we could find room for them too."

When she smiles up at Cage, his tough facade finally crumbles a little and he gives her a softer stare, brushing his thumb over her cheek as he cups her face. This more affectionate side of Cage is something I never got the chance to witness until coming to Green Valley.

I know he had a serious relationship when he was at Harvard, but he never brought that girl home. When he left Harvard and came back to Erickson MMA, we all lived the bachelor lifestyle, our doors revolving with the latest flavor of the month... or week... shit, sometimes, night.

But monogamy looks good on him.

"We'll have to buy another fucking storefront," Cage grumbles, turning his attention back to the rest of us. "If we keep this up, we'll own the whole damn block."

"Think we could get Mr. Jones to sell his appliance store?" I ask. "That building he's in has a sweet balcony on the backside. I've always wondered what was up there."

Cage just huffs his annoyance and walks over to the coffee pot for a refill.

Since I've been here, we've remodeled the space on the other side of the gym, making another apartment. For a brief time, Gunnar and I shared it, but now he's living with Frankie and I have the entire place to myself.

And thank fuck for that.

No one wants to share walls with Cage and Tempest.

"Ozzi called yesterday," I mention, reaching over for the last muffin— Folsom Prison Blues, my favorite. After I take a large bite, chewing and swallowing, I add, "He mentioned something about coming to Green Valley to see what all the fuss is about."

"Sounds like that Erickson invasion might happen sooner than later. I hope Green Valley is prepared," Cage mutters.

On that note, Gunnar, Frankie, and Cage leave the kitchen and head down the stairs that lead into the studio, leaving me and Tempest alone.

She starts to tidy up the space, putting a few dishes in the dishwasher and humming to herself, but then she stops and turns to face me. "I can tell you have something weighing heavy on your mind," she says matter-of-factly, letting out a deep sigh. "I also know how it feels when you think you don't have anyone you can confide in. So, I just want to put this out there and tell you if you need someone to talk to, someone who's family, but not, I'm your girl. Zero judgment."

Pushing off the counter, she walks over to stand on the opposite side of the table. "I'm at the bakery every morning until eight, except on Wednesdays," she continues, pausing to smile. "Come over any morning and I'll serve you up a muffin of the day and a fresh cup of coffee… and a listening ear, if you need it."

I think about what she's said for a minute, trying not to let my face tell on me. My mom always says I can't lie because my face always tells the truth. "I might take you up on that offer," I finally say, averting my eyes to the table, running my hand over the weathered wood. "If for nothing else than the muffins."

She gives me a knowing smile and shakes her head. "All of you Ericksons are alike," she teases, walking toward the stairs.

"Take that back," I call out, but smirk, because she's right. We are alike, which is what makes us love each other fiercely, but also annoy the shit out of each other on a daily basis.

6

I always wondered what it would be like to have a sister. I'm glad to now know what that feels like and I wasn't lying when I said I might take her up on her offer. It would be nice to get some shit off my chest, but I'm not sure I'm ready just yet.

Just the thought of Dallas and everything that transpired before I tucked tail and ran to Green Valley still makes my stomach turn and my anger boil. Out of all the brothers, I'm the least aggressive, which is probably what made me not as good as Cage or Gunnar in the ring.

Growing up, I loved the sport, still do, but I didn't have what it takes to make me a prodigy.

I wasn't the oldest, so I didn't get to call the shots.

I'm not the youngest, so I never got the attention Ozzi and Gunnar got.

I'm the middle child, often overlooked, and most of the time it's okay with me. But lately, I've felt the force of my position in the family. As a matter of fact, being in the middle is a good euphemism for my life.

I'm not happy, but I'm not sad.

I'm not wildly successful, but I'm not sinking.

I'm not content, but I'm not completely dissatisfied.

I'm just in the middle and I'm trying to hold on until something better comes along.

But this is the beginning of a new year, so I'm hoping for a fresh start.

CHAPTER 2

MAGGIE

"*M*argaret," my dad calls from the back room that doubles as a break room and office. "These numbers aren't adding up."

His tone is full of confusion and frustration, and I know if I don't hurry in there and figure it out for him, there will be a full-blown meltdown in about five, four, three...

"This computer isn't working right," he grumbles, louder than the first time.

I smile and hand Mr. Beardsley his change and receipt. "Thank you for coming in today," I tell him with a smile.

"Sounds like you better get back there and help your daddy," he says with a knowing smile.

Most people who come into our feed store have been regular customers my entire life. They've watched me grow from a baby who played in a fenced-off area behind the counter, to a little girl who helped dust the shelves and greet customers, and eventually, to a teenager who earned her keep by doing it all.

I was homeschooled, so I spent every day of my life in this store, learning the business from a young age.

"Tell Mrs. Beardsley I said hello and thank you for the rhubarb jam."

The Beardsleys have one of the best gardens in the valley. They set up at the local farmer's market, but during the winter, Mrs. Beardsley spends her time making jams and baked goods. And she's always so sweet to send something for us when Mr. Beardsley picks up their monthly feed order.

"Coming, Daddy," I call out once I place the invoice in the box.

When I walk in, his glasses are pushed up past his bushy, gray eyebrows and he's rubbing his hands over his face. I smile and go over to the computer, nudging him out of the way. "Let me finish this," I tell him. "Mama left you a sandwich in the fridge and I just brewed a fresh pot of coffee."

"Have I ever told you you're my favorite daughter?" he asks, standing and giving his shirt a fresh tuck in the back.

"I'm your *only* daughter," I say with an eye roll he can't see. "Now, go eat your lunch."

When I finished my homeschooling, I enrolled in online college classes. Since I'm needed here at the feed store, I thought it was the best bet for me. Plus, my mama and daddy are old school and extremely protective. Some would say overprotective, but I say they just love me and want what's best for me.

However, their love is suffocating at times.

For instance, I'm twenty-four years old and still live at home. The furthest I've ever been from Green Valley is Nashville for a family vacation. My closest friend is a pen pal I've had since the second grade. I've only been on three dates. And my only job experience is in this feed store.

Well, and the column I write for the *Green Valley Ledger*, but no one knows about that except the editor of the newspaper.

It's the only secret I've ever kept from my parents.

And occasionally, it makes me feel so guilty my stomach hurts. But I'm afraid they wouldn't approve, and I can't risk it, because I love it too much to give it up. Besides, there's the part of my job at the paper where anonymity is key.

Plus, I'm an adult and should be able to do whatever I want.

In theory.

After I fix the spreadsheet and make it balance, I peek into the front of the store and see that my father is whistling away as he straightens shelves. This is typically our downtime, right before closing, when we stay open because it's what the posted hours say on our door. My father is a stickler about honoring your word, even in the small things.

In all my life, I've never seen him close the store early or late. He's always here and always does what he says he's going to do, practicing what he preaches. It's one of the things I love the most about him.

Smiling to myself, I quietly slip back into the office and resume my place at the computer, but this time, instead of balancing accounts or working on spreadsheets, I open up my secret file titled: Backlog. Another thing about my father, he's technologically inept. I'm not saying that to be rude or indignant. I'm only speaking the truth. He knows it too, which is why he insisted on me getting my bachelor's degree in business and accounting.

It's my parents' wish and dream that I take over this feed store one day, and in the meantime, and in the end, be better at it than they've ever been. Don't get me wrong, my parents have done well for themselves, making this feed store more stable and prosperous than my grandfather ever thought about it being.

But that's the thing, every generation wants the next to do even better… go further, be more.

I want that too.

Just not at O'Neal Feed and Fodder.

As the file opens, I scroll down to a document that's titled: APR1095. It has nothing to do with inventory or sales and everything to do with my real dream, journalism.

At the top of the page, there's the beginnings of my weekly column.

Greetings, Good People of Green Valley.

Sure, it's not a piece in the *New York Times* or *USA Today*. It lacks mystery and grit. No one will ever mistake my little corner in the *Green Valley Ledger* for a big-time journalistic creation, but it's something. It's my chance to use my voice and give back to my community, in a small way, the only way I'm allowed.

And for now, it's enough.

At least, that's what I tell myself.

Cracking my knuckles, I pull the rubber band out of my ponytail and retie it at the top of my head, gathering up all the strands. It's my routine. It's the way I go from Maggie O'Neal, feed store employee, to Maggie O'Neal, columnist for the *Green Valley Ledger*.

Or, I guess I should say, *Trixie and Tess*, but that's my little secret.

My big secret, actually.

The only people who know I'm the voice behind the gossip and advice column—and not two people, but one—is Sarah Clark, my editor, and Everly, my pen pal and confidant.

It's the perfect job for me. No one would ever suspect Maggie O'Neal. Besides, most people think the article is written by two people anyway, and I fly so far under most people's radars, it'd take an act of God for me to be found out.

Literally, God would have to come down and speak through Reverend Seymour from the pulpit.

Please, God, don't speak through Reverend Seymour from the pulpit. I mean, do speak through him, but not about me.

Amen.

Now, what am I going to write about this week? My covert inbox, stealthily titled *Junk*, has been full of trivial gossip and complaints lately.

Why is there not more parking in front of Donner Bakery?

Have you seen the state of the flower beds near the Green Valley city limits sign?

Florence Goodman stole my carrot cake recipe and I'd like a written apology.

How do I get my husband to help around the house without nagging?

But just like every week over the past few months, my attention turns to the same topic: the Viking Invasion.

At least, that's what I call it. And let's be honest, there hasn't been something this exciting going on in our small, quiet town since Jethro Winston's exes formed a club. And then he went and married a movie star. As exciting as all of that was, it didn't pique my interest quite as much as the Erickson brothers infiltrating Green Valley.

Maybe that's my lack of social interaction talking.

Or the fact I've never been so enamored by the male species as I've been in the last few months.

Or maybe the way my mouth goes dry when I pass one of them at the Piggly Wiggly or bump into them leaving Donner Bakery or Daisy's Nut House.

Do I intentionally put myself in their paths? Maybe. Okay, yes, yes, I do. But it's for research.

Which brings me back to my article.

This week, I feel like the good people of Green Valley need to know there's even more excitement coming. Last week, on one of my walks around downtown, I noticed an addition to Viking MMA. As I was peeking into the windows, I saw the brothers working on putting the finishing touches on a large ring, like the ones you see on the wrestling shows on television. Not that I've ever been interested in wrestling or fighting or any of that.

Until now.

The word around town is there's a new addition to Viking MMA.

CHAPTER 3

VALI

*W*alking down the stairs, I'm caught off guard when I see Gunnar on the mats. Typically, I'm up at least thirty minutes before he and Cage start their morning training sessions. When he hears my footsteps, his head pops up and he catches me in the mirrors.

"What's up?" I ask, joining him on the mats to stretch before my run.

He lets out a heavy sigh and I pause to look at him. Gunnar is your quintessential baby of the family. He's laid-back, fun-loving, and outgoing. The X factor for him is his drive. I've never seen someone so committed to their dream.

Well, except Cage.

But sometimes, I think Gunnar's got him beat in that arena. He took the harder road by biding his time and going to college. The entire time he was in school, he was also training and keeping up his skills. He could've followed in Cage's footsteps and jumped straight into the ring, but he didn't. There's always been an element of patience to Gunnar. It's admirable.

But fuck if I'd ever tell him that.

It'd go straight to his oversized head.

"Nothing," he finally says, letting out another sigh. "Just wanted to get a jump start on the day and have a few minutes of quiet before Cage starts in on my ass."

I chuckle, because I'm glad it's him and not me.

Cage is one of the hardest trainers I've ever witnessed, and growing up in a gym, around top athletes, I've seen my fair share.

"Are you nervous about New Orleans?" I ask, stretching out my hamstrings.

Gunnar shrugs, but I can see it all over his face. He wants this. If he can win this fight, it will be huge for him… for Cage, for this gym… our family. It will mean another Erickson has claimed a belt. Shit, Gunnar's success will reach all the way to Dallas. Viggo is even coming to the fight.

All five of us will be traveling to New Orleans to be in his corner.

It's what we do—what we've always done. Even when we don't all see eye to eye or our goals don't exactly match up, when push comes to shove, we're always there for each other.

"Just wanna win," Gunnar says, jumping to his feet and walking over to where his gloves are stored.

Following him over, I grab the tape and help him out, dressing his hands and getting him ready for the ring. "You're gonna kick ass."

His eyes meet mine and things that neither of us will say cross between us. When he's all taped up, we bump fists and he makes his way over to the new, state-of-the-art ring. Honestly, it's better than anything we've had at Erickson, and when Viggo sees it, he's going to be jealous as shit.

"Going for a run," I call out across the open space. "And for muffins."

Gunnar laughs and then flips me the bird, because muffins are not part of his pre-fight diet.

"I'll have one for you," I add, opening the door and walking outside. Taking a deep breath, I let the clean, crisp Tennessee air fill my lungs before I start bouncing on the balls of my feet to warm up. Winter here is different than it is in Dallas. We get cooler temps back home, along with the occasional snow flurries, but in Green Valley, it's just down-right cold. It's also quiet, which is something I'll miss when I go back to Dallas. It's barely light outside and there isn't a soul around. The birds are chirping and it's like I have the whole town to myself.

One thing I never felt in Dallas, or pretty much my entire life, is solitude.

Coming from a big family and falling in the dead center of five brothers, I never had time to just be in my own head. I came out of the womb sharing my life—rooms, clothes, dreams, jobs, goals.

And the last thing I shared that sent me to Green Valley—a woman.

Not with my brothers, that's where I draw the line, but with someone else… which is also where I draw the line and what landed me here, in this peaceful setting. At first, I thought I'd made a mistake by coming here, it was too quiet, too slow. But now, I'm wondering how I'll leave and go back to the hustle and bustle of a big city.

After a few miles, sweat begins to drip off my forehead and I feel the desired burn in my legs. Pouring on the speed, I run it out for the last two miles and then slow it back down as I come back into view of the gym… well, actually, my destination is the storefront on the other side of the street where cars are beginning to crowd the once-empty parking spaces.

Donner Bakery has become my kryptonite. And it doesn't help that my brother's girlfriend works here—girlfriend? That doesn't seem right. It's not significant enough for what Tempest is to Cage or to our family. She's already become a part of our tight-knit group. It's odd to imagine a time when she wasn't one of us. Which is why my brother needs to hurry up and put a ring on it.

But I'm definitely not the one to give advice on that.

Groaning at the memory flashing in my head, I stop just before I get to the door and pull off my gloves and headband. When I look back up, an older lady is leaving the bakery and holds the door open for me with a smile. I offer her one in return and dip my head in her direction. "Thank you."

"You're welcome, sweetie."

Sweetie.

God, I love this place.

Stepping inside, the smell of sweet deliciousness fills the air. But before I get a muffin, I have to get my other fix. Pulling out the two quarters I keep in the small zipper pocket of my sweatpants, I place them into the newspaper dispenser.

Taking the newspaper with me, I get in line, and while I wait, I open it and flip to find the new ad I placed a week ago, announcing the new women-only self-defense class Tempest has been teaching in the evenings. While I'm here, I've tried to make myself as useful as possible, helping establish a few marketing strategies that can be easily maintained after I'm gone.

The ad looks good—eye-catching, but not over-the-top. I tried to word it in a way where anyone reading this would feel like it's something for them. We're trying to ingratiate the gym to the good people of Green Valley and make it more of a place everyone feels welcome than a sideshow.

Cage has done a pretty good job so far, offering free classes for the local police officers and firefighters. The women-only self-defense class was actually Tempest's idea and it's been well-received, but not enough people know about it, hence the ad. Which I strategically asked to be placed right next to my favorite column, *Trixie and Tess Tell All*.

"Good morning, Vali. What can I get you?"

Popping my head up from the paper, I smile at my favorite muffin maker. "I'm hoping for a Folsom Prison Blues," I whisper covertly, using the folded paper as a shield, because these muffins are basically the equivalent to gold... or street drugs. The second they hit the case, they're gone. But Tempest always puts one back for me, because secretly I'm her favorite.

"So, that's one Sweet Dream and a coffee," she calls out, giving me a wink.

We gotta play it cool. Otherwise, there could be a mutiny. A muffin mutiny.

After I pay and step to the side, I go back to the newspaper and see what my favorite gossip columnists have for me this week.

If I had one suggestion for the *Green Valley Ledger*, that would be to have a daily paper. This once-a-week bullshit is for the birds. Tempest claims it's because there's not enough news to fill a paper on a daily basis, but that doesn't help my need to be entertained.

Just as I'm getting ready to dive in, only getting to the now-familiar opening of *Greetings, Good People of Green Valley*, Tempest peeks around the newspaper with a piping hot cup of coffee and a bag with the goods.

"I stuck a Hey, Good Lookin' in there for Cage," she says. "They're his favorite. And I would've put one in there for Gunnar, but I know he's on his fight diet, so make sure you sneak Cage his. Gunnar's working so hard. I don't want to tempt him. Which reminds me, I need to make sure to bake a batch just for him once he wins his fight."

If the power of positive thinking could win someone a title belt, we'd definitely have this shit in the bag.

"I'll be stealthy," I promise. "And mine will be gone before I even make it down the sidewalk."

"Any good gossip?" she asks, gesturing to the paper.

Taking a tentative sip of my coffee, I pass the paper to her. "I haven't gotten to the good stuff yet, but I did find the new ad for your self-defense classes. Take a look."

She opens the paper and smiles. "Looks great."

"I was thinking, I could help out with the classes, if you need an extra body... someone to beat up on or whatever."

Tempest laughs, folding the paper and handing it back to me. "Actually, that'd be great. If the class grows any more, I'm sure I could use some assistance."

"Have you convinced Frankie to join the class yet?"

Her smile grows even wider. "I think I have. She told me last week she thinks she's ready to give it a shot."

"That's progress," I tell her, bringing my cup up for another sip of coffee. Gunnar's girlfriend, Frankie, is as opposed to violence as one can be, which makes all of our sport and occupations a hurdle for her. When she and Gunnar first got together, it was almost a deal-breaker, but they made it and she's really coming out of her shell at the gym. When I first got to town, she wouldn't even step foot on the mats. Then, she started visiting on off-hours and watching all of us horse around. That turned into observing classes, which was recommended by her therapist, and now, she's a familiar face at Viking MMA.

Most people know her as Nurse Frankie, although she's more than that. She's practically a doctor, with all of her extra schooling and experience. And she really comes in handy around the gym. It's kind of perfect, actually.

Who knows, maybe one of these days, she'll be ringside.

Someone from behind the counter calls out Tempest's name. "Gotta go," she says, glancing over my shoulder. "The muffins need me."

Chuckling, I wave her off and then head out.

The muffins need me too, I think as I dig into the bag and devour half of one of the mammoth baked goods in one bite. By the time I approach the gym, it's history.

When I walk in the front door, Cage is working with a group of local law enforcement personnel, guiding them through some tactical skills. Tossing the bag at him, he catches it deftly with one hand and gives me a nod of appreciation.

I head upstairs for a shower because I fucking stink. As I pass by the new ring, I see Gunnar sparring with Vince and he's looking good. The kid has moves most people have never seen before. Some of those are thanks to our big bro, but some of them are all his own. He's a natural.

"Kick his ass, Sea Bass," I call out on my way up the stairs, earning me a colorful greeting from both of them that makes me laugh.

As I take the steps two at a time, I unfold the newspaper and flip back to the page with my favorite article.

Greetings, Good People of Green Valley.

How is it that one sentence puts such a pep in my step? When I leave to go back to Dallas, I'm going to have to get Tempest or Frankie to mail me a *Green Valley Ledger* once a week. In secret, without Cage and Gunnar knowing about it, because I'd never live that shit down.

The word around town is there's a new addition to Viking MMA.

I smile, loving that the feeling is mutual. My good friends Trixie and Tess can't get enough of me either. Well, us… the Vikings, so they call us. That term isn't new. Cage was always known as The Fighting Viking. With our Scandinavian blood, we all look the part. Cage, Gunnar, and Ozzi have lighter blond hair and pale blue eyes. Where Viggo and I took more after our mother and have darker blond hair and deeper blue eyes, but there's no missing the fact all five of us are related.

Well, butter our butts and call us a biscuit, the Ericksons have been busy!

Word on the Main Street is there's a new state-of-the-art ring inside Viking MMA. Not the kind you put on a finger, although many of us wonder if that's also in the works for one of the Fighting Vikings, but we digress. The ring we're referring to today is the kind most of us have only seen on television, think WWE or UFC.

Our question is what are they planning? Other than an invasion, are they intending on bringing more than a healthy serving of Eye Candy to little ol' Green Valley, Tennessee?

I smirk at their insightfulness.

Well, Trixie and Tess, you'll just have to wait and see.

After I've showered and am fresh as a baby's butt, I pull on some clean workout clothes and then make myself a smoothie. The muffins and coffee are great, but it's all about balance.

With the sounds of the gym filtering up the stairs, I park myself at the wooden table in the kitchen and open my laptop.

The awesome thing about what I do for both Erickson MMA and Viking MMA is that most of it can be done from anywhere. As long as I have my laptop and my phone, I'm good to go. It makes this little sabbatical a hell of a lot easier and keeps my brothers out of my business for the most part. They don't really care what's going on as long as business is handled.

However, Viggo and Ozzi know why I'm here. They're the ones who encouraged me to get out of town for a while. And they also agreed to keep my need to flee on the downlow, letting me have some time to come to terms with my shitshow of a life.

In return, I promised to keep up with all the promo and marketing for Erickson MMA while I'm gone.

Thankfully, Cage hasn't been too pushy about getting answers, and Gunnar is so wrapped up in his next big fight and Frankie Reeves he hardly notices other people.

It's been nice to fly under the radar. Most of my life, I've felt overlooked. Being in the middle means I'm not the oldest and I'm not the baby. I'm not as talented as Cage and Gunnar. I'm not as driven as Viggo. I'm not as charming as Ozzi.

I'm just... Vali.

Typical middle child.

Up until six months ago, I was happy with my life, content even. I was starting to really love my position at the gym, doing something I felt passionate about. The promo and marketing side of things is definitely more my speed. Even though I'm not competing or fighting on the regular, I'm in the best shape of my life, finally finding a balance between living and breathing the sport and enjoying it as a hobby. And my personal life was great.

At least, that's what I thought.

Assumed, maybe.

And we all know what happens when you assume.

Or better yet, when you trust someone.

"Val," a voice calls up the stairs pulling me out of my thoughts. Shutting my laptop, I stand and stretch and then make my way down to see what's up.

"Hey," I say, seeing Vince standing there, obviously spent from his time in the ring. "Cage wants to know if you can spar with Gunnar for a few more rounds. I've got somewhere to be and he needs to get in at least another hour's worth of punches."

I smirk, shrugging. "If he can catch me."

Gunnar might be stronger than me, but he's not faster.

After I get some gear on, I duck under the ropes, and Gunnar and I go a few rounds, falling into an easy rhythm. And just like I said, he has to work to catch me.

"Fuck," he groans as we come to the end. "Can you just stay in one spot for one damn second?"

Laughing through my mouthpiece, I shake my head and feel the sweat dripping down my face. God, this is good. I really do love this sport. And giving my punk-ass little brother a run for his money. Title belts, my ass.

"You gotta work for it, fucker," I taunt, going for a cheap jab and then hauling ass to the opposite side of the ring.

Once we're finished torturing each other, we hop down and dry off. Cage shows up just in time to help us with our gloves and give Gunnar some pointers. When the door opens, all three of us turn to see who's coming in. It's an off time of day. Most people are at work, so when a woman walks into the gym, everything else stops.

Like the whole fucking world stops.

Or maybe that's just me.

Gunnar and Cage seem to be going about their business while Tempest greets the woman and they begin to talk, but not before I catch her looking at me.

She's gorgeous. But she's not what I'd normally go for. Most of my past relationships have been with petite blondes. It's not like I searched them out or anything, but that's always what I've gravitated toward. But maybe that's because I've never seen *her*.

Instead of being obvious about my ogling, I kneel down and take off my shin guards while watching her in the mirror. There's nothing petite about her. Or blonde. She has long, dark hair that falls in waves down her back… not too far from her luscious ass. Her curves are *all* woman and in *all* the right places.

I know I said I didn't want a hookup, or even a one-night stand, but maybe it wouldn't be so bad… maybe it's what I need?

Maybe I should ask her for her number?

Before I can make a decision, she's gone and I exhale. *That's right, walk away*, because I definitely don't need that kind of distraction.

CHAPTER 4

MAGGIE

Okay, Maggie. Pep talk time.

I inhale a deep breath, hold it for a beat, then let it out slowly. I repeat this process a second time, and then again. As I exhale for the third time, I open my eyes and look at my reflection in my rearview mirror. I was just here yesterday, but now that I'm actually here for a class, my nerves are getting the best of me.

You can do this. You're only observing the class, not participating. It's important and your readers are counting on you. Don't let the fact you're at Viking MMA freak you out. It's a class for women, being taught by a woman, so the odds you'll run into any of the Erickson brothers, much less Vali, are slim to none.

Pull up your lace panties and get in there.

Without another thought, I step out of my car and walk into the building. See? Easy. No big deal.

"Hi! Are you here for the self-defense class?" A young woman with a cute and spunky hairstyle greets me immediately. I already know she's

Frankie Reeves, girlfriend to Gunnar, but I can't let her know I know her.

The life of a small-town gossip and advice columnist, who writes under a secret pen name—or two—can be tricky. I have to stay on my toes so I don't blow my cover.

"I am, but I'm just here to observe." I motion to my body, showcasing the dress and boots I'm wearing instead of the typical workout clothes I imagine are required.

"Totally fine," she assures me. "I'm Frankie. I'll show you around and get you settled so you can watch Tempest teach the class. She's really good. What's your name?"

My eyes are wandering around the room, taking in my surroundings but also looking out for any Vikings who may be milling about, so it takes me a few seconds to realize Frankie has asked me a question.

"Oh, I'm, uh, Margaret. You can call me Maggie, though. Everyone does."

"Nice to meet you, Maggie," she says, giving me a genuine smile that somehow puts me at ease. "Make yourself at home and sit anywhere you want in this section." Frankie points to a few chairs set up by a wall of mirrors. "The bathrooms are just down the hall over there, as well as a couple of vending machines if you need anything. If you have any questions, I'm sure Tempest will answer them after the class is over."

"Okay, great. Thank you."

"Have fun," she says as she walks back to the front of the building.

Have fun, sure.

I mean, I'll definitely try to enjoy the class but I don't know if I can relax enough to *have fun,* knowing I'm breathing the same air as the Erickson brothers. My reasons for being here are twofold. One, I've always wanted to take a class like this. My dream is to move away to a big city and I believe a woman should know how to protect herself at all times. Two, it's my duty to my readers to get them firsthand information. Even though I write under the ruse of a gossip columnist, I tend to lean more toward the advice part. One of these days, I hope to be given an opportunity to write something more important and have a greater influence. Until then, I'm perfecting my craft and giving the people what they want.

Since I predict I'll be writing about the Ericksons and their studio quite a bit, I need to be where the action is.

Okay, so my reasons are threefold, I guess, because let's not forget the huge crush I have on Vali Erickson. Just the thought of possibly seeing him today has my stomach in knots and my palms sweaty. Those jitters that left are back and they brought friends.

Thank goodness my dress has pockets, so I can secretly wipe my hands off.

"Hey, everyone! Thanks so much for being here," Tempest calls out, greeting the class. Her enthusiasm is contagious. There are twelve women of varying ages and all of them seem excited to be here. "Let's get started, all right?"

The class begins with a few simple stretches and I find myself following along to the guided breathing portion, allowing it to soothe me back into a calm state. After about five minutes of warm-up, Tempest begins to instruct the class on proper ways to block and dodge attacks, as well as what to do if an attacker lands a hit. There's way more to this class than I initially thought and Tempest is a natural when it comes to teaching. The Duchess of Muffins and a kick-ass instructor, she's your modern-day Renaissance woman.

There's so much to learn, I want to whip out my notepad and pen to take notes. I refrain, though, because I must keep my secret safe at all costs. Plus, I know for certain I'll be back to take the class. I'm regretting I didn't just jump in, feetfirst, per usual.

As Tempest walks around, correcting stances and giving encouragement, I take the opportunity to slip away and scope out the place. As I'm walking toward the hallway Frankie pointed out earlier, I try to nonchalantly catch a Viking in the wild. Sadly, my hunt is in vain, so I walk into the ladies' room and wash my hands, while checking my hair in the mirror.

When I'm on my way back to my seat, I practically halt in my tracks at the sound of a familiar male voice. It's deep, kind of gravelly, and so sexy.

Vali Erickson.

Trying to play it cool, I slip into my seat, but damn if I don't misjudge my trajectory and place myself where my chair and the one next to it are joined. I let out a squeak when I feel the cold metal through the fabric of my skirt and quickly slide onto the plastic, praying no one noticed my outburst. Swallowing hard, I smooth down my skirt and sit up straight, trying to appear as normal as I possibly can, before raising my head and looking straight at Vali.

And he's looking back at me.

And, holy hell, I want to die of embarrassment because I'm sure he just got a front-row seat to the awkwardness that is Maggie O'Neal. At least he's not laughing at me. He's not laughing at all. Actually, he seems kind of frozen in place.

It looks like he's helping a student from Tempest's class, but his eyes are still on me... like he likes what he sees, which is totally crazy and absurd and a sign I've lost my mind and need to leave as soon as possible.

Grabbing my bag and coat, I decide I've observed enough for one evening. Walking briskly toward the front door, I keep my head down and try not to bring attention to myself because I don't want it to be weird when I come back next week. But I've got to get out of here before I inadvertently make the situation worse.

"Hey, wait," a voice calls out.

I'm so close to freedom, but before I can get through the front door, Frankie catches up to me.

"Hey," she says, eyeing me closely. "Is everything okay?"

"Yes, everything is perfectly fine. Just wonderful. I'll be back for a class, I promise!" My words are rushed and probably unintelligible, and as if I haven't had enough embarrassment for one night, I see Vali walking up behind her.

"Ma'am, you okay?"

Ma'am?

Did he just ma'am me?

Why is that so hot?

Ohmygod.

Be cool, Maggie.

"Who, me?" I huff out a laugh as I back toward the door, my hand searching for the handle. "No, I'm fine. I just realized I need to be somewhere... else."

Vali visibly relaxes and then he freaking smiles.

Why did he have to smile?

"Good," he says with a nod. "I hope you'll come back and give the class a shot."

Searching again for the handle, I grab on to it and twist. My fight-or-flight mechanism is working and I feel the need to flee the scene—a virgin trying to escape a Viking. That sounds like a historical romance book I'd find in the local library, *The Virgin and the Viking*. I'd totally read that. Hell, maybe one of these days, I can write it instead but only if I can make it out of this building without causing more of a scene than I already have.

"I was planning on it, yes," I reply, trying to sound calm but feeling anything but. "And, um, thank you for checking on me, Vali. That was very, uh, nice of you."

For the love, Maggie, walk out the door!

Vali's eyebrows meet in the middle in a confused expression and that's when I realize my mistake. I just said his name, the name he doesn't know I know because this is the first time we've ever interacted.

Not knowing how to make this situation any better, I force my body to move and practically hurl itself out the door. I don't say goodbye and I certainly don't look back; I just haul ass to my car. Once inside, I lean my forehead on the steering wheel and close my eyes.

I wish I could say I'm surprised by the turn of events, but that was pretty standard Maggie O'Neal material. My eyes begin to well up with tears, but when my mouth opens and I prepare myself for a good cry, laughter comes out instead. Deep belly laughs fill my car as I replay the entire scene between me and Vali. Of course, I feel ridiculous, but it could've been so much worse.

At least I have a whole week to recover before I have to face him and the studio again. *I will*, I promise myself. My readers demand it and so do I.

The entire drive home, I wear a smile so wide it makes my cheeks hurt, all thanks to Vali Erickson.

CHAPTER 5

VALI

"Hey, man," Cage says, walking by me at the desk and tossing an empty coffee cup at my head.

"Jackass," I mutter.

He just laughs and keeps walking. "What's got you all serious and quiet?" he calls back over his shoulder. "You've been sitting there staring out the window daydreaming for the past hour."

"No, I haven't," I argue, standing from the seat as if to prove my point. But he's right, I have. Shit, I may have been sitting here longer than an hour. Ever since I came back from my morning run and caught a glimpse of the woman from last week leaving the bakery, I've been thinking about her. I can't help it.

It was bitter cold this morning, but the second I saw her, I was anything but cold.

She knew my name, which I admit is kind of bothering me, but I figure she probably overheard someone in the gym talking to me. But that doesn't add up because when I first walked downstairs to help Tempest with the last half of her class, she wasn't there, and then she just appeared, like a siren emerging from the sea.

"You're fucking doing it again," Cage grumbles, passing by me and throwing a punch, which I dodge, thank God.

I shake my head, trying to clear it. "I just have a lot on my mind."

At this, Cage pauses, going serious. "You know you can talk to me, right?"

"I know," I mutter, crossing my arms. "But there's nothing to talk about. I'm good."

And really, that's not a lie. There isn't anything talking can fix and nothing I care to discuss. What's done is done and I'm trying to move the fuck on, end of story.

"You're a shit liar, you know that?"

Flipping him off, I turn to the desk and gather my laptop and notebook and head upstairs.

I need to shower, rub one out, and make myself a smoothie.

While I was occupying the front desk yesterday, I might've snooped in the sign-up sheets. I found one from a few days ago—the same day *she* walked into the studio—Margaret O'Neal.

It's kind of an old name for a younger woman, but somehow it just fits her.

Classic.

Unassuming.

Beautiful.

And I can't get her out of my head. I'm blaming it on being in this small town with little to no distractions. That's gotta be it. Also, the fact that no one has ever caught my attention like that. From the second she looked up at me, I felt this weird pull.

I can't even put a name on it—attraction, chemistry, voodoo. Who the fuck knows? All I know is that even though I haven't seen her in person since last Friday, she's all I can think about.

Casually, I mentioned her to Frankie and Tempest last night, bringing her up in conversation to ask if she'd been back since she bolted from the studio like her dress was on fire. Tempest said her parents own a feed store. Like, food for animals and shit, which is odd and doesn't really fit the mental image I have of her.

But I'm definitely curious to know more.

Maybe I should buy a goat or some other small farm animal so I have an excuse to check out O'Neal Feed and Fodder. Yeah, I've done my research.

Did I just think about buying a goat to get a girl?

Yeah, okay. That's where I draw the line. This town is obviously getting to me. Maybe it's time to tuck tail and run back to Dallas before I'm trading in my slacks for overalls. I came here to clear my head and get some space, and I've managed to do that, but there've been other side effects of living in this small town.

For fuck's sake, I used to run on a fancy indoor track and stop by Starbucks for an Americano on my way to the gym. And after work, I'd hit up high-end bars in downtown Dallas for craft cocktails and tapas. Now, I'm pounding the backroads of Green Valley, Tennessee, getting my coffee fix at Donner Bakery, and tipping up beers at Genie's on the weekends.

And I like it.

What's happened to Vali Erickson and who is this imposter enjoying the fresh mountain air and thinking about buying a fucking goat?

Maybe Cage is right? Maybe I need to talk to someone.

The thought of dredging up all the bullshit that transpired before I left Dallas always leaves me feeling angry and physically ill, so I've buried it pretty deep, hoping it just shrivels up and dies.

But I'm not stupid and I know ignoring things doesn't make them go away. In fact, most of the time, it only makes them worse.

* * *

THE NEXT MORNING, I'm up even earlier than usual. Slipping on my warmest hoodie and extra thick socks, I make my way downstairs and out the front door, being quiet as a mouse. Not that there's anyone who I can really wake up. Since Gunnar moved in with Frankie and Cage and Tempest's apartment is on the other side of the studio, it's just me over here, but it's early and I feel the need to creep.

Instead of stretching and heading out for my run, I walk the short distance over to Donner Bakery. There's only a faint light filtering through the front window, but I know Tempest is back there, baking away, so I walk to the alley and knock on the side door.

"Who is it?" she asks through the door.

"Vali," I call back, glad she's smart enough to not open the door for just anyone, even though everyone seems to know each other in this small town.

A second later the lock clicks and the door opens. "Hey," she says, giving me a puzzled look as she wipes her hands on an apron covered in flour. "What's up? Everything okay?"

"Yeah," I say, running a hand through my hair and glancing over my shoulder, second-guessing my decision to come here and spill my guts to Tempest. Deciding to get the fuck over myself, I say, "I was just wondering if we could talk?"

"Sure." Backing up, she gives me space to walk through and then she closes the door behind her, locking it back. "Have a seat," she says, motioning to a stool on the other side of the workstation that's covered in ingredients and bowls of batter.

Clearing my throat, I suddenly feel nervous. This was a bad idea. Tempest doesn't want to hear about my drama and she's obviously busy. "You know," I say, hesitating at the table. "I should probably go. This isn't that im—"

"Sit," she demands, turning to give me a death glare over her shoulder as she pulls a fresh batch of muffins out of one of the large ovens. "I know what you were getting ready to say and it is important. Cage and I were just talking last night and we decided if you didn't open up to one of us soon, we were going to stage an intervention, so it's good you're coming willingly."

She makes it sound like there would've been an apprehension or something. Like, this is the mob. I chuckle to myself. "Fine."

"Muffin?" she asks, holding a hot one out to me.

I raise my eyebrows in question.

"Sweet Dreams," she says. "Straight out of the oven, they're to die for."

As I inhale the muffin, Tempest begins her inquisition. "So, what's her name?"

I choke on a bite but manage to wheeze out, "Who?"

"The girl... woman... girlfriend... whoever made you go off the grid and escape to Green Valley."

Have I mentioned how intuitive Tempest Cassidy is? She's a lot like my mother, or any mother, I would guess. That saying about them having eyes in the back of their heads must be true, because they always know things they shouldn't. And it's obvious Tempest has already figured out part of what brought me here.

"Chloe," I say, happy I have a delicious muffin in my mouth to cover the bitterness of her name on my tongue. It used to be one of my favorite names to say, always followed by a smile… or a moan, or a…

No.

Not going there.

Tempest continues working away in the kitchen. "Girlfriend?"

"Yeah," I bite out, still thinking I'm not ready to go there, but knowing I need to just rip the Band-Aid off and get it out in the open. "You could say that."

"I'm guessing it ended badly?" she asks, turning from the tray where she's been lining muffins up perfectly, getting them ready for the display case out front.

Taking a deep breath, I exhale… trying to let the bullshit go, but feeling parts of it still trapped in my chest. As much as I hate talking about my feelings, this might be the only way to make things better. Eventually, I'm going to have to go back to Dallas and live my life. I can't hide out in Green Valley forever.

"Did you end things with her or did she end things with you?" Tempest asks when I don't respond to her initial question.

I grunt, because fuck if I don't want to talk about it.

"Was it mutual?" Her eyes rise up to meet mine and there's nothing there but easy listening… like that oldies station my dad used to play in the gym all the time when we were kids—not too hard, not too soft, just open and honest.

Running a hand through my hair, I stand from my barstool and pace the kitchen. "That's the hard part," I admit, hating that we're diving right into the thick of it. "It's complicated and messy… I'm not sure if I even want to talk about it."

"But you're here." Tempest goes back to her muffins and a casual, conversational tone.

She's right. I am. And I wasn't forced. I walked here on my own accord, so deep down I want to talk this out. "I was going to propose," I start, figuring that's as good a place as any.

"And she turned you down?"

God bless the look of astonishment on her face. I could kiss her for it, if she wasn't my brother's girl and if I didn't already love her like a sister.

"Turns out, she's married," I mutter, fighting off the rush of hurt and embarrassment from that admission. To say my heart and ego took a beating that day, and for many days to follow, would be the understatement of the century. "Or was... I don't really know. I mean, if I was her husband and found out she'd had an affair for over a year that ended with another guy proposing to her, I'd have sent her packing, but that's me."

My words and tone are gruff, but they're just a cover for the sheer betrayal I feel every time I think about Chloe and how she lied to me. For over a year, I thought she was mine, and I was ready to give her more than my heart. I was planning on giving her my last name... and forever.

"The worst part is she didn't even have the guts to tell me initially. She let me go all out... a weekend together in the mountains, roses, wine, the whole nine yards. When she cried as I slipped the ring on her finger, I thought it was because she was so overcome with love for me, mirroring the way I felt for her... but that was a lie too."

When Tempest is quiet, I turn toward her to make sure she hasn't left the kitchen and I'm not standing here giving myself an account of my worst failure. But she's listening, and all that's on her face is a look of understanding.

"I know what betrayal of that caliber feels like and I know what it does to your psyche," she begins, wiping her hands on a towel and then walking over to a coffee pot and pouring two cups. "It's where I was when I met your brother. I was broken and questioning every life choice I'd ever made... wondering how I was ever going to trust myself again, let alone other people."

As she slides the cup over to me, I nod and swallow. That's exactly how I feel.

"The first thing I'm going to tell you is," she says, taking a tentative sip of the steaming hot liquid that's honestly better than any Starbucks in the city. Again, I have no clue what's happening to me, so I'm just going to roll with it. "It's not your fault."

Letting out a rueful laugh, I run a hand down my face and then back up through my hair. "I don't know about that."

"Love is blind, Val," she says sternly. "Ever hear of rose-colored glasses?"

I smirk and take a drink of my coffee, enjoying the burn and the warmth as it travels down.

"It's meant for people like us... we see people the way we want to see them, letting their flaws fall by the wayside and only focusing on the things we love about them." She pauses, giving me a small smile. "It's not a bad quality to have... it means we love without limits. But it also means we might not see things in black and white."

"Like a husband and a life I had no fucking clue about?"

Her smile turns sad. "Yeah, like that."

"How did you learn to trust yourself again?" I ask, both wanting to know the answer and doubting it'll ever happen.

"It wasn't easy," she says, glancing down at the counter and then back up at me, and I can see the ghosts of her past—the heartache and betrayal. "I thought I was ruined forever, but someone told me the biggest thing you have to understand is we're all human and there's no one hundred percent guarantee we won't fail ourselves or other people will fail us. It's going to happen."

I nod, knowing she's right.

"But we're always stronger than we realize, and as horrible as what happened was, you survived it… maybe you'll be more guarded next time, but you're not dead. Your heart is still beating and one day it will beat for someone else again."

Letting out a deep breath, I try to let her advice sink in as I rub a hand over my chest.

"One day, you'll wake up and the cut won't feel so deep and you'll move on. You'll find someone who will make you want to trust again… in yourself and in them."

Cage was that person for her. As much as I don't like dwelling on my brother's love life, I'm happy about that. "I'm glad he makes you happy… and that you were able to bring him out of his funk."

"It was mutual," she says with a laugh as her cheeks turn a light shade of pink. "He was exactly what I needed even though I didn't realize it at the time. When fate steps in and lends a hand, there's really not much we can do, except buckle up and enjoy the ride."

She winks, like she's involved in some kind of conspiracy with fate, but maybe it's just the fact she's been in my shoes.

Been here.

Done this.

And has the T-shirt to prove it.

When I chuckle, it sounds nervous, and I can't help it when my thoughts drift to Margaret O'Neal.

"I better get going," I say, suddenly feeling the need to run.

Tempest gives me a consolatory smile. "It was good talking to you, Val. You know I'm here anytime, right?"

Nodding, I run a hand through my hair as I make my way to the door. With a hand on the lock, I pause. "Thanks, Tempest, not just for listening, but for not judging me."

"Never," she says softly.

"Lock the door behind me," I instruct, heading out into the early morning breeze.

After more miles than I can count, I find myself back at the gym just in time for Gunnar's early training session with Vince. Cage is hanging over the ropes, belting out instructions. Instead of heading up the stairs for a shower and work, I hang out for a while because if I'm by myself, I'm only going to dwell on the past—Chloe, the proposal, her tear-filled "yes," and then the implosion of my life.

Around noon, I take my ass upstairs and move quickly through a shower and get dressed. Cage has me helping out with a group of kids from Harper House, a nearby boys' home, and later today, I'm assisting Tempest in her self-defense class.

I can't deny the thought of seeing Margaret O'Neal again has put me in a good mood. I try not to dwell on her soft curves and innocent smile, but fuck, it's hard.

And so is my dick when she walks through the door, long dark hair whipping around her face like a vixen on a movie screen.

"Val," Tempest calls, getting my attention. "Want to help me fix these mats?"

"Sure," I tell her, turning my back to Margaret and taking a moment to collect myself. *Saved by the almost-sister-in-law.* She's already trying to pull the edge on one of the heavy mats and I scoot her out of the way. "I got this."

I know she wants to argue with me about being able to do it herself, but I don't let her. "Go greet your class," I say, nodding toward the growing group of people. This self-defense business was a great idea and I can tell by the look on Tempest's face every time she leads a class she's proud of all this—proud of the studio, and my brother, and everything we're building here.

"Welcome," Tempest says behind me, clapping her hands to get everyone's attention. "I see we have a few new faces. Let's go around and introduce ourselves, give a few facts, and say why we're here, so we can all get to know each other a little better."

Going about my work of adjusting the mats for our lesson today, I tune out the chatter behind me. But when I hear a sexy, somewhat gritty voice for a woman, speak up, I can't help but give it my full attention.

"I'm Margaret O'Neal," she begins and I keep my back to her because I'd totally give myself away if she saw the look on my face right now. Also, I hear the edge of nervousness and it makes me want to wipe it away, tell her there's nothing to be scared or nervous about. "You can call me Maggie." She pauses again as I throw another mat down, lining it up with the one beside it. "Uh, I'm twenty-four. I work at O'Neal Feed and Fodder. And I love collecting travel guides. This is my first time here and I really want to travel. Ha... obviously. Anyway, I thought it'd be a good idea to know some self-defense since I'll probably be traveling alone." There's that nervous laugh again and then, she adds quietly, "I'm also an oversharer."

Maggie.

I like that. It fits her even more than her given name, but both totally do it for me and I can imagine using them while in compromising positions.

Head out of the gutter, jackass.

41

The entire class then laughs, not *at her*, thankfully, but with her and I take that opportunity to ease myself into the background, hoping I can blend in and watch Maggie without her knowing I'm lurking.

And I manage to succeed until it's time for everyone to pair off and practice what they've learned. I watch as the entire class quickly finds a partner, except for Maggie. She stands in the middle of the back row like a deer in headlights, glancing around her and not moving.

I've never been socially awkward, quite the opposite actually. Being in the middle of a big family, I didn't have the chance. From a young age, I was thrust into the public eye and forced to find my footing when it came to interacting with people.

Maggie, on the other hand, is the poster child.

Tempest, being the intuitive person she is, notices it before anyone else, and walks up to her with a smile. "Need a partner?" I hear her ask and I'm grateful for her stepping in and coming to Maggie's rescue. Then, she turns her eyes to me. "Vali, will you be Maggie's partner?"

She phrases it as a question, but her look says *you're Maggie's partner.*

My look back to her says *are you fucking kidding me?*

We go back and forth like that for a few seconds, but in the end, I lose.

Or do I win?

Walking up to Maggie, our eyes meet and I smile at her to hopefully ease her nerves... and mine. "Hi, I'm Vali, but you already knew that, didn't you?"

Tempest snorts and walks away, leaving us to it.

And I want to kick myself for that greeting, because even though it's what I would say to any other woman, I shouldn't have thrown that little tidbit back in Maggie's face. At least not at first. She obviously needs a little warming up before I unload the full Erickson charm on her.

As she's gaping, trying to come up with a reply, I decide to save her. "And you're Maggie O'Neal... well, Margaret, but everyone calls you Maggie, so I'm assuming I can call you Maggie." I don't know why my voice drops an octave and I keep repeating her name, so don't ask me.

But I do love the way she swallows hard and lets out a small squeak as a reply.

"How about we try out these moves, huh?"

She nods and then licks her bottom lip.

Fuck.

I felt that little move go straight to my dick.

Clearing my throat, I hold out my hands, silently asking permission to touch her. The move we're supposed to be practicing requires me to grab her from behind. When she gives me the go-ahead, I tentatively step behind her and lightly wrap my arms around, closing my eyes at the sensation of her softness under my skin and trying not to imagine her in a more compromising position.

Shit.

Without warning, Maggie brings her hands up to my wrists and executes the move.

One second, I'm inhaling her sweet scent and memorizing the feel of her skin.

And the next, I'm flat on my back, wheezing for air.

CHAPTER 6

MAGGIE

*L*ooking down at my feet in shock and horror, I gasp.

"Oh my God," I sputter, my hand covering my mouth. "I'm so sorry... I—"

"Executed perfectly," Vali forces out, his face pulling together in a wince, but then he smiles and breaks out in a glorious laugh. It's a struggle at first, but then he twists onto his side and hops to his feet, all of those rippling muscles on display. And suddenly, I'm not so regretful about my knee-jerk reaction.

Besides, I couldn't help it.

He was touching me.

And I was feeling things.

And I was sure if I allowed it to happen much longer, I would spontaneously combust or he would hear the way my heart was pounding in my chest.

Or God forbid, I'd moan at how good his strong arms felt wrapped around my shoulders.

"I'm sorry," I repeat, offering him an apologetic smile. "Really..." I can't help the nervous laugh but swallow it down quickly. "I just reacted."

Vali's eyes are dark and hot and I can hardly stand being this close to him.

You know that saying about if you can't stand the heat, get out of the kitchen... or if you can't run with the big dogs, stay on the porch? Yeah, well, I'm not a big dog and I can't handle the heat. I'm Maggie O'Neal, a twenty-four-year-old woman who's only been kissed twice and never by lips that look like Vali Erickson's... so full and plump and *oh God*, I'm staring.

Averting my gaze, I swipe my hair behind my ear and talk to the mats at my feet. "Do we need to do that again or am I good?"

"You're good," he says, and that heat I felt in his eyes is now flooding my body and I don't know what to do with myself. Thankfully, Vali winks and walks off.

I'm really only thankful about the fact he walked off because the wink nearly did me in. My eyes involuntarily roll in my head and I turn to find something else to direct my attention to, finding Tempest giving me a small smile.

"Great class," she calls out, clapping her hands together. "Thanks for coming. If you feel like you need to work on the move we learned tonight, feel free to stay as long as you'd like. I hope to see y'all next week!"

Letting out a breath of relief, I walk to the corner where I stashed my bag and retrieve it. I'm glad I put a towel in here, because my forehead is covered in sweat. And my mouth is parched.

As I'm guzzling some water, I overhear a conversation that the reporter in me won't allow to be ignored.

"Drinks at Genie's tonight," Gunnar, the younger one, says, and I hear a loud smack like he punched someone or slapped a back.

There's a grunt and then a responding *whack*. "You keep that up and you'll be buying all the rounds," Cage replies gruffly.

These Ericksons are very hands-on.

I like it.

"Vali, you in?" a voice I don't recognize asks, but I'm very much interested in anything and everything pertaining to the person in question.

Scooting just a few inches over, I use the large mirrors to get a visual without being noticed.

I'm really good at this—observing, watching, noticing, but never being seen. It's what makes me good at my secret side job. Pathetic, I know, but it's mine and it's what makes me happy. So, sue me for being a low-key stalker.

"Where else would I be?" Vali asks, that thousand-watt smile blinding me, practically knocking me on my butt, even in a reflection and twenty feet away.

"Thanks for coming to the class," Tempest says, making me jump. I barely catch myself from crashing into the mirror in front of me and Tempest grabs my shoulder. "I'm sorry." Her laugh is contagious and I can't help letting one of my own escape.

"It's okay," I tell her, standing to my full height, at least four inches taller than her. That's not unusual, I'm taller than a lot of women, even my mother. I took after my dad in more ways than one—taller, *bigger boned*. I've heard that my whole life... *bigger boned*. When I was little it bothered me because I knew it was people's nice way of saying I was chubby. But now, I'm cool with it. I am who I am. All I can do is embrace my curves and the fact I'm not a petite person and roll with it.

Tempest chuckles again and rights my bag on my shoulder. "Well, as I was saying, I'm really glad you came to class tonight. I hope you'll come back."

"Definitely," I tell her, nodding as I try to not look over her shoulder at Vali and his brothers cutting up on the other side of the gym.

She swats behind her. "Don't pay attention to them. They're basically twelve-year-olds dressed as giants. And I also wanted to tell you I'm sorry about matching you up without asking you if you were comfortable with it. I should've asked first."

"Oh," I say, shaking my head. "Don't worry about it…" That nervous chuckle is back and I'm swiping my long hair behind my ear. "It was fine… I just hope I didn't hurt him."

"Ha!" Tempest slaps her leg. "Do not worry about that. Vali might not be as big as Gunnar and Cage, but he can definitely take a hit. Actually, next time, you should try a little harder."

She winks and I swallow, trying not to let my true colors shine through. "Well, I better get going…"

I almost say because my parents will send out an APB if I'm not home in the next thirty minutes, but that makes me sound like a child. And I suddenly want to be included and seen as an equal with Tempest and the rest of the people at the studio… Vali, most of all.

"See you next week?" Tempest asks and I feel like she's asking on more of a friend level than an instructor to a student.

Nodding, I smile. "I'll be here."

Fighting the urge to turn back to Vali, to say something to him… make a connection… something I absolutely don't understand, I turn and walk out of the studio.

Ten minutes later when I walk in the front door of my home, my parents' house, I hear my mom call out from the kitchen. "Margaret, is that you?"

Rolling my eyes, I chuckle to myself. Of course, it's me. If it's after eight o'clock on any given night, my father is in his recliner in the living room and my mother is puttering around the house. The only other person who could just walk through our front door is me.

"Yes," I call out. "I'm home."

I'm it—my parents' only child.

They tried to get pregnant for fifteen years and had given up hope. When it finally happened, they were shocked to say the least. My mother went to her doctor every week for almost three months so they could guarantee her she was still pregnant.

To say they've doted on me my entire life would be an understatement.

"How was your class?" she asks, sounds of pots and pans banging around following her question. My mother is a multitasker. She's always busy. If she's not cooking and cleaning, she's helping out at the store. And when she's not doing those things, she's volunteering at the church or participating in a community project.

She's a real go-getter, to put it in my father's words.

"It was great," I say, finally making my way into the kitchen. Leaning against the counter, I smile at the sight that greets me. Along the counter are freshly washed jars lined up and ready for some sort of jam or jelly. Whatever it is, I know it will be the best I've ever tasted. She's a jam-making genius. With her beautiful brown hair tied up on the top of her head in a scarf, she looks like one of those fifties housewives.

When she looks up, cheeks flushed and looking happier than a bird with a French fry, her smile grows even wider. That's my mom, she always has a smile for me. "Did you learn something new?" she asks. "Meet anyone?"

My stomach flutters and I try to quell the blush that is trying to creep up on my cheeks. "Uh, yeah... I did. It was really fun."

She cocks her head, trying to read between the lines, always using her mother's intuition.

"I'm going to go back next week."

"That's good, sweetie. I'm glad you enjoyed it."

Glancing down at myself, I pull at the T-shirt and feel the need to shower. Even though it wasn't an intense workout, I definitely worked up a sweat. "I'm heading upstairs," I tell her.

"Okay, honey," she says, going on about her business.

When I get to my room, I hang my bag on the hook by my door and flop onto my bed. My mind is still reeling with the way my body responded to Vali. I've never felt anything like that. The rush of... heat and electricity... I can't wrap my head around it.

I knew he was handsome.

I knew I had a bit of a crush on him, as much of a crush as you can have from a distance.

But seeing him up close and personal... *wow*. That's all I can say. For a person who's usually good with her words, I'm lost for an explanation. It's not that I'm immune to the male species. Of course, I notice if a handsome man comes into the store or I pass them on the street. I mean, I noticed Vali's brothers long before he showed his gorgeous face around Green Valley. But no one has ever caught my attention like Vali Erickson.

In this week's Trixie and Tess article, I referred to the brothers as *eye candy*. But Vali is so much more than that. He's strong and astute, aware of his surroundings with a confidence that oozes from his pores.

And I'm totally smitten.

Taking a deep breath, I close my eyes and allow myself a few moments to relish in today's events.

Before I pull myself out of bed and go shower, I grab my laptop and open up my email. If I don't get out some of this pent-up excitement, I'll never sleep.

So, I went to the self-defense class tonight and HE WAS THERE.

And he touched me.

And I threw him to the ground.

SMH

But still, he touched me and I felt THINGS. And it was amazing and confusing and oh my God what am I doing? Also, why can't you live closer because I could really use someone to talk to face-to-face.

Oh, on that note. I think I *might've* made a friend.

Hope everything is good there.

Maggie

Closing my laptop, I toss it on my bed and go shower, trying to not think of Vali and failing miserably, so much that I accidentally put conditioner on my loofa and get an extra moisturizing treatment unintentionally.

After I'm dressed in leggings and a big T-shirt with my hair combed out and air drying, I climb back up on my bed and open the laptop back up to work on my article for next week, but I see a notification for my inbox. Everly's response is short: *TELL ME MORE.*

Shooting her an email back, I tell her all the details, giving her a play-by-play of the entire self-defense class and the interactions with Tempest and Frankie.

This would probably be better over the phone, but I know how you are about your secret life, so I'll do my best to express all of my thoughts and feelings in this email.

First, I need you to pull up a chair and listen closely.

I chuckle and shake my head. So many times over the last thirteen years I've wished she was my next-door neighbor or a girl in Green Valley. Shoot, even Tennessee would be nice. At least then I might've had a chance to meet her in person over the years. From the first email, when we were matched up during a homeschool project, I knew she was a kindred spirit. Well, it was a homeschool project for me. Everly, on the other hand, went to public school, and thanks to her, I got a first-hand account of how the other half lived.

Like she can see me, I pull the screen closer and snuggle down into my pillows.

Okay, I need you to know everything I say comes from a place of love. I would never let anyone say these things to you, but it's okay coming from me because I'm more like a bestie-sister than anything. One of these days we're going to meet and realize we were separated at birth.

I stop reading to snort. Yeah, not even. I've seen plenty of pictures of Everly and the only thing similar about us is our height and hair color. Other than those two things, we're polar opposites. But maybe we could be fraternal twins… who are a few years apart. She's also uber-successful and owns a wedding planning business in New Orleans and still manages to do these secretive, invite-only matchmaking sessions with the elite crowd. Basically, she's every Instagram influencer I follow, but also my friend.

You're twenty-four years old.

You're an adult.

Again, I say this in love, but you need to stop living in your bubble and get out there and LIVE! I'm super proud of you for taking this self-defense class and for getting out of your comfort zone. But you can't wait for happiness to land in your lap. When you email me tomorrow, I expect something juicy or dangerous (not too dangerous… safe-dangerous) or daring! Go paint Green Valley red, or green, or what-ever color suits your fancy. You mentioned overhearing them talking about going to Genie's… do that. Put on some tight jeans and a cute sweater... swipe on some lipstick and GET OUT THERE and get you a man... or in this case, a Viking.

XOXO,

your Nola Bestie

My heart is pounding when I get to the end of the email. Ever is right, I know she is. But I can't do that. I can't get up at... Pausing, I glance at my phone and check the time. It's eight forty-five. I can't get up at eight forty-five, get dressed, and tell my mom and dad I'll be back later.

Can I?

No, that's crazy... and so not me.

My computer dings with another email notification.

You're sitting there thinking of all the reasons you're not going to do what I told you to do. So, this is me figuratively pushing you out the door. GO! DO IT! THANK ME LATER!

Letting out a pent-up breath, I shoot her back a response.

FINE.

Already feeling the nerves, I push myself off the bed, and before I can second-guess my decision, I grab the first pair of jeans I see and pull them on. Then, I browse through my tops and pick the first one that isn't a T-shirt or looks like it came from my mother's closet. To finish it off, I slip on a pair of cute flats. Not heels. I'm tall enough on my own, thank you very much.

Bracing my arms on the side of the vanity in my bathroom, I try to slow my breathing as I look at myself in the mirror. "You can do this... you're a twenty-four-year-old woman... you're an adult. It's not like you're going to commit a crime."

My pep talk does very little to calm the jitters I feel through my body, but I don't let them stop me. Using the blow dryer, I finish off my hair, making it fall in line as much as I can and hoping I can pull off the freshly showered look. Swiping on some mascara, I pinch my cheeks and finish the look with a coat of berry red lip gloss.

There, that's good.

"You're good," I whisper to the girl in the mirror, thinking back to when Vali said those exact words to me and feeling the heat again, which solidifies my decision.

Yeah, I'm totally doing this.

When I walk down the hall, I peek into the living room and see my dad still in his usual evening spot. Bypassing him, I head into the kitchen. "Hey, Mom."

"Hey," she says, eyes trained on the last few jars she's dipping into a pot of boiling water.

Clearing my throat, I bite the bullet. "I'm, uh, going out for an hour or so," I tell her, trying to sound confident and in charge of my life. "I'll be home by ten thirty… eleven at the latest."

At that, her head snaps up and I watch as her eyes go wide when my words register. "Going out?" she asks. "With who?"

"Uh, some friends." It feels a bit like a lie, but I try to sell it. Besides, I'm sure there will be people I know at Genie's. I mean, I've never been there, but I know pretty much everyone in Green Valley. They're not my friends, per se, but they're at least acquaintances. "From the self-defense class," I add, grasping at straws. "They mentioned going out tonight and I decided it sounds fun… and it's Friday. I'll be back in plenty of time to get in bed and be at work in the morning."

Eventually, my mom nods her agreement. There's an expression of reluctance, but it's like she's warring with herself, knowing she can't really tell me no. Sure, I live under her roof, but I am an adult. And even though I haven't exercised many of my adult rights in the past, I am old enough to leave the house by myself at nine o'clock at night and go somewhere besides the Piggly Wiggly.

"Okay," she finally says. "You have your phone, right?"

"Yeah." Holding it up, I show it to her.

"Okay," she says again. "Be careful and call if you need anything."

Giving her a reassuring smile, I nod. "I will. Love you."

The next thing I know, I'm in my car driving to Genie's.

On a Friday night.

Like a normal twenty-four-year-old.

And, *oh my God, I'm going to Genie's on a Friday night.*

What if Vali and his brothers aren't there? Or what if they are and Frankie and Tempest aren't with them?

What if I trip on my way in the door?

What if they ask for my ID?

No, that's stupid. Again, I know everyone and they know how old I am.

Letting out a maniacal laugh, I shake my head. "Stop it, Maggie. Get over yourself. It's just a bar… in Green Valley, Tennessee. It's not like you're jumping off a bridge or flying over the ocean."

Mentally, I continue to make a list of things that are scarier than walking into a bar by myself—spiders bigger than a quarter, shadows in the dark, clowns... By the time I pull into the parking lot, I'm so distracted by list-making that I'm out of my car and in the bar before I know it.

CHAPTER 7

VALI

*F*riday nights at Genie's have quickly become one of my favorite rituals since moving to Green Valley.

We Ericksons have our Friday nights down to an art. First, we show up at eight thirty to ensure we get a coveted booth. Then, we order a few pitchers of beer and some food, so we can relax and bullshit and blow off some steam before the crowd picks up.

Back home in Dallas, nights out on the town are way more stressful. You have to decide where you want to go, which causes more grief than you'd think, thanks to all of the establishments to choose from. Second, you have to make a reservation, knowing you'll still be waiting on your table even though you show up on time. If the reservation times don't work for everyone in your group, you go back to step one and pick a new place. And don't even get me started on the traffic you'll encounter to get to the final destination.

It's a shit-ton of stress for something that's supposed to be relaxing.

Genie's is another surprising reason I actually prefer Green Valley to Dallas. I didn't realize life could be so much easier in a small town.

Don't get me wrong, I'm still a city boy at heart, but I can definitely appreciate small-town living.

"Cheers to another successful week." Cage holds his mug of beer above the middle of the table and we—Tempest, Gunnar, Frankie, and me—do the same, clinking our mugs together before taking large celebratory gulps.

"Let me be the first to congratulate Tempest on her kick-ass class, which saw a seventy-five percent increase in attendance this week," I say, tipping my beer in her direction before draining it and pouring a refill.

"Well, thank you, but I have no doubt the increase was due to your brilliant ad in the paper. So, thank *you*, Vali, for your marketing help."

Even though I completely agree with her statement, no one likes a braggart, so I wave off her praise like it's no big deal. And it really isn't one. It's basic marketing I'm happy to do while I'm here. I like doing my part and feeling useful, but I admit, hearing how Tempest appreciates my work is pretty cool.

"Who else has something to share?" Gunnar asks. I notice his elbow nudging Frankie, causing her to blush and mouth the word "stop" to him. Tempest must notice, as well, because she pounces before I'm able to.

"What? What's going on here?" she asks, pointing back and forth between them. "There are no secrets here, so spill."

"This is the first time in two years the shelter has only had one family to take care of. I know it may seem weird to celebrate a loss of... business or whatever you want to call it but it's pretty amazing. We haven't had any new cases all week and we were able to find permanent housing for the family we have." Frankie is always reluctant to bring attention to herself but it's easy to see the pride on her face as she shares her news. "Give us another week and Gunnar and I might have to find somewhere else to volunteer our time."

She lets out a laugh and leans into Gunnar's side. I watch as he tips her chin up and kisses her, not giving two shits who's watching. That boy is so head over heels for her it's not even funny.

Sitting at this table with a bunch of lovebirds isn't easy to swallow. It's a stark reminder of what I don't have—love, trust, someone who's mine—and probably won't anytime soon. In an effort to keep my feelings to myself, I drain my second mug of beer.

"Well, I for one prefer this to our boring-ass weekly meetings. Who's with me?" I ask, raising my mug just like Cage did a few minutes ago.

"Put your beer down, asshole."

Before the verbal blows start to fly, Tempest quickly redirects the conversation. "Well, I propose we start finalizing plans for our trip to New Orleans! We have flights and hotel rooms to secure and I'm ready to start planning my food tour."

"Food tour? I'm intrigued," Gunnar encourages. "Tell me more."

"New Orleans is known for its amazing food, right? So, I want to try it all! Gumbo, beignets, muffulettas or however you say it. I can't wait." Tempest gets this dreamy look on her face and starts rubbing her stomach. I assume she's imagining the food baby she's gonna create as she eats her way through the Crescent City and I can't say I blame her.

Gunnar groans. "I should've known better than to ask. Promise me you'll save some of your tour for after my fight." Tempest nods her head in agreement while Gunnar continues. "I can't wait to celebrate my win with one of those famous Hurricane drinks. It has to be better than this one light beer Cage allows me to drink." He wrinkles his nose as he looks at his half-full mug.

"Be thankful I allow that instead of making you drink non-alcoholic beer," Cage grumbles.

I share a horrified look with Gunnar and we both shudder at Cage's words.

"I've been thinking of making some Nola-themed muffins," Tempest says, as though the last exchange never happened. "I could make a praline muffin... oh, a bananas Foster muffin... and what are those cakes that are made only during Mardi Gras?"

"King cake," both my brothers and I answer in unison. Dallas, technically, isn't that far from New Orleans and we've known a few Louisiana transplants over the years, so we've had a few of the things Tempest has mentioned. I'm sure getting the real thing in Nola is much better, though.

"Yes! I'm definitely making a king cake muffin," Tempest declares, the excitement in her voice impossible to miss. "Just thinking about the trip has my creative juices flowing."

"Well, you know we're at your service to taste test anything and everything you make," Cage assures her.

"Hear, hear!" Frankie and I clink our mugs together to show our agreement, while Gunnar crosses his arms over his chest and pouts.

"I'll freeze some for you to eat after your fight," Tempest promises.

As my family continues discussing recipes, the studio, and everything in between, my attention is caught by a woman walking through the front door.

Not just any woman, Maggie O'Neal.

She looks a bit like a fish out of water as her wide eyes take in the bar. While she's taking inventory of Genie's, I can't help but do the same to her—jeans that hug her curves, a V-neck sweater that shows just enough cleavage to pique my interest, gorgeous brown hair that frames her fresh face. She's not made up, overdone or trying too hard.

Maggie O'Neal is just right... the perfect amount of everything.

The way she clutches the strap on her purse, fingers locked around it in a death grip even though she's wearing it across her torso, it's obvious she's not comfortable being here. If I was a betting man, I'd bet this is her first time at Genie's, which makes me wonder why she's here in the first place.

What would make her step out of her comfort zone and come to a bar by herself?

She is by herself, right?

Craning my head as inconspicuously as possible, I look behind her and back toward the door.

Maybe she has a date?

That thought instantly makes my stomach sour, which is ridiculous because why shouldn't she be dating? She's a gorgeous, young woman who should be out having the time of her life. Just because my love life sucks doesn't mean hers should too.

Fuck, I need to stop projecting my shit onto other people. Chloe and I are done. I need to suck it up and move on.

It's not like I want Chloe back. Fuck that. I just still can't believe I was *the other guy*. She made me a cheater and I'm not sure I'll ever be able to forgive her for that. Any time I think about it, I want to erase the last two years of my life.

Maggie has found a seat at the bar, and when the bartender sets down a drink in front of her, it looks like she ordered water.

Maybe I should order her a drink and have it sent over. The way she's sitting with her back straight, still gripping her strap to her purse, she looks like she could use a drink. My hands are itching to touch her and rub the tension from her shoulders.

I can't help the low chuckle as I replay our interaction from earlier today.

When she threw me to the mats… *shit.*

The crotch of my jeans gets tighter just thinking about how she manhandled me. I'm not sure who was more surprised, me or her. All I know is I'd like a repeat. I mean, I'd love the opportunity to wrap my arms around her without the threat of being knocked on my ass, but I'm okay if she gets rough with me. More than okay, in fact.

My mind starts conjuring images of me and Maggie... in the studio, all hot and sweaty... I'm on the floor again but this time, she's on top of me and—

"Dude, that chick is checking you out big-time," Gunnar whispers to me, pulling me out of my fantasy.

When I glance at him, he tips his head toward the bar, pointing in the direction of my so-called admirer. I follow his line of sight and am caught in Maggie's gaze. As soon as she realizes she's been caught staring, a look of terror washes over her beautiful face and she goes rigid, spinning around on her barstool.

I don't like that. Not one bit.

It's one thing to feel a bit sheepish for being caught but to look down-right afraid doesn't sit right with me. I try to tell myself not to care, to ignore her, and the feelings she's stirring up in me because that's not what I'm here for. I didn't come to Green Valley for a rebound or a hookup or anything more than that. My brothers came here and found the peace and direction they needed, so why can't I? Of course, they also found their soulmates but I'm ignoring that part. Not everyone is cut out for long-term relationships, and if that is my fate, I'll have to accept it.

But, first and against my better judgment, I'm gonna go talk to Maggie.

CHAPTER 8

MAGGIE

Oh, God. He sees me.

Yeah, he's totally looking at me.

And now he's standing up.

Spinning around on my barstool, I pick up the cold glass of water and take a drink because my mouth is now as dry as the Sahara Desert. It must be the nerves or the way Vali Erickson makes me drool. That must be it.

I'm dehydrated.

Which could also be why I'm breathing erratically. Glancing over my shoulder, I see him walking away from the booth where his brothers and Frankie and Tempest are sitting.

For the love of all things good and holy, please don't let him walk over here... no, let him walk over here. Please, God. Let him walk over... okay, yeah, he's definitely walking over.

I know I came here to see him but now that I'm here and he's here and he knows I'm here, I can't do it. With shaky hands, I pull out a five-dollar bill and slap it down on the table. I realize the water is probably free but I don't feel right dirtying up someone else's glass and just walking away without ordering anything else.

Standing, I grip my purse strap even tighter and turn for the door.

"Maggie."

Oh, God. Ohgodohgodohgod.

Closing my eyes, I swallow hard and try to gather all the strength and cojones I have. Girl balls, as Everly would call them. She claims I have them but they're buried under all of my manners and good intentions. Before I can turn around to face him, I can actually feel his presence. Don't ask me how. I have no clue. Which isn't a surprise because I'm feeling pretty clueless these days, especially when it comes to Vali.

"Maggie," he repeats. His voice is now closer and low, so low it hits me straight between my thighs. When I turn around to face him, his eyes lock with mine and it feels like time stops.

During the strange time lapse, it dawns on me Vali knows my name. I've never even really liked my name. I mean, it's okay and serves its purpose, but it's never been one of my favorite attributes. Until now.

"Vali," I breathe out in response and greeting, brushing my hair behind my ear. "Hey."

I hope that came off as cool-casual as it sounded in my head, like *oh, hey, fancy meeting you here.* Except cooler, because who says that? *Get it together, Margaret.*

When he unleashes a full-fledged smile on me, I'm glad I had a chance to say those two words because they might be my last.

"Hey," he says as his eyes scan my face and then trail down my body, leaving a wake of heat in their path. "Do you want to come sit with us?" Motioning over his shoulder, I catch Gunnar and Frankie looking this way and my heartbeats triple.

Bringing my wrist up, I glance at my watch. I've already been gone over half an hour... but also, I've *only* been gone half an hour. In half an hour, I drove here, parked, found a seat at the bar, ordered water, and now I'm standing here talking to the hottest guy I've ever met.

"Sure," I manage to squeak out, looking back up at Vali and giving him what I hope is a nice smile... not as nice as his, of course, but as long as I'm not competing with the Joker, it's fine.

Everything is fine.

"Great," he says, exuding that cool-casual I was going for as he smiles, showing me all of his straight, pearly-white teeth.

Have I mentioned he has gorgeous teeth? I know that might sound crazy. How can teeth be gorgeous, right? But they so are. Not too big. Not too small. Straight, but not fake. And now that I've seen them up close, I see he has a small chip out of one of the front teeth and I wonder how that happened?

In a fight, maybe?

When I don't follow right away, he turns back to me and cocks his head. "You okay?" he asks, his voice rising above the noise of the bar that actually seems to be getting louder as we stand here.

"I'm good."

He then places his hand on my back to lead me over to the table. Yeah, his big, strong hand is on my back and there's only a thin layer of wool between my skin and his. When I almost trip over some guy's boot, I feel him tense as he grabs my waist to keep me upright and I have to force my eyes from rolling into the back of my head.

Did his hand just slip under the hem of my sweater?

Oh, God.

"Hi, Maggie," Tempest calls out from the booth, interrupting my errant thoughts.

"Hi," I say, giving them all a small wave. "Vali invited me over." My fingers are still gripping the strap of my purse so tight they're tingling. *Relax, Maggie. Relax.* An awkward laugh escapes me and I'm getting ready to make an excuse to leave when Vali's hand settles even heavier on my back, reassuring me, silently telling me to stay.

"I'm glad he did," Tempest says, her smile growing as her eyes move to Vali. "Would you like a beer or something else to drink?"

I look back over my shoulder at Vali who's waiting for me to slide into the booth. "I'm just having water."

Being the oversharer that I am, I want to tell her I've never had alcohol. There's no way I'd start tonight, especially since I told my mother I'd be home in an hour and I have to be at work early in the morning.

As a waitress walks by, Vali calls out to her, getting her attention. "Can we get an ice water?"

My cheeks heat up when she gives me a judgy glance and then winks at Vali.

I am so out of my league.

"I've never seen you here before," Tempest says, obviously just trying to make conversation but I literally want to crawl under the table and out of this bar. My cheeks that were only a light shade of pink a moment ago, flame.

Thankfully, the flirty waitress is back with my water and I eagerly accept it, taking a drink and draining half the glass. When I realize everyone is still waiting for my response to Tempest's statement, I give a small smile and swallow. "Uh, no... I've never been here before."

"Well," Vali says, his arm brushing against mine and sending an electric jolt through my body. "I think you should do it up right."

My eyes widen and I try to read into his words. As much as I might know about the world at large, I don't have a lot of real-life experience. "What?" I ask, feeling my palms begin to sweat.

"We should take a spin around the dance floor."

I feel my shoulders visibly relax. Dancing is something that I actually know how to do, not because I read about it or watched YouTube videos, but because I've done it. My mom and dad love to dance in the living room. When I was little, they'd put on old records and dance the jitterbug and the two-step and everything in between.

"Yes," Tempest says, turning her attention to Cage. "Let's dance."

Even Gunnar and Frankie start edging their way out of the booth to head to the dance floor.

"What do you say?" Vali asks quietly, dipping his head down toward mine. *So close... so very close.* As the song playing turns slow, he slides out of the booth and stretches his hand out to me. "Can I have this dance?"

Placing my hand in his, I feel that same electricity, a low hum that flows from him to me.

"I'd love to," I finally manage to say, standing to my full height and realizing something else.

For once, I'm going to dance with someone who's taller than me. Maybe that's one of the reasons I've been attracted to the Vikings since they invaded all those months ago. I'm not one of those petite girls who fit under every guy's chin. Out of the two real boyfriends I've had in my life, one was shorter than me and one was the same height.

This is different.

Everything about Vali feels different.

With a confidence I've only read about, he spins me out and then pulls me back to his body in a smooth motion before bringing our joined hands up and holding them to his chest.

Even this dance is different.

So different that I completely lose track of time and one dance turns into four. By the time the music breaks, my cheeks hurt from smiling so much and my body is somehow tense and relaxed all at the same time.

"You're a great dancer," Vali says, leaning down and placing his lips by my ear. I tell myself it's just so I'll be able to hear him over the crowd, but when he lingers, I'm not so sure. And he's still holding my hand close to his chest with his other hand wrapped around my hip and I never want to leave this spot.

Maybe Genie would let me rent it out?

I open my mouth to respond, to tell him he's a great dancer too—best partner I've ever had—but my phone rings and jolts me out of the moment.

"What time is it?" I ask, my eyes growing wide as I pull away from Vali and dig into my purse. Because, of course, I'm still wearing my purse. I obviously forgot while Vali was sweeping me off my feet.

He chuckles. "Are you Cinderella?"

Popping my head up at him, I frown in confusion, feeling my heart rate spike as I silence the call. It's my mother and I'd rather not speak to her in the middle of Genie's with Vali looking at me with those bedroom eyes and smiling at me with those wicked lips.

"What?"

"Cinderella," he repeats, running a hand through his luscious hair. "You know, she has to leave the ball at midnight before her carriage turns back into a pumpkin... and the glass slipper... and the footmen that are mice. That was always my favorite part."

I let out something resembling a chuckle. "I'm definitely not Cinderella." But I do have to go. I promised my mother I'd be home twenty minutes ago. "Thank you for the dance... or dances, rather. I had a really great time."

I'd love to do it again.

I'd love to do so many things with you, I think as my eyes go to his lips and he leans in toward me. *Is he going to kiss me? Does he want to?*

Before I can find out, my nerves get the better of me and I turn and walk swiftly toward the exit, waving over my shoulder and calling out, "Thanks again."

CHAPTER 9

VALI

I'm being tortured.

I've never been much of an angel, to be sure, but I didn't think I deserved to suffer like this, with blue balls the size of Texas.

That Maggie O'Neal is a fucking vixen.

I was completely lost in her as we danced last night. Her soft curves, sweet smell, and gorgeous smile captivated me in a way I've never experienced, and I was stunned when she hauled ass out of Genie's like the floor was on fire. That didn't stop my body from reacting to her, though.

Later, when I crawled into bed lonely and buzzed, I tried to ignore my throbbing dick but, eventually, I had to rub one out, fantasizing about Maggie the entire time. Apparently, my dreams were about Maggie too because I just woke up with another raging hard-on.

The effect that woman has on my body makes me feel like a damn teenager again.

Maybe I just need to get laid.

I told myself I wasn't going to hook up while in Green Valley but I can't be jacking off all the time either. I suppose I should feel relieved I can still get it up after ending things with Chloe. That whole situation really messed me up and I'm not sure I'm mentally ready for any kind of intimacy, even though my body has other ideas. All of this is just another reminder of why I need to get Maggie out of my mind. She certainly doesn't need or deserve to put up with my bullshit, especially if I'm not planning on sticking around. She's too sweet to string along.

From now on, it's strictly professional between us.

I can't wait to see how long it takes me to break that vow.

Gunnar and Cage agreed, as we said our good nights last night, to sleep in this morning and pick up training after lunch, so I decided to spend my morning getting a little pampering. Self-care is important, which is why, after showering and fixing my coffee to go, I find myself standing in front of The Beauty Mark.

The Beauty Mark is Green Valley's one and only salon, and at nine thirty on a Saturday morning, it's already bustling with customers.

When the large bell hanging on the front door announces my entrance into the salon, everything stops. There's no talking or hair cutting. In fact, only the large hairdryer in the back seems to be making any kind of sound. Even the young woman at the front desk has stopped talking to whomever she's on the phone with as she blatantly stares at me.

Everyone is staring.

I'll be honest, I'm used to turning heads but this is a bit unsettling.

Maybe they don't let guys in here?

After an awkward minute of not knowing what to do, I take a step back, assuming I should just leave. The barber in town can't be bad, can it? I mean, I see a lot of long beards around here but that doesn't mean the men of Green Valley don't care about their appearance. I guess if I really feel the need for some big-city pampering, I could always drive to Maryville.

"Oh, don't go!" the woman closest to the door calls out. She lays down her scissors before walking over to me with her hand reaching out for me. "Hi, I'm Missy, please come in. And, please forgive all of us for being so rude. It's not every day someone like yourself... you know, a... um, *man*... comes into the salon."

"Especially one so cute!" Missy lets out a gasp while turning her head toward the older lady she left in her chair before greeting me. "Miss Faye, you better behave yourself." I don't think Miss Faye cares about the admonishment, though, because she simply shrugs before winking at me.

Thankfully, this causes the rest of the workers and clients to resume what they were doing before I walked in, taking their attention away from me.

"I'm Vali, and no worries," I assure Missy. "I wasn't sure if I needed an appointment or not, so I thought I'd stop by. I didn't realize you'd be so busy this early in the day."

"Oh, yes, Saturday mornings are our busiest times. We have a lot of regulars who come in for their weekly wash and sets." She says this like I should know what she means. I don't but I try to smile like I do.

"Well, I can make an appointment for another time. It's no problem." I'm disappointed I won't be getting any services today but I really should've known better. It's not like I'd ever be able to waltz into a salon in Dallas and expect same-day service. Something about Green Valley not only relaxes me but also my expectations.

"No!" Missy, and what seems like everyone else in the shop, yells, causing my body to freeze in surprise.

Missy laughs nervously. "I'm sure we can fit you in. What were you wanting to get done?"

"I'd love a trim and a deep-conditioning treatment, if you have time. You don't, by any chance, do facials, do you?" If I'm here and she's gonna fit me in, I might as well get the works.

"We can do all those things, no problem!"

"Are you sure? I don't want to put you in a bind."

"Honey, if they run out of chairs, you can sit on my lap," Miss Faye offers.

Missy turns to Miss Faye. "Don't make me call Mister Ralph on you!"

Faye waves her threat away. "Oh, please. He'd love for someone else to put up with me for a while. I wore him out years ago!"

I try to mask my laughter with a cough before walking over to Miss Faye and introducing myself. "Nice to meet you, Miss Faye, I'm Vali Erickson. I appreciate your offer but, hopefully, we'll all get to keep our seats today. If we run out, though, I promise, we can share."

When I give her a wink, she flutters her lashes, totally eating it up.

"Oh, I like you, Vali Erickson. You're just what this place needed today." Faye reaches out and pats my hand.

"What do you mean by that?" Missy questions Faye with her hands on her hips.

"Nothing, dear. It's just after coming here every Saturday morning all these years, it's nice to have a change in scenery, if you know what I mean. Especially one as good-looking as Vali."

Missy mumbles "good Lord" before turning toward me. "Let's find you a cape and we'll get started. Miss Faye, you don't mind waiting a few minutes while I wash Vali's hair, do you?"

"Not at all, dear. I still have the rest of my *People* magazine to read."

Chuckling, I follow her to the back of the salon, where she hands me a black cape to put over my clothes, before sitting at one of two sinks.

Missy begins washing my hair and I close my eyes, allowing the feel of her fingers gently scratching my scalp to lull me into deep relaxation.

This is exactly what I needed.

When she's finished with my thorough shampoo—I'm talking world-class, moan-inducing action—she moves on to the deep-conditioning treatment. While that's working its magic, she works magic on my face.

Just as she starts with the purifying mask, a familiar voice grabs my attention, pulling me out of my state of deep relaxation. Peeking out of one eye, I see Maggie O'Neal talking to Miss Faye at Missy's station. Immediately, my dick twitches and I force myself to close my eyes.

Out of sight, out of mind, right?

However, my dick doesn't need any visual reminder—his imagination is stellar. Being the only guy at a salon, sporting a chubby, is *not* how I planned to spend my Saturday morning.

"Vali, is that you?"

I crack my eyes back open and turn in the direction of Maggie's voice. There she is, standing closer than she was before. Fresh-faced with her hair pulled back by a headband, she's breathtakingly beautiful. My dreams pale in comparison to the real deal.

"Oh, hey, Mags. You stalking me?" I ask. I'm joking, of course, but the way she flinches at my words makes me wonder if I haven't hit a nerve. This is a small town, I'm sure our meeting here is purely coin-cidental.

Maggie huffs out a laugh while brushing back an invisible strand of hair off her face. "No, of course not. I—I would never do that."

"Maggie, I'm kidding. I don't really think you're stalking me. But, on the other hand, if you are, I think I'd be okay with it." The wink comes naturally and I hope it puts her at ease. "Are you here for an appointment?"

Again, she fusses with her hair and it seems as though I've made her self-conscious. Man, I can't win here. Things felt so natural between us last night but are awkward now. I don't like it.

"No," she answers. "I'm here to deliver some feed to Tammy, the nail tech."

"I didn't realize the local feed store made deliveries."

"Well, we don't do it often but I had some errands to run anyway, so I told Tammy I'd bring her order. The better question is, what's going on over here?" she asks, pointing to me. "Do your brothers know you're here getting prettied up?"

My face mask cracks a bit when I bark out a laugh. "No, they do not, but they wouldn't be surprised to find out. I've wasted many years trying to convince them of the benefits of this kind of self-care. They're lost causes, I'm afraid." This time, it's Maggie's turn to laugh loudly and it's music to my ears.

I watch her as she slowly stops laughing, her eyes traveling over me from my head to my toes. It's only now I realize just how ridiculous I must look but, really, I don't care. I may have my secrets but I'm willing to be open for Maggie. At least, I think I am… to an extent. Besides, maybe seeing me like this will stop her from being so nervous around me. I'm not opposed to dancing with her again, if that'll help, as well.

No, I'd like that very much.

"I should go," Maggie says, pointing toward the door. "It was, uh, good seeing you, Vali."

"You too, Mags."

I swear I hear her mumble, "Please don't cut your hair," before she quickly walks out of the salon.

Once my face and hair are clean and I'm seated in Missy's chair, I see that Miss Faye is sitting nearby.

"Looking good, Miss Faye. Is your husband taking you out on a date later?"

Faye lets out a cackle before rolling her chair close to me. "Heavens, no. This is just my weekly upkeep. I have a reputation to uphold, you know."

"Is that so? And what kind of rep is that? Wait, let me guess… heart-breaker?"

"Ha! You're a flatterer, Vali, and I love it. No, my reputation is what I like to think most Southern ladies aim for: sweet and feisty. Sweet to most but feisty to those who know better. I'm definitely not as sweet as that precious young girl you were speaking with earlier. She's a precious little lamb and, from what I hear, as innocent as one too." Faye quirks an eyebrow, causing me to chuckle.

It also causes me to pause because if what Faye just said about Maggie is true, then I should definitely stay away. If she's a lamb, then I'm a fucking wolf and she deserves better than that.

CHAPTER 10

MAGGIE

Hey, Ever!

*I ran into Vali at the hair salon today. He was getting a facial.
You don't think he's gay, do you? I feel like my gaydar is usually
spot on but maybe I missed the signal with him because he's SO
FREAKING HOT.*

*Wow. That would be about right. The one guy that's really got
my attention and made me feel things and he's gay. Batting for
the other team. Not just out of my league, but out of my whole
freaking sport.*

*How much do you charge for your fancy matchmaking services
again?*

You might be my only hope.

Maggie

P.S. We're on a nickname basis now. He called me Mags.

CHAPTER 11

VALI

Tonight is Tempest's self-defense class and I've been waiting all week for it—not so much for the class, but to see Maggie. After our run-in at the hair salon last Saturday, I expected to see her around town but, unfortunately, our paths haven't crossed.

Not on my morning runs.

Not during my daily trips to Donner Bakery.

Not at the Piggly Wiggly.

However, the thought did cross my mind to stop by her family's feed store, but seeing as how I never bought the goat I jokingly considered a couple of weeks ago, it might be a bit obvious. Besides, I'm still not sure what my intentions are with her. For someone who is generally decisive, I find myself waffling when it comes to her.

On one hand, I'm attracted and turned the fuck on.

On the other hand, I promised myself no hookups or relationships.

Bottom line, I still don't trust myself or other people. But something inside me tells me Maggie is different. The best part, nothing about her reminds me of Chloe. Actually, quite the opposite. Everything about Maggie makes me forget—Chloe, the lies, the distrust, the hurt... why I've sworn off relationships.

"Vali," Tempest calls up the stairs, practically scaring the shit out of me.

"Up here," I call back, closing down my laptop and organizing the papers I have scattered around the table. Even with my thoughts on Maggie, I've still managed to get a lot done. I worked on advertising for Ericksons and Viking MMA, contacted a couple of managers about our exhibition fight, and finalized the graphic we're going to use for merchandising. All in all, it's been a great week.

"Hey," she says, appearing at the top of the stairs. "Can you still help me with the class tonight?"

Wild horses couldn't drag me away.

"Sure," I say, keeping my eyes on the stack of papers so I don't look too eager. "If you need me."

"I do. A few of my mama's friends signed up for the class yesterday, so we'll have at least three newbies. And if everyone who's signed up comes, we'll have an odd number again, so I'll need you to pair up with someone." She winks, and I know she's conspiring. "Think you can take another beatdown?"

"Is that a challenge?"

"You know you like her."

My immediate response is *no I don't*. But that's juvenile and would make me a liar, so I don't say it. Instead, I shake my head and tuck my chin to my chest to hide my smile.

"It's okay, you know?"

"What?" I ask, playing dumb as I stuff my laptop into its case.

Tempest laughs and it sounds endearing and sympathetic. "To like her."

When I finally glance up at her, I know she sees everything from the way her smile grows and then fades. "You know," she starts, pulling out one of the chairs at the table and sitting down. "When your brother first came to town, I was in a horrible place. The first night I met him, I was celebrating my divorce and my name change."

"And you danced on the bar."

Her eyes grow wide and so does her smile. "He told you? Oh my God. I'm going to kill him."

I laugh, running a hand through my hair. Thanks to Missy's deep-conditioning treatment, it feels amazing. "I think that's one of the things I love most about you."

She blushes a little but continues. "Anyway, I was in a bad place and definitely not looking for a man, even though the thought had crossed my mind. There's no way I would've ever gone through with a one-night stand or anything like that. It's just not me. And I'm not suggesting that for you, but maybe having a female companion while you're in town wouldn't hurt."

Sighing, I rub my eyes. "I promised myself I wouldn't," I admit. "Beyond that, Maggie seems like a really good person and I don't want to string her along or give her false hopes."

"Maybe she's just looking for a companion too?" Tempest asks, shrugging nonchalantly, but I can see it all over her face that she knows better.

We sit in silence for a moment and I let myself wonder what could it hurt?

She's an adult.

I'm an adult.

No harm, no foul, right?

"She was the one who was married," Tempest says quietly. "Not you. You didn't lie. She did. You didn't cheat—"

"She made me a cheater," I say, cutting her off, feeling the familiar punch in my gut every time I think about it. One thing I always said I'd never do was cheat. I had a girlfriend in high school who was screwing the captain of the football team the entire time we were together, behind my back. When I found out, I was more pissed than anything, but it also made me feel like shit and I swore I'd never do that to anyone. I also didn't plan on dating another cheater, but here we are.

"Don't let your past dictate your future."

Smirking, I shake my head. "Did you read that in a fortune cookie?"

"No," she says, chuckling. "It's a piece of wisdom someone gave me and I think you need it, so I'm giving it to you. It's yours now."

"Thank you," I say, feeling grateful. After years of having asshole brothers, it's nice having women around to talk to who aren't my mother. She's great and all, but she's a bit biased, so her advice is often skewed.

"One last bit of wisdom," Tempest says, standing from her seat and walking toward the stairs. "Sometimes the second chance is better than the first time ever dreamed of being."

A few moments later, I follow Tempest downstairs and watch Gunnar and Vince spar for a few before women start filing in for the class. Keeping my eyes on the mirrors, I watch for Maggie's tall form and gorgeous dark hair.

There she is.

Of course, all my body parts take notice, but it's the warmth in my chest that catches me off guard. I just met this woman, so why am I reacting this way? I watch and she walks over to the back wall and places her bag down, eyes scanning the gym until they come to rest on me.

And then they find mine in the mirror staring back at her.

She smiles and then turns to do something with her bag, giving me a fantastic view of her ass.

Oh, the things I'd love to do with that ass. It's luscious and full. Perfectly grippable.

Pretending like she doesn't know I'm watching her, she walks over and joins the rest of the women who have started congregating on the mats.

When Tempest greets everyone, I decide it's time for me to stop being a voyeur and join them.

Standing in the back of the class, I continue to watch Maggie under the ruse of assisting Tempest. When she started out, she was unsure of her movements, which is understandable. For a lot of people, the act of defending themselves is a foreign concept. Even if they've seen it in movies or television shows, they've never actually done it. Some can get it with a simple explanation, where others have to actually do the movements to understand.

Maggie isn't entirely in tune with her body, which is obvious from watching her. Well, obvious for me, because I grew up in a gym and watched my dad turn average people off the street into world-class fighters. My understanding of the human body goes a bit further than most. Even though I didn't choose to train or fight for a living doesn't mean I don't know how to do those things. So when it's time for Maggie and me to pair up, I don't hesitate.

Going to her, I immediately switch into training mode, giving her instruction specific to her.

"You're not turning your hips enough," I tell her, silently asking with my eyes if it's okay for me to position her where she should be. She doesn't hesitate, but I do notice the slight blush as I place my hands on her waist and shift her hips. "Like that," I continue, fighting my body's natural responses to her the entire time.

She practices the movement a couple of times and then her eyes lock with mine.

"Feel the difference?"

Nodding, her eyes dart to my mouth and I can't help darting my tongue out to lick my bottom lip, imagining what it would feel like to kiss her full lips. She doesn't wear lipstick, I've noticed, but her lips are a natural shade of pink.

"Yeah," she finally breaths out, causing my dick to twitch.

When Tempest asks the class to come back together, I clear my throat and step away, but the connection between me and Maggie doesn't sever. It's crackling like a live wire.

I notice Maggie takes her time after class. First, she gets a drink of water. Then, she uses a towel to blot her face. Last, she glances behind her to find me, and when she sees the rest of the class has dispersed, she finally stuffs everything back in her bag and stands up.

Walking toward her, I make a split-second decision, not leaving any time for second-guessing.

"Come to Genie's with us tonight."

It's not a question or even a suggestion, it's more of a demand, but I can't help it. I want to spend more time with her. I want to spin her around on the dance floor again and hold her close. And if she looks at me again, like she did in class—with hungry eyes and wanting lips—I'm going to kiss her.

I need to kiss her.

CHAPTER 12

MAGGIE

Hey, Ever,
Okay, you're right. He's definitely not gay. At least, I don't think
he is. Unless he ASKED ME TO GO TO GENIE'S TONIGHT
because he wants to hang out as friends. But I don't think so.
Because I caught him staring at my lips and butt... I mean, a
gay guy would not be interested in my lips and butt, right?
Also, I think he wanted to kiss me.
Admitting that makes my stomach do all sorts of funny things
because GOD I WANT TO KISS HIM TOO.
I'm meeting him and the rest of the Erickson clan in thirty
minutes, so I've gotta run. Just wanted to say, thanks for the
advice and always listening to my rambling nonsense.

Your Tennessee Bestie,
Maggie

CHAPTER 13

VALI

$\mathcal{T}$onight, Maggie is still a little nervous but she's also engaging and funny and so interesting. She's spent the past half hour regaling us with tales from the feed store, which might sound boring but when it involves people who don't own animals buying harnesses and rope? Well, let's just say, we're all ears.

"No way," Tempest says, her hand coming up to cover her mouth. "He asked for a bit too?"

"Bit, reins, the whole nine yards," Maggie confirms with a nod as she reaches for a peanut and cracks the shell. I watch as her mouth opens and then as she chews.

Why is that intriguing?

Fuck if I know.

Every single thing Maggie O'Neal does is either a turn-on or the most interesting thing I've seen. I'd like to blame my response to her on my limited exposure while residing in Green Valley, but I feel like it wouldn't matter where I met her, I'd still be attracted.

Tempest is right, *I like her.*

"You have to tell us who," Gunnar demands with a chuckle, one arm around Frankie who swats at his chest for being so damn nosy.

Maggie takes a drink of her water and shakes her head. "Nope, I'm not a gossip."

See, she could spill this guy's name, but she won't, not even for the sake of the story.

I really like that about her.

"Who wants to lose at darts?" Cage asks, picking up his mug of beer and downing it.

Frankie slides out of the booth and stands. "I don't mind handing your ass to you."

Cage's grin widens because he knows she can back up her claim and he's obviously hankering for a challenge. Cage and Gunnar taught her how to play and now she wipes the floor with them both anytime she gets the chance.

"I was kind of hoping for another spin around the dance floor," I whisper in Maggie's ear and notice the way she shivers. It's slight, but it's there and it lets me know I'm getting to her too.

When I stand and offer her my hand, she doesn't hesitate.

"Gunnar and I will hold down the fort," Tempest calls out, smiling like a loon when I wrap an arm around Maggie's shoulders and literally spin her onto the dance floor.

Her laugh is contagious and one of the best sounds I've ever heard.

Just like last Friday, she surprises me with her moves. Honestly, the first time I asked her to dance, after her admission she'd never been to Genie's, I thought she'd tell me she didn't know how, which wouldn't have deterred me. But unlike so many things, she's an old pro on the dance floor.

"Who taught you how to dance?" I ask, pulling her close as a slow song comes on.

She leans her head into my chest and I can't help but hug her to me a little tighter.

"My mom and dad always danced in the living room growing up. When my mom would get tired, I was her backup. My dad taught me everything I know."

I hear the love in her voice as she shares that part of herself and it's sweet, just like Maggie.

Running a hand down her hair, I gently grip her neck and place my lips at the crown of her head.

God, I want her, but my brain and body are still battling it out. Except now, it's not just about me and my past, it's about Maggie. I don't want to hurt her. And if she's as innocent as Miss Faye said, I fear I might.

Maggie tilts her head back to look at me, determination in her gaze. "Do you want to kiss me?"

I chuckle, biting down on my lip before responding. "I want to do so many things to you," I admit, my voice dropping low as I keep my eyes on the people around us, but my attention fully on her. "Kissing you is at the top of that list, but I'm worried once I get started, I won't want to stop."

When I look down into her stunning brown eyes, I see the same desire I feel shining back at me and take the opportunity I'm offered.

I kiss Maggie O'Neal.

CHAPTER 14

MAGGIE

*H*e's kissing me.

Vali Erickson is kissing me.

And I'm kissing him back.

As my fingers find purchase in his shirt, I pull myself closer. Our lips are pressed together and my entire body feels like it's on fire, melting under his touch.

When Vali's tongue swipes across my bottom lip, I open my mouth on instinct. His taste is minty mixed with a hint of beer and it's my new favorite flavor. Moving my mouth in tandem with his, my heart feels like it's in my throat and I'm not getting enough air to breathe.

But if I were to die, right here on this dance floor, I'd die happy.

My mind feels detached as my body takes over—hands roaming, hard muscles tensing, lips tingling. There's no thinking or overthinking, just feeling.

So much feeling.

"Maggie," Vali whispers against my lips, bringing me back down to earth. His hand slides from my jaw into my hair as he presses our foreheads together, breathing deeply. "God, I want you."

My eyes flutter open and I realize we're still in the middle of the dance floor at Genie's, and even though everyone is doing their own thing, I know we've caught a few people's attention and it's enough of a wake-up call to make my heart start to pound again.

"I should go," I say quietly, but my grip doesn't loosen on his shirt.

When my lips brush his cheek, he chuckles and it's low and rumbly and vibrates through my body. "You sure about that?"

"Yes," I say, closing my eyes and leaning into him. "No."

I'm not sure my legs even work at this point, but if I don't leave, I'm liable to do something completely inappropriate, far more inappropriate than kissing a hot Viking in the middle of Genie's.

"How about I walk you to your car?" Vali asks, his lips at my ear. "Then I can kiss you again without an audience."

"Okay," I manage to say, but I'm pretty sure it came out more of a moan than a verbal response.

Escorting me back to the table, Vali retrieves my purse. Thankfully, everyone else is off playing pool, so I don't have to be cordial or make complete sentences. Instead, I offer them a smile and wave as we make our way toward the door.

Once outside, I feel a warm, strong hand on my waist as Vali anchors me to his side.

The cold night air is a vast contrast to my overheated skin and I use the opportunity to take in deep, cleansing breaths as we walk the short distance to my car.

"I had a great time tonight," Vali says, dipping his head down to nuzzle my neck.

Oh, God.

"Me—me too," I stutter, my words matching my breathing that's now coming out in choppy pants.

Is this real life?

Am I really here?

I've always heard the phrase *one thing leads to another* as an explanation of how two people ended up having sex. I never understood that completely until now. For the first time in my life, I realize how one thing—like kissing on a dance floor—could lead to sex.

At this point, all of my blood has left my brain and is pulsating between my legs.

Get ahold of yourself, Maggie.

Deep breaths.

When we get to my car, I distract myself and my erratic thoughts and breathing by digging through my purse for my keys. Before I can even make a move to unlock my door, Vali snatches them out of my hand with a wicked grin.

Oh, God. Ohgodohgodohgod.

Have I mentioned how far out of my league I am?

Backing me against the door, he braces his thick, strong arms on either side of me, caging me in. "You're so gorgeous," he mutters, his mouth bypassing mine and going for my neck. My eyes fall closed as my arms snake up between us and wrap around his shoulders.

When his teeth scrape against the skin at my collarbone, I almost combust.

But then he presses his long… hard… *body* against mine. And I feel everything.

Oh, God.

He chuckles again, his head tilting back up and our eyes meet. For a moment, he just stares at me, his teeth coming out to work his full bottom lip. I swallow and try to control my breathing but it's useless. I'm a lost cause.

"You're nervous," he says softly. It's not a question, but an observation, and he's right.

I nod.

"Don't be nervous." His voice drops even lower and he leans in to brush his nose against mine. "I'll never do anything you don't want me to."

I nod again, letting out a shaky breath.

"Do you want me to kiss you again?"

Nod.

That glorious laugh echoes out over the parking lot. "I'm going to need a little more than that... just to make sure I'm not reading you wrong."

Swallowing again, I reach deep for those lady balls. "I really, *really* want you to kiss me again."

"That's what I thought."

This time it's not subtle or sweet. Vali dominates my mouth and caresses my body like he's claiming it for his own and I willingly give it to him. My toes curl in my boots as his tongue swipes against mine. When I feel his hand slip down my back and grab a handful of my butt, I suck in a gulp of air and hold back a groan.

Never.

I've never felt this turned on—out of my mind, feral, carnal.

"Vali," I moan, when our mouths part and he begins to nip and kiss my neck. "Please... I don't..."

I don't know what I'm saying. I don't even know my name.

"What do you want, Maggie?" Vali asks, his voice deep and smooth, pouring over me like warm honey. "Anything you want... just tell me."

"I—I..." Pulling back, I take a deep breath and try to focus, scrambling for an answer. As the cold air hits me, my reasoning starts to come back in full force and I realize how close I was to telling Vali I want everything—more kisses, more touching, more of his body... anything and everything he's willing to give me.

Brushing a strand of hair behind my ear, Vali stands up to his full height, putting an inch of distance between us. "Can I kiss you again sometime?"

Swallowing hard, I nod and then respond with a, "Yeah."

"Yeah?"

More fervently, I shake my head. "Yes, you can kiss me again sometime." And other things, hopefully, but not tonight. Tonight, kissing is enough because I need a chance to process what's happening.

"This was the best first date I've ever been on," Vali whispers, leaning forward to brush his lips against my cheek. "You, Maggie O'Neal, are making me rethink everything I came to Green Valley for."

"And what's that?" I ask, the journalist in me sparking to life.

He smiles, swiping his thumb over his bottom lip and then running a hand through his hair.

I wish I would've spent more time with my hands in that hair.

Next time?

Yeah, there will definitely be a next time.

"I came to get away," he finally says and I feel the equal parts of truth and evasion. "And I promised myself I wouldn't get involved."

That admission feels like a bucket of cold water. "Oh," I whisper, touching my lips as if I'm trying to hold in the heat from our kisses, just in case they're the only ones I get.

"But that was before I met you."

"Oh."

We stand there for a few more moments, our eyes locked and unspoken conversations passing between us. I appreciate his honesty, but I'd love to know more about what brought him to Green Valley. However, I can tell he's not ready to share more about that, so for now, I'll accept the small truths he's given me and be happy that something about me has caught Vali Erickson's attention.

It's a heady feeling, to say the least.

"Good night, Maggie," Vali finally says, leaning around me and opening my door for me.

"Good night, Vali," I reply, sliding into my car and instantly missing his touch and heat.

When I get home, my parents are in bed, but I can see the dim light from my mother's lamp switch off when she hears my bedroom door open. Smiling, I quietly step into my room and shut the door, sliding down to the floor and leaning my back against it for support.

I kissed Vali.

Vali kissed me.

And he wants to do it again.

And I want more—things I've only read about. His hands on my body. His skin on mine. I want to experience what it's like to lose control of myself and give in to the desires building inside me.

I want all of that with Vali.

Exhaling, I press my fingers to my lips together and try to breathe deeply through my nose to relax my racing heart. After a few minutes of reveling in the aftermath of the most amazing night of my life, I pull myself up off the floor and head to the bathroom to wash my face and slip into my comfy pajamas.

Later, when I'm lying in bed staring at the ceiling, I let my mind replay every touch and caress, trying to recall every second with as much detail as possible. In the quiet darkness, my phone dings from my nightstand and startles me.

Swiping across the screen I see it's an email from Everly.

Okay, it's midnight and I know you, so you're home by now. TELL ME EVERYTHING.

Biting back a smile, I hit reply and spare no details.

CHAPTER 15

VALI

*I*t's been five days since my date with Maggie and I've spent the entire time wanting to kick my own ass for not getting her phone number. I hate that we shared the two most amazing kisses of my life and haven't spoken or even texted since. Such a jackass move on my part, even though it was purely unintentional.

I thought about digging into the files and getting her number from there, but that's not technically ethical and I only want it if she wants to give it to me. It's been crazy busy at the gym this week, but whenever I've had free time, I've walked around downtown, hoping to bump into her somewhere. Unfortunately, I've had zero luck.

Gunnar loved reminding me that, if she really wanted to talk to me, she knew where to find me and that our first date must not have been *that* great. Of course, he's a little shit who loves to get a rise out of me, which he does.

The crazy thing is I don't ever remember feeling this intensely about someone this early on—not even Chloe—and it's kind of scary.

Since there's no way I can wait two more days to see her, later this morning I plan to make a trip to O'Neal Feed and Fodder. But, first, it's time for another Erickson Family Meeting.

I make my way downstairs and fix myself a cup of coffee while I wait for everyone else to show up. I'm thinking about a second cup when Cage, Gunnar, and Frankie finally walk in.

"It's about time," I greet them. "I was about to call it good and go run my errands. The only reason I stayed was because I assumed Tempest was bringing muffins."

"Lay off Tempest. She'll be here when she gets here," Cage grumbles.

"Sorry we're late. We stayed up watching scary movies last night and then overslept. Can you believe Gunnar has never watched *A Nightmare on Elm Street*?" Frankie pauses pouring her coffee to give us a look of incredulity.

"Yeah, he'd try to watch horror movies with us when we were younger and would always get too freaked out. He'd run and tattle to Mom and get us in trouble, even though we were old enough to watch." Cage gives Gunnar a look like he's still annoyed about the movies but Gunnar shrugs it off.

"Whatever, bro. You're just bitter I've always been the favorite." Gunnar sips his smoothie, looking like the smug bastard he is.

"Anyway," Cage redirects. "Let's get started. Vali, what's up with the grand opening for the ring?"

"I'm glad you asked, big brother. Everything is pretty much ready to go. I have our sponsors all lined up and I'm ninety-nine-point-five percent sure we're getting a solid 'yes' from Michael 'Maneater' Mancini as our special guest. His manager is supposed to call me later today to confirm. And, lastly, we're set to raise a nice chunk of change for the women's shelter again."

Gunnar nudges Frankie and her smile grows. "That's awesome, Vali, Thank you."

"I'm here! I'm here!" We all turn our attention to Tempest as she barrels into the kitchen. She places a box on the table and lets out a large sigh. "Sorry I'm late. I was trying out a new muffin recipe and lost track of time."

Cage pulls her onto his lap and kisses the side of her head. I watch as he whispers something in her ear, causing her to blush while nodding her head, and my thoughts immediately turn to Maggie. Cage and Tempest have this deep connection and intimacy I envy. I'd love to share something like that with Maggie one of these days, but I honestly don't know if it's possible. As much as I'm enjoying getting to know her, I don't know if I'm ready for that... and I don't know if she is either.

"Go on, y'all." Tempest points to the box of muffins. "Eat 'em while they're still warm. Remember, this is a brand-new recipe, so you're my guinea pigs."

"Say no more." I grab the box and open it, releasing a sweet but delicious aroma into the air. Tempest has the gall to look nervous as I take a muffin out, then pass the box to Frankie and Gunnar, who reluctantly passes. I don't know what she's worried about; she's never created a muffin less than amazing. There must be something special about these.

"Gunnar, you need to try one," Cage says, surprising us all.

Gunnar eyes Cage suspiciously. "But I'm training. You said I couldn't have any until after my next bout."

"Well, as your coach and your brother, I'm telling you to try one." Cage gives Gunnar a look that shows he means business, causing Gunnar to quickly grab one and shove it into his mouth.

Fucking animal.

I bite into my muffin and my eyes roll back as the sweet strawberry filling hits my tongue. Tempest has struck gold again, not that I ever doubted her. "Tempest, this is delicious. You have another hit on your hands, for sure."

Frankie chimes in. "OMG, it's so good. What are these called again?"

Tempest looks at Cage and smiles before answering. "They're called Having My Baby."

We're so into our muffins, it takes a few seconds to realize what she's said. Gunnar is the first to put two and two together and literally jumps out of his chair, glaze smeared all over his chin.

"Wait a damn minute," he says, a small bite of muffin still in his meaty paw. "Is this your way of telling us you're gonna have a baby?"

My eyes widen as I watch Cage and Tempest look at each other and then yell in unison, "We're pregnant!"

Frankie screams and rushes over to hug them both, followed closely by Gunnar.

I wait for the commotion to calm down before joining in. My last bite of muffin must've gotten stuck in my throat or something because it's burning and my eyes are watering a bit.

Yeah, it's the muffins.

I'm sure it has nothing to do with the fact Tempest has wanted a baby for so long and thought she struggled with infertility before she met Cage.

Damn, when did I get so soft?

"I'm so happy for you both." I kiss Tempest on the cheek before hugging my brother. "First grandbaby in the family. Mom is gonna lose her mind."

"Yeah," he chuckles. "It'll be worth it, though."

I look at Tempest, her glowing face so obvious now. "It sure will be."

"So, do you know the sex? This strawberry muffin makes me think you're having a baby girl." Frankie is clearly over the moon as she excitedly asks her question.

"No, it's still a little early to tell. I already have a blueberry muffin in rotation, so I thought I'd try strawberry this time."

"Well, it's perfect and you know I'll answer any questions you may have, if you can't get a hold of your OB-GYN."

"I was hoping you'd say that!" Tempest says, looking relieved. "Is it normal for my boobs to be this big when I'm barely out of my first trimester?"

"On that note," I loudly declare, "I have some errands to run, so I'll see you all later."

"Aww, come on. I didn't have you pegged to be a fuddy-duddy, Vali," Tempest laughs.

"I'm no such thing; I just don't need to know... well, anything about the ways my sister's body is changing."

It's sweet how Tempest's face softens when I refer to her as *my sister*.

"I agree," Cage chimes in. "Frankie is the only family member allowed to discuss Tempest's body besides myself. Meeting adjourned."

As I make my way to Cage's truck, the cool air is welcomed as it refreshes me, giving me clarity.

A baby. Wow.

Things will be very different once it's here but only in the best of ways. I wonder if Tempest has been sick this whole time and just not said anything about it. I know I'm pretty clueless when it comes to things like this but, thinking back, I don't recall ever noticing her behaving any different than usual. Even in her self-defense class, she hasn't left any clues. Eventually, I imagine, she'll need to adapt her class around her pregnancy. I'm hopeful Frankie will be ready to step in when that happens but, if not, I will.

A short drive later, my GPS leads me down a road just out of town, straight to O'Neal Feed and Fodder.

Why am I nervous?

I'm just here to ask Maggie for her phone number and to see if she'd like to go out on a real date, where I pick her up and we go out, just the two of us. It's not a big deal. She can say no and I'll survive. I may have to move back to Dallas sooner than I'd planned but it'll be fine.

Lies.

I mentally roll my eyes at myself while getting out of the truck and walking inside the store. I locate the cash register immediately and am disappointed to see no one behind it. Hopefully, she's just in the back of the store or taking a break. I decide to look around the store to distract myself. Patience is not always a virtue of mine.

There are so many things here I've never seen before. Who knew farm animals needed so much shit?

As I reach out to take an item off a shelf to get a better look at it, I hear the voice I've missed since Friday night.

"Vali, is that you?"

I turn around and see Maggie looking at me curiously. At least she doesn't look angry that I'm here, invading her work life.

"Yeah, hi. How are you?"

"What are you doing here?" she asks, stepping closer to me.

"Well…" I pause to look around, making sure no one can hear. "I realized I never got your phone number the other night at Genie's and I wanted to ask you out again."

"You came out all this way to ask me out?" For some reason, this information seems to surprise her but it shouldn't. I think I've made it clear how much I want her.

"Not just for that, but yeah. I didn't want to wait until your next class and this was the only day I could get away. Sorry I took so long."

"Why else did you come here?"

I love that she's tall enough for me to look into her gorgeous chocolate-brown eyes without needing to bend over. I have a perfect view of them sparkling back at me, eager for my answer.

"As you know," I say, my voice lowering, "we shared quite an incredible kiss Friday night. Well, two to be exact." Maggie blushes and her reaction causes me to chuckle. "And I really did hate not being able to call you the next day and see how you were doing; I didn't want you to think I was ghosting you."

I don't want to break eye contact with her because I want her to know I'm being sincere, but her full lips are trying their damnedest to distract me. If I look at her lips, I'm liable to do something that could get Maggie fired and me arrested, or at the very least banned from the store.

"Don't worry about it. I didn't think you were ghosting me. It's probably best we didn't talk until now. The store has been busy and I needed time to, uh… process."

"Process? Process what?"

"Our date, the kiss… us." She starts fidgeting with the hem of her shirt, showing how nervous she is. "That was not typical behavior for me and I was feeling a lot of… well, *feelings,* so I needed to process them. It's what I do. I'm a processor," she says with a shrug.

She's too fucking cute.

"I respect that. Have you finished processing? Is it too soon to ask for another date or your phone number?"

"No, I—"

"Maggie, can you come help at the register, please?"

We both look to where the voice came from and I see a woman who looks just like Maggie, only older, waving at us.

"Be right there!" Maggie yells back before facing me again with pink cheeks. "That's my mom. She looks pretty swamped up there. Don't leave, okay?"

"You got it," I tell her, giving her my best smile.

Maggie's eyes go a bit dreamy before she turns to head toward the counter. While she helps her mom, I continue browsing the store. Something catches my eye and I immediately start laughing, remembering the story Maggie told us while at Genie's.

Catching her attention, I hold up the metal horse-bit I found and quirk my eyebrow at her. Her eyes widen and she mouths *oh my God* before schooling her features and turning back to her customer.

Oh, yeah, this is fun.

Next, I grab a set of reins. When I feel Maggie's gaze on me again, I move my arms up and down, pretending I'm riding… a horse. Yeah, a horse, that's it.

Her eyes are practically bugging out of her head now but I'm the one in trouble. Even though I was only trying to be silly with the reins, that didn't stop fantasies of Maggie in my bed flooding my brain. Images of her under me, over me, tied to the bed, and on all fours have me cussing my lack of control.

Please don't let anyone think I get turned on in feed stores.

I can see the headline in Trixie and Tess's column now: "*Vali Erickson's Dark Secrets Revealed… It's Fillies over Females for one Viking Invader!*"

Deciding I need to refocus my efforts to entertain Maggie, I take a crop off its display on the wall. I admire it for a few seconds before I quickly pop it in the air.

Without looking, I already know that surprised yelp coming from across the room was made by Maggie. She's made that sound before. Like the time she sat in the chair wrong while she was observing Tempest's class for the first time. This time, though, the sound she made is clear but deeper, maybe? She kind of sounds intrigued, and I hope I'm right. I'd love to treat her luscious ass to some sexy spanking one of these days.

I give the whip one more crack before I hear a throat clearing behind me.

"May I help you?"

Laying the crop down, I turn to face the man talking to me. *Shit*, I bet this is Maggie's dad.

"Oh, no, sir. I'm just looking around." I give him a charming smile, but not too charming. Parents can smell a bullshitter from a mile away, and at first glance, Mr. O'Neal seems like a straight shooter.

"Mmm-hmmm," is all he says before eyeing me up and down with a very scrutinizing gaze. When he stands in the aisle with his arms crossed, watching my every movement, I decide it's time to make my exit.

Giving him a tight smile, I nod my head and tell him to have a good day as I make my way to the front door.

On my way out, I make eye contact with Maggie, she looks mortified. I'm not sure if that's because of me or her dad or both but I think we can all agree this was not the best first interaction.

I'm almost back to the truck when I hear Maggie yelling for me to wait.

"Here," she says, slipping a piece of paper into my palm. She's breathing heavy, hair blowing, cheeks still flushed. Before I can say anything, she grabs my shirt and pulls me toward her, kissing me quickly. Just as I'm getting a taste of her, she pulls back and offers me a gorgeous smile before running back inside the store.

I get settled into the truck and start it up before opening the note. Opening it, I see it's a receipt from the register and on the back, in neat handwriting, is exactly what I came here for.

Yes, I want to go out with you again.

Here's my number.

Use it.

Hell, yeah. Mission accomplished.

CHAPTER 16

MAGGIE

Dear Trixie and Tess,

I think I'm in love with two people.

One is someone my parents approve of and we have a nice time together but he doesn't get my juices going, if you know what I mean. *wink*

The second is someone I'm secretly dating but I know my parents would never approve of, but he just does it for me.

On one hand, I can see myself marrying the first guy. Our life together would be secure and my family would accept him with open arms, but would I regret it down the road? When the kids are grown and out of the house, is a nice guy enough?

And then there's the other guy who would be a gamble, but I know our life would never be boring. Would my family grow to love him? Would we stay so passionate?

Help! I don't know what to do.

Torn in Tennessee

* * *

Dear Torn in Tennessee,

Our short answer is: go with your heart.

Our long answer is: you have some questions to ask yourself.
Are you attracted to both men? Man #1 might be a family
favorite, but is he yours? Even though physical attraction isn't
everything in a relationship, it is an important element. Without
attraction, your relationship will more than likely lack passion
and intimacy. A marriage without passion and intimacy is
nothing more than a friendship bound by a contract.

Another thing you might ask yourself is are they both ready for
a relationship? Man #2 might be fun to be around, but is he
husband material? If you're ready to commit yourself to
someone for life, make sure they're ready to do the same.

Our last piece of advice may sound juvenile, but when we have
a tough decision to make, we often make a pro and con list.
Now, we might get to the end and choose the option with the
most cons, but at least we're choosing it with eyes wide open.
The decision might not be easy, but it's better to make the hard
choices now so you don't have to live with the wrong choice for
the rest of your life.

We'll leave you with this quote from Shakespeare, "The course
of true love never did run smooth."

Best of Luck in Love,
Trixie and Tess

*E*xhaling, I sit back and read over the words on my computer screen. Relationship advice is my favorite kind to give. That might sound crazy because I haven't been in many relationships, but it's true. I've read a lot about love and observed a lot about love. What can I say? I love love.

Whoever Torn in Tennessee is, I really hope she thinks long and hard about these two men before she makes a decision that could affect the rest of her life. If I really gave her my full advice, I'd tell her to break it off with both of them. The first guy is obviously not a love match and the second guy sounds like he's a good time, but maybe not marriage material. But part of being a good advice columnist is being unbiased and giving the advice seeker something to work with so they can draw their own conclusion.

Before I can close my laptop and call it a night, an email from Everly pops up.

> *Hey, Mags,*
> *Are you up late writing your article?*
> *E*

I smile because she knows me so well, probably better than anyone.

> *You know me too well… or maybe just the right amount. ;)*
> *What's up?*

For a second, I appreciate the connection Everly and I have. But that thought leads to someone I'd like to know better and have more of a connection with. Ever since Vali stopped by the store earlier today and asked for my phone number, I've felt like I'm floating on cloud nine.

Then, he texted me.

Who knew a few little words on a screen would feel so good?

It was sweet and simple, just him telling me thank you for giving him my number and agreeing to go out with him again. I replied with a simple, "You're welcome." Glancing over at my phone, I wonder if it's too late to text him, and if I did, what would I say?

Everly's next email pops up.

> *I need some advice from the advice columnist.*

*There's a client who came to an event I hosted last week, and
instead of making a match for him, he's decided to set his sights
on me.*
The down and dirty…
*He's handsome and totally someone I'd notice in a bar or club.
He's employed and owns a house in the Garden District. There
isn't an ex-wife or children. But something in my gut tells me
not to get mixed up with him. Am I being too guarded? Using
my policy of not dating clients as an excuse to not explore my
options? Help!*

Squaring my shoulders, I put my advice columnist hat back on and
give her my knee-jerk response.

Ever,
Always trust your gut. Always.
*Playing the devil's advocate here, but if he's so wonderful, why
is he single?*
Also, how old is he?
Mags

After I hit send on the email back to Everly, I pick up my phone and
open up the text messages from Vali. As I wait for Everly's response, I
type out a new message to Vali.

**Me: I know it's late, but I just want you to know I'm thinking
about you.**

The next email from Everly comes through, so I put my phone back on
the nightstand and try not to overthink it. Maybe it's the mood I'm in
or the advice columnist but being open and honest feels right tonight.

Mags,
*You're right. I know I should always trust my gut, which is
exactly why I'm going to turn him down for the gala he invited*

me to. As for your other answer, he's at least ten years older than me, but that's never been an issue with me before. And in his defense, he's very career-oriented, so I'd have to guess he's been busy for about twenty years. But you're right, if he's so great, why is he using my services for matchmaking? That's definitely something to think about.
Thanks for always being a voice of reason.
Speaking of, how's Vali?
E

Biting back a smile, I type out a response, filling her in on him dropping by the feed store and asking for my number and another date. After exchanging a few more emails, we say good night and I put my laptop on my desk and finish getting ready for bed.

After I turn out my light, I grab my phone and open it up to a response from Vali.

Vali: It's never too late for you.

When the little dots pop up to signal him typing, I wait to see what else he has to say.

Vali: And I've been lying here wondering if it was too late to text you. So I'm glad you texted first. :)

Vali: I've been thinking about you since the first day you walked into the gym.

After that, something scary happens. I start typing a response to Vali, telling him I was up late writing my article, like he knows about that part of my life. Thankfully, I catch my mistake before I hit send and erase it and start over.

Me: Then we're even. ;)

Vali: Go out with me this Saturday?

Vali: Or, actually. I want to cook dinner for you and maybe watch a movie?

My stomach flips and I have to fight back a ridiculous scream of delight.

Me: Yes to all of that.

Yes to everything with you.

CHAPTER 17

VALI

"So, what are you making?" Tempest asks, taking another hot pan of muffins out of the oven.

Sighing, I take a sip of my coffee. "I was thinking something simple like pasta or chicken. I really just want to have a chance to talk to her and get to know her better."

"Now, that's the sweetest thing I've heard in a while," Jennifer, the owner of Donner Bakery, says from her spot over at the opposing counter where she's decorating one of her famous banana cakes.

Tempest chuckles, pulling off her oven mitts and tossing them down beside the cooling muffins.

"What?" I ask, raising an eyebrow in challenge.

She smirks, shaking her head. "Oh, nothing."

"You think I'm trying to get in her pants," I deadpan.

This gets a chuckle out of Jenn and the two women share a look.

"I'm being serious," I say, sounding as affronted as I feel. "I mean, sure, I wouldn't mind getting to know her in every sense of the word, but I really am looking forward to learning more about Maggie, the person."

Tempest's expression softens and she gives me a small smile.

Jenn sighs. "I knew you were a good egg."

"Thank you," I tell her.

"Well," Tempest says, grabbing a box and setting it down in front of her. "I'm glad to see you moving on and getting out there…"

Her slight hesitation has me cocking my head and asking, "But?" I notice the way she swallows and glances away from me. "What?"

"Don't take this the wrong way," she begins, meeting Jenn's gaze and then looking back at me. Squaring her shoulders, she continues, "Maggie is sweet and smitten. You can see it in the way she looks at you and hangs on every word you say."

For some reason, I feel my cheeks heat up a little under her observation.

"I guess what I'm trying to say is be careful."

"With her?" I ask, not really needing the clarification, but seeking it anyway.

Tempest nods and wipes her hands on her apron.

"I know you're not planning on staying," she huffs out. "And I just don't want to see either of you get hurt, that's all."

Taking a sip of my coffee, I let that sink in and slide down along with the hot liquid. She's right, I don't plan on being in Green Valley forever. So, what am I doing getting involved with someone? I know I should stick to my original plan—no sex, no relationships. I should finish what I came here to do, which was flying under the radar and staying away from Dallas until the storm blew over, then get back to my life. But, at this point, how can I not explore the attraction I feel to Maggie O'Neal?

She's all I can think about.

All I want.

"I see your wheels turning," Tempest says, stepping away from the counter and crossing her arms. "I'm not telling you to not *get to know her*." Pausing, she gives me a smirk. "All I'm saying is be upfront with her and don't lead her on. If you're both on the same page, everyone's hearts should stay intact."

Swallowing the sudden lump in my throat, I nod. "Geez, Dr. Phil," I quip, needing a change of subject. "I came for a box of muffins, not a therapy session."

"Oh, hush." Tossing an oven mitt at me, she walks over with a box of muffins in hand. "Islands in the Stream," she says. "They've always been good luck for me and will make a great dessert regardless if you have chicken or pasta."

Leaning forward, I place a quick kiss on her cheek. "Thank you."

"Be careful out there," Jenn calls out as I leave the back exit.

I shake my head, laughing as the door closes behind me.

This is Green Valley. The worst thing that could happen is I trip on my shoelaces. Before I take another step, I glance down at my feet to make sure I didn't just jinx myself. When I see they're still tied tight, I take off across the street.

After I stop back by the studio to run the muffins upstairs, I grab my beanie and a pair of gloves and head out for my run. It's brisk, but the burn feels good. My thoughts are a bit scattered as all of Tempest's advice filters through my mind. I play her words over and over for about five miles.

At one point, I almost have myself convinced to call this whole thing off, but then Maggie's face pops up in my mind and, for a second, I think about what it would be like to never see it again. I have to stop and take a few cleansing breaths before continuing my run. My chest hurts at the thought and not in a way that feels good… not the kind from a good run.

I don't have any answers, but I'll take Tempest's advice and be upfront with Maggie. Hopefully, we're on the same page and we can just see where this thing goes.

But if she doesn't want to risk getting hurt, I'll understand.

Shit, that was me before I met her. I was done taking risks, at least when it came to relationships. I thought I was over it. On a break. A hiatus. But what the hell do I know?

Obviously, nothing.

Absolutely nothing, except Maggie O'Neal is the most intriguing person I've met in a long time, maybe ever. She's sunshine and a breath of fresh air. And if I don't follow my instincts and get to know her better, I'll regret it for the rest of my life.

Before I head back to the studio, I make a lap around the park to make up for all the time I spent breathing on the side of the road.

As I'm passing back by Donner Bakery, there's a line outside the door that goes down the sidewalk. People around here are serious about their baked goods, and rightly so. They're easily the best bakery in the state.

An hour later, after a quick shower, I borrow Cage's truck and head for Piggly Wiggly to buy the ingredients for chicken pomodoro.

Last night at Genie's, Maggie mentioned loving Italian, so this way I don't have to choose between chicken or pasta. I'll make both.

"I've always loved a man who can cook," the cashier says with a wide grin as she scans my items. Her tone is a bit too seductive for the checkout at the Piggly Wiggly, so I give her a small smile and pretend to count my money.

"I've seen you in here a few times," she continues, trying to make conversation. "Are you planning on staying in Green Valley?"

Her question catches me off guard and I'm not sure what my expression looks like, probably something along the lines of why-the-fuck-are-you-so-nosy, but it doesn't deter her as she begins to talk even more.

"Not that it's any of my business, but you're one of those Ericksons, right? The Viking Invasion? I've read about y'all in the gossip column. Seems you've got the attention of pretty much everyone in town with your new fancy gym and all those muscles."

I watch as her eyes scan my body and immediately want to hide behind the rack of glossy magazines. Normally, I like the attention, but she's laying it on a bit thick.

Clearing my throat, I plaster on a fake smile. "Yeah, I'm one of those Ericksons," I repeat with a chuckle. Hoping a little admission will satisfy her enough that I can get out of here without more than her eyes assaulting me.

"Well, if you're ever looking for somewhere to go or something to do," she adds, bagging my last item. "I'm always up for a good time."

"I have a girlfriend," I blurt out. It's a knee-jerk reaction, probably similar to how women feel when they try to go out and have a good time, but douchebags are coming at them from every angle, so they wear a fake wedding band to ward them off. This is my version of a fake wedding band.

After that, she gives me my total and I pay. Based on the sly grins she's giving me, I'm afraid the girlfriend comment seems to be a challenge for her. I might need to bring Maggie with me the next time I buy groceries.

"Have a nice day," she calls out as I walk away with only a wave.

Tempest let me use her kitchen to cook dinner since I don't have all of her fancy-schmancy pots and pans over on my side. Just as I'm finishing up the sauce, she walks up the stairs.

"Something smells amazing," she says, a hand on her belly.

Since they made the announcement about the baby, I've started noticing little things, like her touching her still flat stomach and her appetite or sometimes lack thereof.

"I'll leave you a bowl, if you want."

"No," she says with a scoff, waving me away. "I'm not eating your special dinner. Besides, this baby changes its mind on the hour. Chicken pomodoro may sound disgusting by the time I get around to eating it."

Laughing, I shake my head. Over the years, I've come to terms with not understanding women, but pregnant women take that to a whole new level. "Well, just in case you or the baby change your mind, I'll leave some in the fridge," I tell her, finding a bowl and dishing up some pasta. "I've made enough to feed an army."

"Let me guess," she says, walking around me and pouring a glass of water before planting herself on a barstool. "Since you can cook, you're used to feeding your bottomless-pit brothers."

"Bingo," I tell her, dipping out some sauce for the pasta. "But I'm not the only one who can cook. So, if Cage is trying to pull that one over on you, don't let him. Our mom made sure we all knew how to take care of ourselves and other people—cooking, cleaning, washing clothes. We did it all growing up. I was just more interested in learning her ways in the kitchen than everyone else."

Tempest quirks an eyebrow. "Good to know."

"I better get this over to my side," I tell her, making sure I have everything cleaned up. "Maggie should be here in about fifteen minutes."

"You should invite her to the fight," Tempest says.

I glance over my shoulder and see her watching me. "Yeah, I'm sure she'll be here."

"No, I mean to New Orleans," she amends. "You should invite her to go with us. It would be fun... she'd have fun. We've all been hanging out, so it wouldn't be weird or anything. She could meet Viggo and Ozzi..."

Do I want that?

Do I want Maggie to meet the rest of my family?

We've kissed twice, hung out a few times, and had one official date. Are we ready for that?

"Don't overthink it, Vali."

Swallowing, I cock my head and lick my lips, trying to wrap my brain around the idea. "Weren't you the one who told me to be careful?" I ask. "I'm not sure if we're at the place where I'd invite her to go away with me for the weekend."

"It wouldn't be just you," Tempest teases. "We'd all be there."

She's seemed to shift gears a little and I want to know what her MO is.

"What's this about?" I ask, deciding to shoot straight.

She shrugs. "I see how much she likes you and I see how much you obviously like her," she says, waving her hand toward the food I've prepared. "Most guys would just take a girl out for a burger and a bang, but you're going the extra mile. You like her."

"But that doesn't change the fact I'm going back to Dallas eventually."

Her expression goes soft and she sighs. "I know and I think that's still okay. I don't want what I said earlier to dissuade you from giving this a go. If y'all are meant to be together, fate always finds a way. Look at me and your brother. He didn't plan on sticking around, but he did. And he's happy and I'm happy and we're having a baby."

Tears shine in her eyes and I have to swallow down the emotion.

"Just remember what I said about allowing yourself to have a second chance and not letting your past dictate your future."

"Yeah, all while being careful with Maggie's heart. I know," I say, chuckling. "Thanks, Tempest. And I'll think about it."

As I'm walking down the stairs, I hear her call out.

"Have a nice date and be safe!"

CHAPTER 18

MAGGIE

"*I* can't believe you made this," I tell Vali as I sit back in my chair, still trying to convince myself this is real life. I'm really sitting in the kitchen of Vali's apartment at Viking MMA. He really asked me out on a second date. We're really eating an amazing meal that he prepared.

It's the best date I've ever been on.

"I'm so glad you like it," he says, watching me from across the table with a look that makes my insides tingle. His long legs are stretched out under the table, and occasionally, his foot touches mine. I'm not sure if it's intentional or not, but I can't help the way my stomach clenches every time. "You mentioned liking Italian, so I figured this was a safe bet."

My smile grows. "You pay attention."

"I do," he says, his voice dropping an octave as he swirls the last bit of wine in his glass. "When I like something, I'm very observant and detail-oriented."

And by something, he means me.

In all my twenty-four years, I've never felt the way Vali Erickson makes me feel.

"Tell me something else about you."

That thousand-watt smile flashes and then fades a little before he finally speaks. "I was in a relationship before I came to Green Valley." With his eyes locked on mine, I try not to let my flinch at that admission show, but I'm not sure I'm successful because he leans forward and takes my hand in his. "I'm only telling you so you'll understand why I said I came here to get away with no plans of getting involved. And because I want to be upfront with you."

My heart settles a little, resuming its normal speed, or as normal as it gets when I'm in Vali's presence.

"What happened?" I ask.

Those amazing deep, blue eyes bore into mine, but I hold firm, letting him know he can tell me. We can do this—be open with each other.

"We dated for nearly over a year and I didn't know she was already married until I proposed to her."

My gasp is audible as I cover my mouth with my hand in shock. "Oh my God."

Vali lets out a humorless laugh, running a hand through his hair. "Yeah, it was bad. Her husband showed up at the gym and the two of us put on a real-life fight night for everyone to see. I had no clue at first who he was. It wasn't until we exchanged a few punches that I realized what he was saying... *she's my wife*." He pauses, his gaze somewhere else, probably back in that gym. "When I finally understood, I just let him get his licks in."

"You let him beat you up?" I ask, still in shock, but now my stomach hurts and my chest is tight. Imagining Vali in any kind of pain—emotional or physical—tears me up inside.

He shrugs. "I was a cheater."

When he finally looks back up at me, there's shame and regret in his expression.

"No, you weren't."

"What would you call it?"

"Someone who was lied to," I tell him with as much conviction as I can muster in hopes he'll believe me, because it's obvious that he's still holding on to a lot of resentment about this.

"You sound like Tempest," he says, a little levity finally coming back in his tone.

I let out a deep breath. "Well, she's a really smart lady, so..."

At that, he finally smiles and I'm relieved. I'm not sorry I asked or that he told me, but I don't want to ruin the nice time we've been having and I'm hoping there's still a lot left to our date.

"Tell me something about you," he says, leveling me with those eyes and sexy smirk. "I know you've lived your whole life in Green Valley and work at your family's feed store and you love Italian food and dancing, but I want to know more. Tell me something about Maggie O'Neal no one else knows."

My pulse quickens and my palms immediately feel sweaty. As I covertly wipe them down the front of my jeans, I clear my throat. "Well, um," I start, buying myself a little time. What can I tell Vali Erickson that will be interesting? *Just be yourself.* Everly's words of advice from earlier come back to me, and so I continue, "I was home-schooled and completed college online. So, you can blame my socially awkward behavior on that."

Self-deprecation is always a good choice.

"You're not socially awkward," Vali insists as he sits up straighter in his seat and leans across the table. His lean, muscular arms crossed, drawing my eyes down to the watch on his wrist and then up to the cuffs of his dress shirt that are neatly rolled to his elbows. "Look at me."

My eyes pop up to his and I swallow. He's looking at me with so much intensity I can feel his gaze on my skin and it makes me squirm a little in my seat. Vali knows how to command a room and it totally works for me.

"You're great," he continues. "Actually, you're so much more than great, Maggie O'Neal. You're quirky and beautiful. Everything I learn about you makes me want to know more. And I'm pretty sure no one has ever intrigued me as much as you do."

The heat on my cheeks is traveling down my body and I don't know how to stop it, so I smile and say, "Thank you," before chugging the remaining water in my glass.

Compliments are often lost on me. I know the proper thing to say and how to respond, but it's only because I've read up on it and trained myself to comply. Being gracious and believing are two different things. But I love that Vali thinks those things about me.

"I think you're really great too," I tell him. Giving compliments is much easier. "And if we're going to compare who's intrigued more with who, it's definitely me with you."

Vali's eyes twinkle when he laughs, reaching across the table and lacing his fingers through mine. "Did you always want to work at the feed store or is that something that was just expected of you?"

"It's all I've ever known," I start with, focusing my eyes on the way my fingers look tangled with Vali's and the way our hands fit together so perfectly. "I love the store and the people. And I love helping my parents because they've done so much for me."

"But?" Vali asks, drawing my attention back to him. The level of understanding I feel in this moment is freeing, so much so I almost tell him everything. Almost. But it's too soon and I'm not ready to let my anonymity go just yet. Holding a few cards still close to my chest, I tell him as much of the truth as I'm willing to part with for now.

"But it's not my dream job," I confess. "Growing up as an only child and then being homeschooled, I had a lot of time to daydream. I found solace in writing. Most of the time, that energy went into corresponding with my pen pal, but when I wasn't doing that, I'd write short stories. So, I guess if I could pick my job, it'd be something to do with that."

"You had a pen pal?" he asks with zero judgment, only mere curiosity.

Smiling, I nod. "Have," I correct. "I *have* a pen pal."

"That's so cool," he says, brushing his thumb over mine and sending tingles up my arm. "I always wanted one when I was younger."

"We've exchanged emails for thirteen years, so she knows me better than anyone."

Vali's eyes soften a little and I feel like he wants to say something, but he's also holding back a little. This is more than I expected coming into tonight's date. In reality, I always keep my expectations low so I'm not disappointed, but I could've set the bar high and still been pleasantly surprised. Vali consistently does that every time I'm with him, regardless of the situation or our surroundings.

"Tell me something funny," I prompt after a few moments of silence, not ready for this strong connection to end.

His smile widens and he cuts his eyes to the side, thinking. "Well, I had an interesting encounter at the Piggly Wiggly earlier today."

"The Piggly Wiggly," I say with a giggle. "Do tell."

He clears his throat and then runs his free hand—the one not still holding mine—through his hair, something I've noticed he does when he's nervous or uncomfortable. It's his tell and I love it. Every time he does it, I want to ask him if I can do it for him.

"I think the cashier was hitting on me," he says thoughtfully. "She mentioned reading about the Viking Invasion in the newspaper and wanted to know if I was one of *the Ericksons*. I've got to say, I'm used to Cage being noticed, but I've never had that happen to me."

I feel my heart hammering in my chest and beads of sweat are threatening to pop out of my forehead at any moment. "Small towns," I mutter, swallowing down my nerves.

"I told her I have a girlfriend," Vali blurts out and now my heart is pounding for a different reason.

"A girlfriend?"

Offering me a crooked smile, he winks and I forget everything—what he was saying, my name, to breathe.

"Don't panic," Vali says, giving my hand a squeeze. "We don't need labels. I kind of hate them, actually. It was a knee-jerk reaction and it was out of my mouth before I could take it back. I just wanted you to know in case it's ever mentioned, because you know… small towns."

"Right," I tell him, my head nodding a little too vigorously. "Of course." The nervous laugh that escapes is undeniable and I want to crawl under the table. *Why can't I be cool?*

"Hey, Maggie." Vali squeezes my hand again and I reluctantly meet his gaze. "I always want to be upfront with you. Lying and evading the truth ruined the longest relationship of my life and pretty much destroyed me. So, I know this might be a little heavy for a second date, but I need you to know that at some point, I'll be going back to Dallas. And when I came here, I wasn't in a place for a relationship and had sworn off women. But I had no clue I'd meet you. I'm not making any promises or asking for any in return, but I enjoy spending time with you and I want to continue to do so for as long as I'm allowed."

My heart both sinks and soars at his words. I've always known Vali probably wasn't a lifer and, at some point, he'll leave Green Valley. But honestly, I haven't given it much thought. Overthinking usually gets me nowhere, so for once in my life, I decide to throw caution to the wind.

When and if Vali leaves, all I know for sure is I don't want to have any regrets. I don't want to wonder *what if*.

"I love spending time with you," I finally say. "You've…" *Given me something to look forward to. Made me feel things I've never felt before.* "You've become a bright spot in my day. So, for as long as you're here." Pausing, I clear my throat as I pull up my big-girl panties and make one of the most adult statements of my twenty-four years. "I want to be with you."

Vali sighs and it sounds like relief and regret wrapped in one. Moving his chair around the table until his knees are brushing mine, he takes my hands back in his. "I don't want to hurt you."

"You won't." *You couldn't. How could you?* "I'm a big girl," I say, mustering all the strength I have to sell these next words as hard as I can. "I know what I'm getting myself into. No promises. Just two people getting to know each other and who enjoy spending time together."

When he reaches out and cups my cheek, my eyes close and I lean into his touch.

"So beautiful," he whispers against my skin. The scruff on his jaw giving me new sensations that shoot through my body. "Tell me what you want, Maggie… anything… but I need to hear it from you."

"I—I," I stutter, unsure how to put it in words. "I want you… I want to feel…"

"Don't hold back from me," Vali mutters as his lips make their way across my jaw and down my neck. "Honesty, remember?" He brings his head up and meets my eyes with his. "Because I want to devour you, but unless I'm reading you wrong, you might not be ready for the full-course meal."

He's speaking in code, but I'm picking up what he's putting down. I try to calm my racing heart so some of the blood that's pumping to other areas will go back to my brain where I really need it right now. "I… I might not be ready for the full course, but I'm definitely ready for appetizers."

That thousand-watt smile nearly blinds me from this proximity and his chuckle reverberates through my whole body. "How about dessert?"

Swallowing, my eyes grow wide and I wonder what he has in mind, but when he reaches a long arm over to the counter and comes back with a familiar box, I exhale. "What flavor?"

"Islands in the Stream."

"My favorite."

Opening the box, he pulls one of the delicious muffins out and holds it up to my mouth for a bite. With my eyes locked on his, I take one. Like that, just a breath apart, we share a muffin and I start to relax into the closeness.

When Vali leans forward and licks the side of my mouth, I laugh, but then immediately wish for more. If his tongue feels that good on my mouth, where else might it feel good.

"You missed a crumb," he says with a wicked grin.

Closing the distance between us, I crash my lips to his and the muffin is forgotten. Instinct takes over and I begin to feast on his mouth like it's the best dessert I've ever eaten. Vali is better than muffins or chocolate… or even chocolate muffins. He's deliciousness personified and I want more.

"More," I tell him between kisses, my hands already moving through his hair, pulling him closer.

He chuckles and stands but doesn't break the kiss. With his hands snaking around my waist and then down to my butt, he leads me to a couch on the opposite side of the open space.

When the back of my legs hit the edge, he guides me down until I'm cocooned in the plush fabric. Bracing his arms on either side of me, he hovers above, not giving me his full weight. But I need it. I need to feel him, so I tug on his hair and urge him down to me. "More."

His long legs tangle with mine and, after a few seconds, every inch of Vali's body is lined up with mine. It's too much and not enough all at the same time.

When I feel his hardness between my legs, I gasp and he pauses his kiss, gazing down at me.

"Is this okay?"

With hooded eyes, I nod.

He gently brushes his lips against mine and then against my cheek... and then the other one, working his way around my face, peppering kisses as he goes. When one of his hands trails up my side, I hold my breath.

For a moment, I'm ripped out of the haze of being with Vali and thrust into my insecurities, because my hands are also trailing up his sides and it's hard to not make comparisons. He's hard. Everywhere.

But I'm soft.

Everywhere.

We're two totally different people.

"Maggie," Vali says, his face buried in my neck. "Breathe."

Letting out a breath, I close my eyes and just feel.

Just be yourself.

That's all you can be.

"You feel so good," Vali murmurs. "I want to touch you... everywhere. But if you want to stop or slow down, tell me. This is your show. I'm following your lead."

Oh, God.

His fingers skirt under the hem of my shirt and then his entire hand is gripping my side. I can't even express the way his skin on mine feels... and it's just his hand... and I want more. Insecurities be damned. *I want more.*

"More."

Vali obliges and works his way up until he's cupping my breast, kneading it through my bra.

"More."

Rising up, he meets my eyes and he looks as drunk on lust as I feel. When his hand leaves my breast, I whimper at the loss. But then he lightly runs his finger around the collar of my sweater and places a kiss at the exposed skin. Pushing it off my shoulder, he kisses his way up and then back down and I'm completely lost to him. To this moment.

When he tugs at the cup of my bra, cool air hits my nipple. Then I feel his mouth on me. Everything that happens after that is a blur.

Vali's hips press between my legs, giving me glorious friction in exactly the right place.

His mouth is sucking.

His tongue is swirling.

I'm writhing.

When he starts thrusting against me, I completely come undone. There's an explosion of white behind my eyelids and I hear a loud keening sound. After a few seconds, I realize it's me. I'm making that sound. But I can't stop because my body is no longer my own.

It belongs to Vali Erickson.

CHAPTER 19

VALI

"*I*'ll make sure this gets in next week's paper," Sarah says, looking over the ad for our exhibition fight we're hosting next Friday night to celebrate the new ring and raise some more money for the women's shelter.

"Thank you, Sarah," I tell her, glancing around the small office. "Say, Trixie and Tess wouldn't happen to be here, would they?"

Her eyes grow wide and then she schools her features. "Uh, no. Why do you ask?"

"Oh, no reason. I'm just a fan of the article and wanted to let them know they've been a great source of entertainment while I've been in Green Valley. We really appreciate the hype they seem to generate for the studio."

She smiles and nods. "Well, I'll be sure to pass on the compliment. *They'll* be thrilled, I'm sure."

The way she says *they* makes me pause. "Are they writing under pen names?"

"They prefer to remain anonymous," she says, smiling again as she clasps her hands under her chin. "It helps people feel more comfortable when they submit requests for advice."

I nod. "That makes sense, especially in a small town."

"Well, thanks again for buying an advertisement from us," she says, placing my ad in a file folder on her desk. With this being such a small newspaper for an equally small town, Sarah is the editor in chief, ad sales, and columnist. She seems to do it all.

Shit, for all I know, *she* could be Trixie and Tess. It never dawned on me until now that the two could potentially be one.

"Absolutely, we want to support any local business we can. And what better way to get word around than through the *Green Valley Ledger*."

It really is a great publication for a small town. So far, the news and articles I've read have been thoughtful and accurate.

"It'd be great if Trixie and Tess could cover the exhibition fight," I tell her on my way out the door. Lowering my sunglasses as the bright Tennessee afternoon sun greets me. "They seem to love us, so who better to report back to the good people of Green Valley."

Me using their opening line gets a chuckle from Sarah. "I'll make sure they're on it."

Before the door closes, a flyer taped to the glass catches my attention.

Valentine's Day Jam Session.

Valentine's Day?

"Hey, Sarah," I say, poking my head back in the door. "When's the fourteenth?"

She glances down at a calendar on her desk. "Monday."

Well, shit.

"You ever been to one of these jam sessions?" I ask, pointing to the flyer.

"Sure, everyone in Green Valley has been to a jam session," she says. "And if they haven't, they're missing out."

Scanning the flyer one more time, I pull my phone out and snap a pic of it so I have all the information. This is probably the best I can do on such short notice. "Thanks again, Sarah."

As I'm walking back toward the studio, I call Tempest.

"Hey, Vali. What's up?"

"What do you know about the jam session?"

There's some rustling on her end of the phone and she sounds a little odd when she answers. "Oh, it's fun. I haven't been in quite a while, but there's good music, dancing, food."

"Did I interrupt something?" I ask, picking up on some heavy breathing and hoping she's not boning my brother while talking to me.

"Yoga," she says, letting out a deep breath.

Chuckling, I shake my head. "Cool. So, do we all want to go to a Valentine's Day Jam Session on Monday or do y'all have big plans?"

"Valentine's Day is a Hallmark holiday."

"I agree, but it's customary to observe it."

"Jam session sounds fun," she finally says, letting out another deep breath. "Let's do it. We'll make Gunnar and Frankie go too."

"Great, I'm going to call Maggie," I tell her, glancing both ways before I cross the street. "Carry on with your yoga."

"Namaste," she says before ending the call.

Instead of going back to the studio, I stop at the park and find a bench. The air is cool but the sun is bright and it feels good to soak in a little vitamin D. Opening up my recent calls, I scroll to Maggie's number and hope she's not busy. I never know when a good time to call is, but she insists it's okay to call her during the day while she's at work. So, I do, because sometimes, I just need to hear her voice.

If I thought I was thinking about her a lot before Saturday night, that was nothing compared to the last five days.

"Hello?" She sounds almost as breathless as Tempest, but with her, it sets my blood on fire and brings back memories from her beneath me on the couch... writhing and moaning.

"Hey," I reply, clearing my throat and trying to redirect my thoughts.

"Vali?" she asks, still breathless and bringing my dick to attention. "Sorry, I'm helping my dad unload a pallet of feed. I didn't even look at my phone before I answered it. How are you?"

Imagining her glistening with sweat and continuing my mental porn show featuring Maggie O'Neal, I cover the phone with my hand and let out a groan, like I'm trying to relieve the built-up pressure and tension caused by just thinking about her. When I pull my hand away, I school my voice before replying. "Great," I start, nearly forgetting exactly what it was I wanted to say. *Get it together, dipshit.* "I was, uh... just calling to see if you'd like to go to a jam session for Valentine's Day."

So smooth.

"Oh," she says, sounding surprised, but pleasantly so. "I love going... I'd love to go."

The way she stutters over her words sometimes makes me smile. It's endearing and makes me want to wrap her in a hug. "That's great. We can discuss the details later, but I wanted to ask you before someone else swooped in and made you their Valentine."

There's a long pause and I wonder if I've said something wrong or if she can't talk.

"Maggie?" I ask, bringing my phone away from my ear to make sure the call didn't drop, but it's still going.

"No one's ever asked me to be their Valentine," she finally says. "Thank you."

"It's my pleasure."

* * *

STANDING outside the Green Valley Community Center, I'm getting a little antsy waiting for Maggie. I really hate not picking her up at her house for a date, but she insists it's better this way. I've told her I didn't care if she lived on the outskirts of town or Timbuktu, I still wanted to pick her up but she just laughed and redirected our conversation.

I have a feeling she doesn't want to formally introduce me to her parents as the man she's dating, especially after my one and only visit to their feed store. I guess I understand. I didn't really make the best first impression but that's on me. How can I redeem myself if she refuses to introduce me to them?

Maybe I need a do-over visit to the store.

Before I can formulate a solid plan, my attention is pulled to the parking lot where I see Maggie walking toward me, looking sexy as fuck. I lean back against a column and enjoy watching her come to me. She's so striking with how she carries herself and I don't think she even knows it. Her height and voluptuous curves paired with her long, dark hair and wide smile command the attention of everyone around her.

And she's mine.

For now, anyway.

When she's close enough for me to touch, I slide my arm around her waist and pull her to me. Capturing her mouth with mine, I claim it, not able to hold back any longer. Even though we made out in the parking lot of Genie's on Friday, it's been too long since I've been able to see her... touch her... taste her.

I want her so fucking much. I want to learn her body and watch her fall apart over and over. I want her to explore my body and have her way with me, any way she wants. I want so much but realize now is not the time or place for my dick to be running the show, so I slowly and reluctantly pull away.

Maggie's lips are swollen and her eyes are dazed as she looks at me and whispers, "Wow".

"Happy Valentine's Day, beautiful." I kiss her forehead, allowing my lips to linger so I can have one last taste before we walk inside.

"Same to you." She bites down on her bottom lip, fighting back a smile as she shakes her head. I'd give anything to know what she's thinking and to replace her teeth with my own. Those luscious lips have made an appearance in every dream I've had for the past week.

And as much as I want to make her come again, it's not going to happen in the parking lot of the community center. My instincts tell me Maggie's a virgin. Even though I don't have a lot of experience in that arena, I know one thing for sure, I want every orgasm I give Maggie to be better than the one before.

I want all her firsts to be worth the wait because she definitely is.

"So, tell me about the jam sessions. I hear they're pretty famous," I say as I grab her hand and lead her to the building's entrance, needing to distract myself so I'm not sporting a semi as we walk into the community center.

"They've been happening for a few years now and they're pretty fun. Typically, they're held on Friday nights and people from all over come to enjoy good music and even better food. You like bar-b-que, right?"

I look at her like she's lost her mind. "Woman, I am from *Texas*. Of course, I like bar-b-que."

She laughs and squeezes my arm as we step inside, where we're instantly greeted by a friendly welcoming committee. After we get the rundown on where to find the festivities, we make our way to where the food is and Maggie continues our conversation.

"I know you're from Texas, which is why I asked. Texas bar-b-que is very different from Tennessee bar-b-que. Some even say your version isn't bar-b-que at all."

I jerk away from her in shock. "Them's fightin' words, Miss O'Neal," I say, laying my Texas twang on thick. "Now, take me to this high-and-mighty food so I can judge for myself."

Thirty minutes later, I'm slumped in my chair, fighting the urge to unbuckle my belt and jeans.

"So, what's the verdict?"

Maggie's expression is smug and I want to kiss it right off her face but I'm too full to move right now. So instead, I give her a shrug, trying to play it off. "It's alright, I guess. If you like that kind of thing."

Her laughter fills the room and I'm mesmerized. It's quickly becoming my favorite sound, second only to the sounds of her orgasm. Shit, I cannot be thinking like that right now, when I'm too stuffed to try and hide a boner.

"One of these days, I'll fix you some Texas bar-b-que," I vow.

She scrunches up her nose, and while the look on her face is absolutely adorable, it's not quite what I was hoping for. "You've had my cooking before. Do you doubt my skills?"

"It's not that," she starts. "It's just that Texas bar-b-que is mainly smoked meat, not cooked over an open flame, and you put your sauce on the side!" Her hand covers her heart to illustrate the horror of her words.

"Listen, good meat is good meat, I don't care where it's from. But, it's only fair that you try my meat since I just tried yours."

The words are out of my mouth before I realize how they sound, and when I look at Maggie's face to get her reaction, I'm pleased to see the same dazed look from earlier. She's also blushing something fierce, which tells me she's just as dirty minded as I am. Well, maybe not quite as much, but close.

"Hey," I say to get her attention.

With flushed cheeks, she meets my eyes. "Yeah?"

"You gonna take me to one of the music rooms so I can finally dance with you?"

Her shoulders relax and she gives me one of her mega-watt smiles. "Are you sure you're up to it?"

"Absolutely. Besides, I need to burn off some of this food."

Maggie giggles and grabs my hand, pulling me out of my chair and leading me to the first music room we find. There are five or six musicians playing some good ol' honky-tonk music, which is exactly what I need right now.

I twirl Maggie around before pulling her flush against my body. "Let's dance."

And, dance, we do. We two-step, we waltz, and we even jitterbug a couple of times before we're worn out and need to take a break.

We leave the room and enter another with a band playing bluegrass music. I'm a little surprised to see both of my brothers, along with their significant others, on the dance floor. Bluegrass is not a genre of music we listened to much back home but it's a slow song and I completely understand the draw of slow dancing with a woman. So much so, I grab Maggie's hand and lead her onto the floor close to my siblings, so we can join in the fun, as well.

What a sight this must be, watching three big-ass dudes from Texas slow dancing to bluegrass music in a refurbished classroom.

"Oh, good, Cletus is playing. He's so good on the banjo," Maggie tells me.

"Who's that?"

"You know Jenn from the bakery, right? Well, that's her husband." She uses her head to point in the direction of a man with wild hair, playing a banjo as if it's the easiest thing to do. Not gonna lie, I'm kind of envious of his long beard. I've never been able to grow my beard out like that.

It doesn't take long for me to get lost in the feel of Maggie in my arms again. She fits perfectly, her soft parts molding to my hard ones, and if it feels this good while we still have our clothes on, I can't fucking wait to be this close to her while naked.

Maggie's head is on my shoulder as we sway to the music, so she doesn't see when Tempest waves at me. I look up at Tempest and watch as she mouths, *"Have you asked about New Orleans."* Drawing my eyebrows together, I give a small shake of my head in reply. She's obviously not happy with my answer because her eyes are now narrowed and her hands are on her hips.

Not wanting to get into it right now, I roll my eyes and sway our bodies so that my back is now facing Tempest. I'm sure I'll pay for this tomorrow but I don't care.

It's not that I don't want Maggie to go to New Orleans with us, with me, because I do. But I can't help but wonder if it's too soon for us. Of course, I wouldn't have any expectations regarding the physical side of our relationship but it'd be our first weekend getaway as a couple, and to me, that's a big deal. Road trips can either make or break a couple and the fact we'd also be with my family, as in my *entire* family… well, it kind of scares the shit out of me. I don't want to pressure her or freak her out but, on the flip side, making that trip without her would fucking suck.

I will ask her, but not tonight.

Tonight, I just want to hold her in my arms for as long as she'll let me.

CHAPTER 20

MAGGIE

"*Maggie*," my mom calls from the register. "When you're finished stocking that shelf, can you run a bag of feed to Mr. Jones? He was trying to make it by before we close today but Sue Ellen is sick and he needs to head straight home after he closes up the store."

"Sure," I tell her, lining up the new boxes of bird seed we just got in. I color coordinated them. "I'm almost finished with this."

My dad scoffs from one row over where he's stocking dog food. "You'd already be finished if you didn't spend so much time turning the shelves into your own personal canvas."

"It's pretty," I retort, keeping my eyes on the task at hand. "Besides, I think it really ups the sales."

I hear him chuckle. Even though he gives me a hard time about beautifying the inventory, I know he secretly loves it. When business is slow, I always catch him walking around the aisles, lining everything up just so. I obviously got attention to detail from him.

Once I'm finished, I step back and dust off my jeans as I admire my handiwork. Glancing at my watch, I see it's already after three and I wonder, not for the first time today, what Vali is up to.

Mr. Jones's appliance store is conveniently located next door to Viking MMA, so that means I'll be close to Vali. I wonder if I should do a surprise visit. I know we're not labeling whatever is happening between us but I assume he wouldn't protest me dropping in at the gym for a few minutes. I mean, why should he be the one to always call or initiate things with me? I'm a grown-ass woman and I can take charge sometimes.

Right?

Right.

That's settled, then.

After grabbing my purse from the back, I find my mom dusting a display by the register.

"Hey, Mom, is it okay if I take a few minutes to stop by and see a friend after I make Mr. Jones's delivery? I promise not to take too long."

"Of course, dear. We can close up without you. Have fun with your friend."

"That's not necessary. I shouldn't be too long," I insist.

"Is this friend the same one who stopped by the store the other day? You know, the one who couldn't keep his hands off the horse crops." My dad enters the conversation, causing my mom to swat at him.

She tells him to stop it just as I huff out a, "Daddy!"

"Hey," my dad defends himself, holding his hands up. "I'm just looking out for my daughter. The way I see it, he's either wanting to use the crop on an animal or my baby and there's only one right answer, got it?" He gives me a stern look before relaxing and giving me a wink.

"You know you can invite him over for dinner any time," my mom says, smiling at me.

"I know, Mom. I'll think about it, I promise."

"It's good that you're getting out and making friends. I always worried you'd struggle with relating to other people your age." My mother's admission makes my heart lurch. She's never said anything like this to me.

"What do you mean?"

"Well, I know your daddy and I have sheltered you and probably coddled you too much but it was only because we love you so much and want to protect you. You always seemed to get along better with adults than kids when you were growing up, so I worried it'd keep you from making friends when you became an adult." I watch my mama dab the corner of her eye with a tissue and immediately feel my throat tighten.

Why is it so hard to see your mama cry?

"Mama, you and Daddy did what you felt was best for me and, I'm not gonna lie, I'm pretty happy with the end results." She laughs at this and I relax.

"We just want you to be happy, Maggie. It's obvious you've met someone you enjoy spending time with and you should feel free to do so." When she smiles up at me, her eyes are still a bit watery but I know what she's saying is genuine. My mama couldn't be phony if you paid her a million dollars.

"What your mother's trying to say is," my dad speaks up. "We love you and we trust you. You're twenty-four years old, for Pete's sake, and you don't have a curfew. Now, go have some fun."

"I love you both so much. I promise I won't be out too late." I hug them both and head for the door.

As I'm walking to my car, my mother calls out to me. "Why don't you take one of those frozen casseroles in the freezer and some of the biscuits I made this morning to the Joneses. That way Sue Ellen won't have to cook while being sick."

"Will do!" I holler back.

I decide to bring some biscuits to the gym as well. I know they're full of carbs but who doesn't love biscuits? Jars of jam my mama and I made this weekend catch my eye and I grab a couple to go with my deliveries.

On my way into town, my mind naturally wanders to Vali, like it seems to do all the time. Especially after our date at his place. *Oh my God*, I can't get that night out of my head. Not that I want to.

I still can't believe I had an orgasm right there in front of him and with my clothes still on! I just knew I'd think about it later and die of embarrassment, but it never happened. It was the most natural and beautiful feeling and he brought it out of me. I can't be embarrassed about that. If Vali was turned off by my inexperience, he definitely didn't show it. Not once did he make me feel ashamed or lesser than, only adored and cherished.

As much as I hate that he was hurt so badly by that Voldemort-lady in Dallas, I'm so glad he's here. And, although he's not sure when he'll be going back to Texas, I want to enjoy every minute with him I can.

And that includes sleeping with him.

But, probably not tonight. I'm not deluding myself, hoping for some grand gesture or empty promises—Vali and I have already set the parameters of our non-relationship—but I don't want to rush things. Since this is my first time, I want to enjoy every moment, including those leading up to the big event. I'm trying not to make it a thing in my head, but it's hard. Everly advised me to let things happen naturally, which is what I'm trying to do, but my body and mind are in a constant state of tug-of-war—just do him already… slow your roll, Maggie.

Regardless of when and how it happens, I know one thing for sure—I want this with Vali.

After I deliver Mr. Jones's order, I hand him a bag with the food. He's so relieved he doesn't have to try and cook for himself and thanks me profusely. I tell him to give Sue Ellen our well-wishes and make sure she gets better, before excusing myself to make another delivery.

I don't know why I'm feeling nervous as I walk into the gym. It's not like I've never been here before, I just haven't been here without a class going on. The door is unlocked but no one's at the front desk, so I continue walking into the class area and that's where I see them. Actually, I hear them first but it doesn't register in my brain what I'm hearing until I see what's going on.

Two very muscular guys sparring in a makeshift ring and, holy cow, one of them is Vali. There's a lot of sweat, as well as grunting, going on, and I can't lie, it's freaking hot. I've never watched any kind of fight before and I had no idea I'd have this reaction to it. Maybe it's because I happen to be dating one of the fighters but still…

I mean, what is my life right now?

A timer goes off and both guys step away from each other. It's not until Vali has his gloves off and his mouth guard out that he sees me and the smile that covers his face when he does, just about kills me.

He grabs a towel and wipes his face with it before jogging over to me.

"Well, this is a lovely surprise. How long have you been over here watching?"

"Long enough…" I hedge.

He steps closer, and even though he's a sweaty mess, he doesn't stink. No, he smells manly and earthy and I'm so freaking turned on right now.

"Did you like watching me spar?" His voice lowers and I have to close my eyes to stay grounded. How does he affect me so intensely... and quickly?

I nod my head, while I'm briefly unable to speak.

"Want to go upstairs to my place?"

I nod again but this time I manage to mumble "mmm hmm" before he grabs my hand and leads me across the gym to the other side of the studio and up the set of stairs.

As soon as we're in his apartment, I'm pushed up against the wall with Vali attacking my mouth.

Oh, sweet Lord Jesus, yes.

"I've missed you," he whispers as he kisses from my jaw to my collarbone. "Can you wait here while I take a quick shower?" He pulls away and it takes me a second to catch up with what's happening.

He's going to kiss me like that and then walk away?

He can obviously tell I'm confused, so he gives me a quick peck on the mouth and promises to be right back.

I have no idea how long he's gone, but when he returns, he must find me amusing because he laughs as he asks, "Why are you still standing by the stairs? Have you been there the entire time I was in the shower?"

"Well, yes, I have. What do you expect? You yanked me up here, kissed me stupid, and then left. I don't even know what day it is anymore!"

He laughs even harder as he walks up to me. "I'm sorry I abandoned you. Please forgive me." He's back to peppering sweet kisses all over my face and, naturally, I melt into him. "Come sit with me."

"Okay." When I start to move, I remember the bag I've been holding for who knows how long anymore. "I brought homemade biscuits and jam."

"Really? What's the occasion?"

"No occasion. I had a delivery for next door and my mom asked me to bring some to Mr. Jones since his wife is sick. I thought the gym might want some too."

"No, the gym does *not* want any, but I sure do." He takes the bag out of my hand and pulls out the food.

"You're not going to share with your brothers?"

"Hell, no. My girl brought me food. Their girls can do the same for them."

Have mercy, he just called me his girl.

I mentally pat myself on the back for making this surprise visit.

"You really made these?" he asks as he opens the jam.

"My mom made the biscuits this morning, but she and I both made jam over the weekend."

Vali sticks his finger straight into the jar, pulls it out, then puts it in his mouth. As I watch him suck the jam off his finger, I feel heat pool in my belly. He's just too sexy.

"Damn, that's good. Want some?"

Maggie, do not think about germs or getting sticky or anything else that would ruin this moment. Your answer is yes and only yes.

"Yeah." My voice is raspy and I'm afraid I've forgotten how to breathe. That's okay, though, because Vali is currently slipping his fruit-covered finger between my lips and I'll probably be dead soon.

I don't let go of his finger easily, loving how it feels when he swirls the sweetness around my tongue.

"Fuck," Vali groans. "Please tell me you don't have to leave anytime soon."

"I'm all yours," I say without thinking. I don't try to take it back either because it's true.

"Come here," he urges, motioning to his lap.

I begin to move but am still unsure of what he wants. Thankfully, he takes pity on me and guides me to where I'm straddling his lap. When I sit all the way down, I realize why this was such a good idea. He's hard and his length is perfectly nestled between my legs.

"Remember the last time you were here... what we did?"

I feel the blush start from my chest and move up to my cheeks as I nod my head.

"Can I see you again?" Vali runs his finger down my throat and over the skin that's peeking through the opening of my shirt.

"Yes."

Vali pulls me to him and dominates my mouth. I've never experienced a kiss like this and I feel it everywhere... feel him everywhere. He starts unbuttoning my shirt but, dammit, he's not moving fast enough, so I help him. I pull the fabric off my arms and onto the floor, ready for the next step.

His large hands cup and squeeze my breasts through my bra, and as much as I love it, it's not enough. I need to feel his skin on mine. I need it like I need my next breath.

"Take it off," I command.

Holy Moses, who am I?

Margaret O'Neal, the wallflower, has left the building, and in her place is a woman who knows what she wants and isn't afraid to get it.

"You sure?" His Adam's apple bobs up and down as he swallows, and I love this is affecting him as much as it is me. That knowledge somehow evens the playing field and boosts my confidence even more. "We don't have to go any further if you're not ready."

"Take it off," I repeat with a little more assuredness than the first time.

Vali's eyes never leave mine as he quirks an eyebrow and releases the clasp on the front of my bra, freeing my breasts from their lacy confines. When I fantasized about this moment, I always assumed I'd feel shy or embarrassed, but nothing could be farther from the truth.

I feel powerful in my nakedness—emboldened.

Finally, Vali looks at me, at my body, and I feel him twitch between my legs. I guess he likes what he sees.

"You are absolutely stunning. You're perfect."

It took me a long time to love my body. When I used to look at myself in the mirror, I was never happy with what I saw. It took becoming an adult to realize my body, while not Hollywood-approved, is still special. My body is strong and healthy and, yes, it's beautiful.

But I've never felt desired until now.

And that's a heady feeling.

"Kiss me," I tell him, loving being in control. When he reaches for my mouth, I put my hand on his chest to stop him. "Not there," I say before looking down at my chest.

He eagerly latches on to my breast while pulling and twisting the nipple on the other one. I cry out when I feel his teeth graze my sensitive skin. After he spends quality time on both breasts, he slowly pulls his mouth off me and levels me with his gaze.

When his expression grows serious, I'm worried he's changed his mind, or I've done something wrong. With my heart starting to pound in my chest, Vali places a soft kiss between my breasts before speaking in a low, soothing tone. "I think I know the answer to this question, but I want to make sure," he says, reaching up to stroke my cheek with his thumb. "Are you a virgin, Maggie?"

Slowly, I nod.

"How far have you been with a guy?"

I shake my head, unsure of what to say. *Nowhere?* That sounds so lame, but this feels like such a vulnerable moment between us. There's not a lick of judgment in Vali's eyes, so I tell the truth. "Kissing... that's it. Until you."

He inhales deeply, raking a hand through his hair and I'm afraid he's going to pull away from me, but instead, he pulls me closer.

"Is that okay?" I ask, needing to hear him say it more than I care to admit. "I mean, if it's not—"

"It's more than okay." His voice is low and deep as he caresses my neck and slips a hand into my hair. "We're going to take this slow... you're calling the shots, got it?"

I nod because if my voice is anything like my insides, it's completely emulsified with little to no substance. Vali Erickson has rendered me a speechless pile of goo with his sweet words and gentle touch.

"Do you trust me?"

"Of course."

Vali grabs the jar again and sticks his finger back inside. This time, when he pulls his finger out, instead of placing it in his mouth, he rubs the sticky fruit across my nipples. The jam is cold, which makes my nipples even harder, but when he sucks one into his warm mouth, I can't help but moan at the sensation.

He continues adding more jam to my skin before lapping it up, until I'm writhing uncontrollably in his lap. My hips move on their own accord, my sexual instinct taking over. Vali grabs on to my ass and pulls me closer, grinding me against his hardness and hitting exactly where I need it. Too soon, we're both coming, holding on to each other as our orgasms blaze through us, leaving us both sticky and spent.

I can't wrap my brain around what just happened, but I do know I want it to happen again.

And, I'll never look at jam the same way.

CHAPTER 21

VALI

*A*djusting my collar, I give myself a once-over in the mirror. Normally, on fight night, I go all out and wear at least a three-piece suit. But tonight—in Green Valley, Tennessee—for an exhibition fight, this will work.

Crisp white button-down.

Gray slacks.

Black shoes.

Grabbing my iPad, I head downstairs to double-check everything. The key objective for the night is to give the good people of Green Valley a show and a better understanding of what Viking MMA has to offer, as well as raise funds for the Maryville Women's Shelter.

Since we didn't sell tickets, that cuts out having people at the door. Instead, we have donation boxes set up in strategic locations where people can drop in whatever amount of money they'd like to give.

Vince and a few of our other regulars are already here, finishing the setup.

We brought in two sets of bleachers, even though we could fit in more. But since a lot of people who will be here tonight have never attended a professional fight, we thought pub-style tables where they can mix and mingle would be better suited.

The new lights Cage had installed over the ring really give the entire place a new look. With the house lights down and only those spot-lighting the ring, it looks fucking amazing.

"Looks great," I call out to Vince. "Thanks for your help, man."

He waves me off. "No problem. Need me to do anything else before I run home to change?"

"No," I tell him, looking around the space. "I think we're good."

"Okay, I'll be back in a few."

Once Vince leaves, I hear footsteps behind me and turn around to see Cage standing in the wide entrance that connects this space to the other part of the studio, where it all started. The look on his face tells me everything I need to know.

He's having a moment.

"You did it," I tell him, unable to fight back a smile. Walking over to him, I clap his shoulder and saddle up beside him as we both take it all in.

"No, brother, *we* did it," he says, sighing loudly. "I know I've given you a lot of shit for sticking around, but I'm glad you have. I'm not sure we'd be to this point already without you."

Swallowing, I let his words sink in. Cage has always been one to give credit where credit is due, but he's not a smoke blower. He'll never tell you something just to make you feel good. So when he does pass out a compliment, it really means something.

"Thanks," I tell him. "And I'm glad it worked out for me to be here… it's been a nice change of scenery and watching you build this place from the ground up is inspiring."

He chuckles, shaking his head. "I honestly can't fucking believe it. When I left Dallas on a bus to Green Valley, Tennessee, I had no clue what was waiting for me. No fucking clue, man. And here I am, staring my Plan B in the face and realizing it might just be better than Plan A."

"Might be?" I question, cocking my head. "If your Plan A hadn't crashed and burned, you wouldn't be with Tempest getting ready to become a dad."

His sigh is deep and satisfied and I'm a little envious. Not that I begrudge Cage his happiness. He went through a lot of shit to get here. But fuck if I don't want that level of contentment.

"Do you think you'll stay?" he asks, changing the subject and catching me off guard.

"What? Here?"

Turning to face me, he nods, a hand smoothing down his beard.

I shrug. "That was never the plan. Besides, Viggo will get tired of not having me to boss around and he'll make up some excuse for me to go back. I can't avoid Dallas forever."

"There's always Plan B," he says, giving me his classic smirk.

Fuck, I bet that used to piss guys off in the ring.

* * *

AN HOUR LATER, as people start to gradually file in, I breathe a sigh of relief. The moment before any big event, I always think, *what if no one shows up?* But I should've known Green Valley would show up. Thanks to our good friends Trixie and Tess, the hype is real for everything Viking MMA.

150

Just as I go to pull out my phone and text Maggie, I see her. Her gorgeous brown hair is up in a high ponytail, making her appear even taller than she actually is. Then, as she steps around a group of people and comes into full view, I practically swallow my tongue.

She's poured into some black jeans that put all her glorious curves on display and I'd like to forget about this exhibition and take her upstairs and have my way with her.

"Hi," she says, her quiet greeting a contrast to her outward appearance. The slow smile on her face as she takes me in is gratifying. I love that she's so transparent. Everything Maggie feels is right there on her beautiful face for the whole world to see, if they only take the time to look.

"Hi yourself, gorgeous."

That earth-shattering smile grows even wider and I have to rein in every instinct to keep from mauling her right here in front of God and all the good people of Green Valley.

Leaning forward, I drop my lips to her ear. "You look delectable. I'm going to devour you later."

She lets out a soft gasp and I bite down on my lip to keep from growling. So innocent, yet so responsive—she's everything I never knew I wanted.

"Vali," someone calls out behind me. "Cage is asking for you."

Backing away, I keep my eyes locked with Maggie's. "Tempest and Frankie saved you a seat."

Eventually, she regains her composure and turns to head for the bleachers.

After I ogle her ass for a few moments, I turn to find Cage. We're about fifteen minutes from go time, so I'm sure he wants to make sure the audio is working properly and the fighters are ready.

As I make my way through the growing crowd, I'm pleasantly surprised at the amount of people who have shown up. With something like this, in a town this small, I wasn't sure what to expect. But the energy being put off is exactly what I like to see—excitement, anticipation, and good old-fashioned fun.

"Hey," Cage says when I approach the booth we have set up for the audio controls. "Everything looks good. Wanna check on Gunnar and Mancini? Then we'll get this show on the road."

I nod, grabbing my iPad and cueing some opening mood music, then reach across to lower the lights. Everyone seems to grow quiet and then the noise builds as they begin to find seats or a spot at the tables where they can see the ring.

Running to the hallway that leads to the dressing rooms, I holler, "Five minutes!"

Adjusting my cuffs, I walk back into the studio and straight up to the ring. As I grab the mic, my eyes find Maggie's, where she's sitting in the front row. Giving her a devilish smile and a wink, I turn to face the crowd.

"Welcome to Viking MMA and our first fight night!"

The crowd roars and I give them a moment, knowing my big brother is basking in the glory of this moment.

"On behalf of the Ericksons, I'd like to thank you all for coming out tonight. If you've never been to a fight night before, you're in for a treat. Since tonight's agenda is a bit different, we'll only have one bout that will go for five rounds lasting five minutes each with a one-minute rest period between each round. All UFC rules apply."

Drawing in a breath, I glance over at Cage who gives me a nod, indicating we're ready.

"You'll notice donation boxes set up around the studio and at the front door. All money raised tonight will benefit the Maryville Women's

Shelter, a charitable cause that is near and dear to our hearts. Any and all donations will be appreciated and put to good use."

On cue, the remaining house lights go off and the music changes and Mancini makes his way up the aisle. Once he's in the ring, the music changes to Gunnar's intro and I can't help the proud smile that stretches across my face as my baby brother makes his entrance.

"Fighting out of the red corner, a freestyle fighter. He stands six foot four, weighing in at two hundred and twenty-six pounds. He holds a professional mixed martial arts record of eighteen wins and three losses, with five wins by knockout. Fighting out of Nashville, Tennessee, Michael... 'Maneater'... Mancini!"

Pausing, I give the crowd a chance to applaud the opponent. Being a Tennessee boy gives him some automatic fans, even though most people in this room have never heard his name before tonight. People love rooting for the home team.

When the crowd dies down, I turn to Gunnar, feeling the weight of this moment. It might not be a title bout or the big times, but there's something special about tonight and I can't shake the emotions.

Clearing my throat, I face the crowd and smile. "Fighting out of the blue corner," I begin, amping up the enthusiasm a little. "He stands six foot three and weighs in at two hundred and thirty pounds. He holds a record of ten wins and one loss, with two knockouts." Gunnar's stats might seem weak compared to Mancini's but that's only because Gunnar is just getting started. Mancini, on the other hand, has been working his way up the ladder for ten years. If I was a betting man, I'd put all my money on the blue corner. "Fighting out of Green Valley, Tennessee, by way of Dallas, Texas, Gunnar... 'THE SHOW'... Erickson!"

The building has never heard this level of excitement. Every person in the building, if they weren't already on their feet, are now, giving it up for my little brother.

Walking to the middle of the ring, I bring both fighters in, giving them a quick rundown of the rules, even though they're both well-versed in them. Checking wrappings and gloves and verifying both fighters have their mouth guards in, I step back and hand the ring over to the ref we brought in from Knoxville.

Even though it's just an exhibition, we want an unbiased, clean fight.

As the bell signals for the round to begin, my eyes drift over to the row where Maggie is sitting with Tempest and Frankie. The latter is who I'm most concerned about. This is her first fight to attend in a while. After a bad experience at Gunnar's fight last year in Maryville, she's kept her distance. But after months of therapy sessions, where she's been actively working on overcoming her aversion to the sport, she decided tonight's exhibition would be a good way to test out her progress.

She seems to be hanging in there.

With Maggie on one side and Tempest on the other, I'd say she has the best support team possible.

Turning my attention back to the ring, I watch as Gunnar bobs and weaves, using good form and lightning speed. For the majority of the first two rounds, he's playing with Mancini, dancing around and letting him throw punches that only find air.

When he comes to the corner between rounds, he's barely even winded.

"Looking good out there," I mutter, leaning over the rings as Cage takes out his mouth guard and squirts some water in his mouth. "Watch out for his right hook. I've seen his films and it comes out of nowhere. It's what he's used to get over half his KOs."

Gunnar nods, his mind focused—*eye on the prize.*

The bell rings and he's back on his feet, bumping gloves with Mancini and then diving in. Within the first few seconds of the round, Gunnar lands two clean hits with a left hook and a right uppercut. Mancini seems dazed, but he's still on his feet, backing away to regain his composure.

There are a few moments during the third and fourth round where I think Mancini is going down and Gunnar is going to get another KO under his belt, but somehow, the big guy manages to stay on his feet.

As the fifth round begins, it's obvious both fighters are getting tired, but Gunnar's stamina is impressive. Unfortunately, Mancini gets in one of those right hooks I warned Gunnar about, but Gunnar answers him with a combination that sends Mancini to the mat.

The ref drops to his knees and begins pounding the mat as he counts down.

Everyone in the arena is either holding their breath or screaming.

Some are chanting Gunnar's name.

A few are yelling at Mancini to get up.

"Six... seven... eight..."

Mancini tries to get up but falls back down as the ref calls out, "... nine."

When he reaches ten, the place erupts.

Cage rushes into the ring and hauls Gunnar up by the waist like he weighs nothing.

My eyes land back on Frankie who, thankfully, is still hanging in there and she's even managed a smile as she looks up at Gunnar. There might even be tears in her eyes and I get the feeling they're more for the emotional battle she just won than the physical one my brother just fought.

After the crowd begins to clear out, I meet Mancini in the back and sit with him while a doctor checks him out. He might have a concussion, but it's nothing severe and definitely nothing he's not experienced before. The life of a fighter is a dangerous one. Everyone knows it and goes into the sport with the knowledge that each fight could be their last.

Most assume that will come late in their career, but every once in a while, something happens that knocks fighters out for good, like Cage.

Once Mancini and his trainer load up and leave, I make my way back out to the ring to find the cleanup crew already getting started. Cage is collecting the donation boxes and everyone else is gone.

"Did Maggie leave?" I ask, pulling my phone out of my pocket to see if I missed a call or text from her. She promised she'd wait for me, and when I left her, she was visiting with Tempest and Frankie.

"She's upstairs," he says, nodding over his shoulder. "Gunnar and Frankie are up there too. Tempest picked up some beer. We thought we'd have a little post-fight celebration with just the six of us. Genie's is packed this time of night and there's no way we'd get our booth."

"Let me have one of those," I tell him, walking up and taking one of the boxes off his hands. "Damn, feels like there's quite a bit in here. Shall we count this up and see how much we got?"

Cage raises his eyebrows. "How about we let Frankie do the honors."

"Even better."

Following him to the stairs that lead up to his and Tempest's apartment, I can't help but smile at the ruckus floating down.

"If I win," Gunnar says, "you have to name the baby after me."

Tempest laughs. "I can't promise that. No way."

"My name is fucking fantastic, admit it."

"Babe," Frankie says. "I thought our first son had to be Gunnar."

"We can have an entire family of Gunnars," he says as we reach the top of the stairs.

Cage grunts, walking over to the table and setting down the boxes before going to Tempest and wrapping her in a hug from behind, resting his hands on her still flat belly. "If this is a boy, he's going to be named Leif."

"You don't even go by that name," Gunnar scoffs. "Why would you name your kid that?"

"Because Tempest loves it."

Tilting her head back, she kisses him, adoration pouring off her. "It's a great name."

"Even though you made fun of it when I told you." Cage tries to sound hurt but he can't hide his smile when Tempest begins to laugh.

"I did not!"

He looks down at her like she hung the moon. "Oh, you didn't? You didn't tell me not to get lost?"

"How could I not take advantage of that opportunity?" she asks, laughing as he leans forward and kisses her again.

I glance over to see Maggie smiling at their banter. God, she's gorgeous. After a few seconds, she feels my eyes on her, and when she turns to look at me, her smile grows.

Setting the other donation box on the table with the others, I walk over to Maggie and urge her out of her seat, sit down, and pull her on my lap. When she tenses, I lean forward and nip her shoulder. "Relax. I just missed you," I whisper. "I need you close."

Rubbing a hand down the side of her leg, I squeeze her knee and she eventually eases back into me.

"Frankie," I say, getting her attention. "Cage and I decided you should be the one to count up the donations from tonight."

"Really?" she asks, glancing over to me and then to Cage.

He smiles, taking a seat and bringing Tempest with him. "Yeah, you do the honors. It's all going to the women's shelter, anyway."

"Okay," she says, swiping a strand of her short hair behind her ear.

Gunnar wraps one of his meaty arms around her shoulders and pulls her to him, whispering something in her ear that makes her smile.

"Proud of you," Cage adds. "You've come a long way."

Frankie's cheeks turn pink, but she nods her head in appreciation. "Thanks. Being at the studio has really helped. And the therapy, of course. But tonight felt completely different than the first fight I attended." Pausing, she locks eyes with Gunnar. "That was a disaster."

He kisses the side of her head. "That's in the past, baby."

Finally opening one of the boxes, Frankie's eyes go wide.

"Well?" Cage asks. "Don't keep us in suspense. How'd we do?"

As she starts to count, Tempest stands up and asks, "Anyone want a beer? I stocked the fridge." Opening it, she leans over and adds, "Oh, and we have sparkling water, milk, and apple juice."

"Beer," Gunnar and Cage both say.

"One for me too," Frankie adds, her attention fully on her task at hand.

"Me too," I add. "Maggie?" She tenses again and I pull her back flush to my chest. "Hey, you don't have to have a beer, but if you want one, I'll drive you home."

Laughing nervously, she fidgets in my lap. "I've never drank before," she finally blurts out and the entire room goes silent, four sets of eyes drifting over to where we're sitting at the end of the table.

It's in moments like these when I realize just how innocent and inexperienced Maggie is. There was a time in my life that might've been a turnoff, but not now, not with her. There's something different about Maggie. She soaks in the world around her, seeing things most people overlook. Even in her innocence, there's an underlying air of confidence.

"Never?" Tempest asks, still standing in the open door of the refrigerator.

"Ha, no… never."

"No pressure," Cage says.

I squeeze her to me, reassuring her. "Absolutely no pressure."

"But I kind of want to see if I like it," she finally says.

With a smile, Tempest pops the top on one and sets it down in front of Maggie. "If you hate it, I'll get you a water."

"If you like it, I'll drive you home," I add.

Frankie pipes up from her stack of cash. "Don't worry if you don't like it right off the bat. I thought it tasted like piss water until about two years ago. Then, all of a sudden, one day I'd been working in my yard and it was hot and a beer just sounded good." She shrugs as she stacks up some twenties. "I've liked it ever since."

"To a successful night," Cage says, holding his beer out to the middle of the table.

"To dreams coming true," Tempest adds, holding up her sparkling water.

"To being one step closer to a title," Gunnar chimes in.

"To overcoming the past," Frankie says.

"To Plan B," I add, grinning at Cage.

Glancing over at Maggie, we all wait to see if she has anything to add. As she lets her eyes roam around the table, her face lights up with the most beautiful smile. There's something else that passes over her features and I'd love to know what she's thinking… I want to know everything about this woman.

"To new experiences," she finally adds.

We all clink our bottles and then drink.

"What do you think?" I ask, turning to see her face scrunched up.

She shrugs, taking another tentative sip. "Not too bad… but not amazing."

"Piss water?" Frankie asks with a laugh.

Everyone goes back to random conversations and Maggie settles back against me, nursing her beer. Occasionally, I catch Tempest eyeing me. I know she wants me to invite Maggie to New Orleans, and I will, but I just haven't found the right time.

Eventually, Frankie slams her hand down on the table, making the room go quiet.

"Three thousand four hundred and seventy-two dollars!"

"Holy shit!"

"That's incredible!"

Frankie's face goes from a wide smile to a solemn expression. "This is so great. I don't know what to say, except thank y'all. For everything."

"Anything we can do to help," Cage says.

"That's what family is for," I add.

Gunnar, who looks like he's finally hit his wall, stands from his chair. "Let's take it home and roll around on it in the bed before we give it to Helen."

Frankie rolls her eyes, stacking the money up and placing it in an envelope Cage gave her. "I'll make sure it gets deposited and you get a receipt for tax purposes."

"Guys, it's been real," Gunnar says, stretching his arms over his head. "Can't wait to do it again in a few weeks."

"That'll be the real deal," Cage adds. "Until then, don't plan on getting any slack."

Gunnar groans and Frankie pushes him toward the stairs. "Good night."

"Good night," we all call back.

Maggie stands. "I should probably go too."

"I'll walk you down."

She's nursed half a beer for the past hour, so I doubt she needs me to drive her home. But I will if she wants me to.

"Thanks for such a fun night," she tells Cage and Tempest. "And my first beer."

When Tempest stands and gives Maggie a hug, Cage gives me a nod that carries a dozen words—*don't mess this up, she's one of the good ones*. I give him a nod back, letting him know I hear him loud and clear, then I escort Maggie downstairs.

"I'll still drive you home if you need me to," I tell her when we get to her car. Leaning forward, I claim her lips and kiss her like I've wanted to all night. "Or even better, you can stay with me."

She pulls back and looks up at me. Her eyes go wide and I see the desire on her face.

She wants that too.

"I'd love to stay the night with you," she whispers. "But I can't tonight."

Without overthinking it, or perhaps not thinking at all, I say, "Come to New Orleans with me."

Her eyes grow wide and her mouth drops open. "New Orleans?"

"Yeah, that's where Gunnar's next fight is in three weeks. We're all going. There will be plenty of room for you to ride with us," I spill out, hoping it's not too soon and I don't scare her away.

"I… I don't know what to say." She sounds stunned and unsure.

"Don't give me an answer tonight," I tell her. "Just think about it, okay?"

CHAPTER 22

MAGGIE

* New Orleans.*

Vali just asked me to go to New Orleans.

With him.

My heart is pounding with a mixture of nervousness, excitement, and anticipation as I drive down the dark streets. When I pull into the drive at my house, I notice the kitchen light is still on which means my mama is awake. Can I tell her a man asked me to go away with him for a weekend? What would she say?

My parents still haven't even met Vali, but I want them to… eventually. I'm just not sure this is how I want to officially introduce them.

Mom… Dad… this is Vali Erickson. We're not using labels, so he's not technically my boyfriend, but we do all the things boyfriends and girlfriends do and he wants me to go to New Orleans with him. What do you say?

Falling forward, I brace myself on the steering wheel and wish my situation was different. If I was a normal twenty-four-year-old and lived on my own, this wouldn't be a big deal. But since I do live with my parents and they depend on me to help them run the feed store, it's kind of a big deal.

But how can I pass up an opportunity like this?

It may be my only chance to spend more than a few hours with Vali. And I want that more than anything. Also, how can I pass up the chance to meet Everly in person? From the moment Vali mentioned it, my mind has been whirling and I don't predict it's going to stop anytime soon.

Eventually, I collect myself as much as I can and get out of the car. When the wind whips my hair around my face, a faint hint of Vali's cologne, mixed with a scent that is singularly *him*, invades my senses and I breathe deeply.

How crazy is it that I miss him only moments after leaving him?

Is that normal?

"Hi, honey," my mom calls out when she hears the door open.

"Hi, Mama," I call back, removing my coat and hanging it on the hook in the hallway. "What are you doing up so late? I hope you're not waiting up on me."

As I walk into the kitchen, I know exactly what she's doing.

The sweet aroma of banana nut bread fills the space and I groan.

"Well," she says, walking over to the oven and bending over to peek inside. "Your dad and I stayed up watching a movie, then I remembered I had some bananas that were going bad, so I sent him to bed and I came in here to bake... you know, a little me time."

Smiling, I walk over and lean against the counter. "Smells amazing," I tell her, wondering if this would be a good time to mention Vali's invitation.

"So, how was the fight night?" she asks, folding a dish towel and laying it just so beside the sink. "Did you have fun?"

I nod, unable to hold back my excitement. "It was amazing and nothing like I thought it would be. The excitement in that room was electrifying." Shaking my head, I muse to myself that I can't wait to write about tonight in my article for next week. That's another thing I've been wondering. When will be the right time to tell my parents about the article?

And Vali, at what point do I come clean to him?

He's already mentioned it a few times when we've been together and, honestly, I'm getting tired of the adrenaline spike every time he does. Sure, I love my anonymity and I know it gives me a level of security. If everyone in town knew who was giving them the advice and gossip, they might not be so inclined to read it or write to me. Without the community's participation, I don't have a column.

"Margaret," my mother says, using my full name to get my attention.

"Sorry, Mama. What were you saying?"

"Who won?"

"Oh," I say, a wide smile breaking across my face. "Gunnar, Vali's younger brother. And you should've seen him. Every move was so precise and calculated. And he ended up knocking the other guy out."

The look of astonishment on my mother's face is priceless. "Well, that sounds... exciting."

"It really was."

And addictive.

Now that I've been to one fight, I need to go to more.

Particularly, one a few weeks from now in New Orleans.

Before I can muster up the courage to mention it to her, she has the banana bread out of the oven and covered in a towel. "We'll slice this for breakfast in the morning," she says, walking around the island and placing a kiss on my cheek. "Sleep well."

"You too, Mama," I tell her retreating form, huffing as I slump back against the counter.

Unfortunately, I don't sleep well. Thoughts of Vali and New Orleans take over my mind. At nearly two in the morning, I crawl out of bed, grab my laptop, and open up my and Everly's last email. I'd promised her an update on the fight and my time with Vali, so I might as well tell her everything.

I hate to get her hopes up about me coming to New Orleans, but she's the only one I can talk this out with and who might have some good advice for me. Although, it will be biased because she's always wanted me to come to New Orleans.

* * *

LATER THAT MORNING, after a few hours of sleep, I open my laptop back up to an overzealous reply from Everly.

Margaret Hope O'Neal.

If you're lying to me, I'll kill you.

And if you're even thinking about not taking this man up on his offer, I'll kill you twice.

Get your ass in that car and come see me! Girl, this is thirteen years in the making. We've always said one day we'll make it happen. Honestly, I always thought it would be me coming to see you. But having you in my city, if only for a couple of days, would be amazing.

Also, I might need a ticket to this fight. It sounds brutal, yet thrilling. Hot guys, shirtless, with loads of muscles? Sign me up.

Ever

Sitting back on my bed, I frown at the screen. There are a couple of things in her reply that give me pause. She's right, we have always said one day we will meet in person. Coincidentally, I have a secret stash of money I've earned from writing for the *Green Valley Ledger* that's labeled my *One Day Fund*—one day I'm going to travel, one day I'm going to see other states, one day I'm going to spread my wings. *When will that be, if not now?*

Then there's the part where she says she always assumed she'd be the one to visit me.

I don't like the way that makes me feel.

And there's one other thing that Everly didn't bring up but I've definitely thought about—*what if we meet in person and it ruins the special connection we've had all these years?*

The magic in Everly's and my relationship stems from the simple, innocent beginning of two preteen girls from completely different walks of life, finding common ground in emails about their favorite things, the weather, what their parents did that made them mad, the latest boy band, and eventually, boyfriends, college, and becoming adults.

Even though we have each other's phone numbers, we rarely use them. I can count on one hand the amount of times I've stepped outside of our normal routine and called or texted her.

She's the one constant in my life that I'd never want to lose.

"Maggie," my mom's voice calls from the hallway causing me to jump and slam my laptop closed.

"Yes?"

"We're going to the store early," she calls out from the other side of my closed door. "There's a shipment coming in this morning. Can you make sure you're there in time to check in the inventory?"

"Yes," I tell her, scrambling off my bed and heading for the bathroom. "I'll be there as soon as I can."

"I left you a piece of banana nut bread and a cup of coffee on the island."

"Thank you, Mama."

After a quick shower, I toss on some jeans and an O'Neal Feed and Fodder T-shirt, pull my hair into a bun, and call it good. Since it's Saturday, the store will be bustling and I always end up sweating off what little makeup I put on, so why waste it?

Grabbing my breakfast from the bar, I hustle out the door and to the store.

From the moment I walk through the front door, I'm busier than a stump-tailed cow in fly season. Between an unexpected delivery truck, two busted pallets of feed, and an argument over the last bird feeder hanger post, I'm swamped. By noon, my top bun is slipping and my brow is covered in sweat as I help one of our regulars load up his purchases. "Thank you, Maggie," he says as I set his last bag in the back of his truck.

"No problem," I reply, closing the tailgate and dusting my hands off on my jeans. "Thank you for your business."

"See you next week!"

When I walk back into the store, my eyes land on the last person I expected to see.

Vali is standing at the counter, his hand outstretched, shaking my dad's and I'm immediately on high alert. My heart starts beating faster and I'm forced to swallow when he turns his deep blue gaze on me. As always, I'm happy to see him. It's like my entire being calls to him.

But what is he doing here?

"There she is," he says, smiling wide, like the cat that ate the canary.

When he steps back, I see my mother standing on the other side of my dad.

"What are you doing here?" I ask, trying to school my features and offer him a smile, but feeling completely flustered. I planned on introducing Vali to my parents, but in my own time. The fact he swooped in here under my nose, and did it for me, is equal parts relief and frustration.

"I was out running errands and thought I'd swing by and see if you've had a chance to think over my invitation."

My mama cocks her head, her smile faltering a bit. "What invitation?" she asks, turning her attention to me.

"Uh, I..." I stutter, feeling the panic set in. "Can we talk outside?" I finally manage, pointing over my shoulder toward the door.

Vali eventually nods, turning toward my parents. "It was really great to officially meet you both."

"You too," my mama says, obviously a bit smitten with Vali, but I can't blame her. He has that same effect on me.

My dad is still standing there with a neutral expression, nodding in Vali's direction. "Thanks for stopping by."

Not wanting to give them any longer to question Vali's statement, I turn and make my way to the door. Once I'm outside, I cross my arms over my chest and begin to pace the sidewalk. When Vali walks out, he pauses, giving me a confused expression before walking toward me.

"Why did you do that?" I ask, feeling my temper rise.

Vali's expression changes from confused to defensive. "I'm sorry. Did you *not* want me to meet your parents?"

"No," I tell him. "I mean, yes, but I haven't had a chance to talk to them yet and you barging in here and taking charge wasn't exactly what I had in mind." I pause, taking deep breaths that make my chest rise and fall. "This whole thing is new for me... not just you, but the idea of having a... whatever you are!"

Vali stays quiet, letting me vent.

"See, that's part of the problem. I don't even know what to call you, so how can I explain to them why I'd want to go to New Orleans with you?"

He nods, his gaze drifting to the ground as he pulls at his full bottom lip.

"I'm sorry," he says, backing away. "I obviously overstepped."

When he turns and walks away, I call out after him but he just waves and keeps walking.

CHAPTER 23

VALI

*I*f it doesn't challenge you, it doesn't change you.

If it doesn't challenge you, it doesn't change you.

If it doesn't challenge you, it doesn't change you.

I continue to repeat my favorite mantra in my mind while starting mile eight of my run. Typically, I keep myself from getting bored while running long distances by listening to music or podcasts but sometimes I have to dig deep and go the mantra route to stay focused. Today, I'm using these particular words to keep my mind off Maggie and our little exchange at the feed store a few days ago.

After I left, I drove back to the gym and laced up my gloves—something I haven't done in months. Then, I proceeded to beat the shit out of one of the bags but it wasn't enough. My body has been filled with energy, pent-up aggression—whatever you want to call it—ever since and it needed to be let out before I started lashing out at people.

Which is why I'm running.

It's my go-to for exercise, especially first thing in the morning, but it's been a while since I've done some long distances and even longer since I've run in the afternoon. The sweat dripping from my clothes makes that pretty obvious.

I just don't understand what I did to upset Maggie so much.

Maybe I assumed too much.

Obviously, I assumed she'd already talked to her parents about going to New Orleans with me. I mean, she lives and works with them. Surely, it would've come up at some point. It's possible she doesn't want to go but doesn't know how to tell me, I guess. I thought she seemed pretty excited about it when I asked her, though.

Maybe I jumped the gun.

I'm just so excited for this trip and the idea of going without her doesn't make me happy. I'd still have fun, I'm sure, but I'd miss her. I know that for a fact.

Also, why was she pissed I introduced myself to her parents? After the way I behaved the first time I went to the store, I felt it was my responsibility to step up and show them I'm really not that much of a douche.

I can't help but wonder if she's ashamed of me or of us being together.

What did she say? How can she explain why she wants to go to New Orleans with me when she doesn't even know what we are to each other or something like that?

I thought we agreed to not label our relationship so we wouldn't have to *break up* when I eventually move back to Dallas. If it really bothers her so much, she could've said something to me about it. If she wants a commitment, she has it. There's no one else I want to be with and fuck me if I don't want to take her and claim her like a caveman, but I'm trying to be respectful of her.

Lastly, why does she have to explain any of this to her parents? I know she doesn't want to do anything to upset or disrespect them, but she's an adult. She makes her own money, and even though she's pretty damn sheltered, she's incredibly smart and mature. There's no reason they shouldn't trust her.

I can also tell their family dynamic is very different than the Ericksons'. Where my brothers and I were raised with many freedoms and sometimes broke the few rules we had, I know Maggie didn't grow up that way.

It's almost as if she's living two separate lives. One is the sweet and perfect daughter, only living to please her parents. The other is someone who's dying to experience the world and everything it has to offer, pleasing herself for once.

When I finish my twelfth mile, I cool off by walking up and down the streets of downtown. I'm feeling pretty shitty that it's been three days since I saw Maggie last, but I decided to give her time to work through whatever was really bothering her. Plus, my feelings were kind of hurt, and if I'm being honest, I've been licking my wounds a bit.

I also have to admit that fire I saw inside her was pretty fucking hot. Although, I shouldn't be surprised because when Maggie lets go of her inhibitions, which I've been privy to a few times now, she's next level. It's not just about her physical attributes, which are stunning, but something inside her, like a contained wildfire.

My gut tells me there's another layer to Maggie O'Neal that has yet to be discovered. And fuck if I don't want to know everything about her and help her experience everything that's out there waiting for her.

But one thing is for sure, we have to communicate better.

If I don't hear from her by the end of the week, I guess I'll be making another trip to O'Neal Feed and Fodder.

* * *

THE ONLY THING I have to look forward to today is getting my weekly fix of gossip through the local paper, which is just sad.

The pit in my stomach grows the longer I don't hear from Maggie but that ends today. Even though I feel she should be the one to reach out to me, I'm gonna use what she likes to call her *less-than-stellar social skills* as an excuse and remove that burden from her. I'm confronting her because I can't seem to stay away. I'm frustrated as hell with her but I still miss her.

I miss her like crazy.

Like clockwork, I finish my morning run and head straight for the bakery. I have the *Green Valley Ledger* in my hand when it's my turn to order, surprising Tempest with "you pick" as my answer when she asks me what I'd like.

"Whoa. Bad day already? You're usually pretty decisive when you place your order. What's going on?"

Sighing, I admit I still haven't heard from Maggie. I haven't been very forthcoming with my family about what happened last Saturday, but it's pretty obvious to everyone we've hit a snag in our relationship, or whatever you want to call it.

"You're going to talk to her today, right?"

"That's the plan. I can't stand the radio silence anymore."

"I'm surprised it's taken you this long. You've seemed miserable all week." Tempest hands me a bag with a variety of muffins, as well as a cup of coffee, waving my money away when I try to pay. "Keep your money. These muffins are made to heal broken hearts and you can't put a price on that." She winks at me before addressing her next customer.

Once I'm situated at a table and have eaten a muffin, I feel relaxed enough to read through the paper. Tempest is right, though, her muffins are fucking magical.

I open the paper and skip to my favorite column.

Greetings, Good People of Green Valley

Elton John says Saturday Night's Alright for Fighting, but in our town, Fridays are even better!

Viking MMA hosted its second charity fight last Friday, paired it with the grand opening of their new ring, and donated all proceeds to the Maryville Women's Shelter.

If you weren't there, you missed one heck of a show and we're not just talking about watching the Erickson brothers strut around the gym. The exhibition fight featured Gunnar "The Show" Erickson and Michael "Maneater" Mancini and ended with an actual TKO! The excitement in the room was palpable and the crowd was on their feet the entire time.

Thanks to everyone who came out and supported our resident Vikings, $3500 is being donated to the Maryville Women's Shelter. And with another win under his belt, Gunnar is even more prepared for his next bout in New Orleans.

We know the Erickson crew will have the love and support of Green Valley as they travel. If you see them around town, make sure you tell them "good luck!"

I pause at the end, needing to read that last part again.

And then I read it a third time.

My brow furrows as I try to remember if anyone said anything about Gunnar fighting in New Orleans, and since I was the MC for the night, I know I didn't. Which makes me wonder where, or rather *who*, Trixie and Tess are getting their information from.

As far as I'm aware, the only people who know about that little tidbit of information is our family.

Also, we haven't had a chance to announce the money we raised for the women's shelter. Since it wasn't counted until after the fight, the only people who know the exact amount are the six people who were sitting at the table Friday night. I find it hard to believe anyone in that room would've blabbed about it to the local paper.

Unless…

The noise from my chair being forcefully scooted against the floor is a jarring clash to the pleasant atmosphere of the bakery and just about everyone in here jumps and looks at me when I stand up.

"Sorry," I mumble as I grab my things and leave.

What else is Maggie O'Neal holding out on?

Either she's feeding insider information to the local gossip columnists or she's hiding something else. Regardless, I don't like it, and there's only one way I can resolve this whole mess.

Twenty minutes later, I'm pulling up in front of O'Neal Feed and Fodder. When I spot Maggie's car parked on the side of the building, I'm equally relieved and apprehensive. I've never been one to look for confrontation, but I also refuse to let things fester.

After what happened with Chloe, I'll never turn a blind eye again. In some ways, she probably helped me become a better person. The further I get from the heartache, the more I can see the lesson in all of it. I might be less likely to trust people, but in return I'm more open and honest than I've ever been.

With the newspaper in hand, I walk up to the entrance and hope the lack of vehicles in the parking lot means I'll be able to get a few minutes of Maggie's time without an audience.

A sixties station is playing in the background and I can hear someone humming along. A few seconds later, Maggie's mom steps out and her smile falters when she sees me.

"Hello, Vali," she says, adjusting her apron. "Nice to see you again."

Offering her a smile and a nod, I reply, "Good to see you too, Mrs. O'Neal. Is Maggie around?"

About that time a door closes in the back and Maggie steps out looking more beautiful than one person has the right to. "Vali," she says, eyes going wide.

I almost laugh at her shock, because surely she knew at some point, if she didn't come to me, I was coming to her. Just because things went a little sideways doesn't mean I'm just going to walk away from her.

"Can we talk?" I ask, motioning over my shoulder toward the door.

She glances at her mom and then back at me. "Sure." Tucking some loose strands of hair behind her ears, she walks around the counter. Letting her step ahead of me, I follow her outside.

Before I can even speak, she blurts out, "I'm sorry." Her back is still to me, but she slowly turns around and I see the regret on her face. Trapping her full bottom lip between her teeth, she closes her eyes and then exhales.

"I'm sorry I lost my temper and freaked out on you like that. You just caught me off guard and I was so nervous about telling my parents about New Orleans. I think I was just really worked up and took it out on you."

Shifting on my feet, I lean into the side of the building. "I'm sorry too. I didn't mean to make things worse. And after my less-than-stellar first meeting with your dad, I wanted to properly introduce myself."

"I was excited," she says, her eyes zoning in on the newspaper under my arm and halting her words. Looking from the paper to me, she clears her throat. "I mean, I am excited. And I really have you to thank for that. After your visit, I was pretty much forced to tell them about the trip."

She pauses, biting on her lip again. "I guess sometimes I need a little push."

"We all do from time to time," I tell her, wanting to pull her into a hug and forget the last few days, but first I have to get the rest out on the table. Clearing my throat, I take the newspaper out and unfold it.

I swear I hear Maggie cringe.

"Would you happen to know how the local gossip columnists know information that only six people were privy to?" I ask, turning to the article in question.

"Uh," she starts, then stops, her eyes dropping down to her feet.

When she looks back up, I see panic all over her beautiful face.

Her usual olive skin has turned ashen.

"Well... I..."

Call it instinct, but I can feel a lie coming and I know if Maggie lies to me in this moment, we'll be over. "Don't lie to me," I plead, not wanting us to end.

Those words sober her and she swallows, glancing behind her and then turning back to me. I watch as she squares her shoulders and prepares for the truth. Dropping her voice to barely above a whisper, she says, "I'm Trixie and Tess."

For a second, I let those words sink in.

She's Trixie and Tess?

"But you're just one person."

"I know," she says with a painful smile. "That's the idea. Everyone assumes it's two people, so no one would ever suspect quiet, sheltered, never-been-anywhere-or-done-anything Maggie O'Neal."

The defensiveness in her tone lets me know I've hit a nerve.

Running a hand through my hair, I chuckle ruefully. "So, you're..."

"Yeah," she says, nervously twisting her fingers. "And I know, you're probably thinking horrible things right now, like I'm a liar or a fraud or numerous other dreadful titles. But I just want you to know that no one else knows... well, except for Sarah. And Everly."

"Who's Everly?"

"My pen pal."

My mind is racing, thinking back to the first Trixie and Tess column I read to the last. Putting Maggie in the place of two strangers, things seem different. And even though she told me the truth, I still feel a bit... I don't know... betrayed? Lied to? Lied to by omission?

"Vali," Maggie says, her hand reaching out to touch my arm. "Please understand that writing that article is my own personal escape. Without it, I'd be miserable. And I've always felt like if anyone found out, my cover would be blown. I know that sounds stupid, because this is a piddly little article in a small-town newspaper, but it's all I have."

"Your parents don't even know?"

"No," she says, shaking her head.

Sighing, I swipe my hand across my face, trying to decide how I feel about this. I mean, I get it, we've only known each other a little over two months and Maggie's been writing this article for a lot longer than that. It's obviously personal and important to her. Besides, it's not like she's writing scandalous things. Also, there's the part of me that's happy Maggie is Trixie and Tess, because now my two crushes in Green Valley can be one.

"It's my favorite part of the week," I admit.

Her face slowly morphs from panicked to something resembling happiness. "Really?"

I nod. "Yeah, I look forward to it every week. It's the first thing I read."

"So you're not mad?" she asks, scrunching up her nose.

Leaning forward, I kiss that nose... and then her lips. "No," I whisper against them. "I'm not mad. And I missed you."

"I missed you too," she says on a sigh, capturing my lips for another kiss as her arms loop around my neck, pulling me closer. "And I'm going to New Orleans with you."

CHAPTER 24

MAGGIE

I can't believe I'm going to see you in person in two days.
What is this life?! And how is it happening to me?
You know what, don't answer that. I've told myself over the last
two weeks that I'm just going to enjoy the moments I'm given,
not overthink them, and appreciate each new turn. I've wanted
adventure my entire life. You, of all people, know that. So, here
I am, nose to nose with adventure and I have to admit, I'm a
little scared, but more than that, I'm excited.
Thank you for always encouraging me to step out of my comfort
zone.
I can't wait to hug your neck.
BUT you have to promise me, that if by some crazy chance we
don't hit it off as well in person as we do online, you'll forget
you saw me and we'll go back to our archaic communication,
because I don't know what I'd do without you.
Your Tennessee Bestie,
Maggie

losing down my laptop, I exhale and glance over at the bag I packed earlier.

This is really happening. At six in the morning, Vali, Cage, Tempest, Gunnar, and Frankie are stopping by here to pick me up on their way out of town and we're driving nine hours to New Orleans.

Not only will I get to see Everly, but I'm also spending an entire weekend with Vali. As of now, I have the option of staying in my own room, but the closer we get, the more I want to forgo that option and stay with Vali. We've skirted the topic, but in true Vali fashion, he hasn't put any pressure on me.

But I want to.

I want to seize the day… the moment… this time with him.

I don't want to look back in a year and think *I wish I would've.*

That's the old Maggie. The new Maggie is meeting new people and going on road trips, she's a different girl. She's willing to put it all on the line and experience life, danger, and heartache be damned.

The last couple of weeks have been both pleasure and torture. My and Vali's make-out sessions have gotten hotter and hotter, each one leaving me wanting more and more. Last night, after a late dinner at his apartment, we settled onto the couch for a movie, but it ended up being background noise to the two orgasms I experienced at the mercy of Vali's fingers.

I've never had anyone touch me like that, ever. It was mind-blowing and next level, something I'd only read about in *Cosmopolitan* and romance novels. And now all I can think about is how euphoric an orgasm would be with Vali inside me.

I'm ready for the clothes to come off.

His and mine.

Sighing, I roll over and turn off my lamp. It's late, and even though I can sleep on the road, I don't want to. I've never been out of the state of Tennessee, so I'm looking forward to crossing state lines and seeing everything there is to see between here and New Orleans.

New roads that lead to new cities that lead to new people and new experiences…

The next thing I know, my alarm on my phone is going off and I bolt out of bed and hit the ground running. After a quick shower, I tie my hair up in a bun on the top of my head, then put on the clothes I laid out last night.

I wonder if this is what the first day of school felt like for people who went to public school.

Or maybe the first day of college…

Or a grand adventure.

"Promise me you'll be safe," my mom says as she hugs me for the tenth time since I brought my bag into the kitchen, where she was waiting for me with fresh biscuits and a cup of coffee.

"I promise," I tell her, closing my eyes as I squeeze her tight. "I'll either be with Vali and the group or I'll be with Everly."

When I sat my parents down and told them about the trip to New Orleans—yes, told, not asked—they were a little shocked, but surprisingly not as much as I thought they'd be. My mama actually seemed excited about the prospect, claiming she'd been to New Orleans once in her twenties and *fell in love* with the city. My daddy, on the other hand, was much more reserved about the idea, per usual.

"Take this," my dad says, holding out a can of pepper spray wrapped in several large bills.

"Dad," I say, leaving my mom's hug and going to him. "I don't need the money, but I'll take the pepper spray," I whisper with a chuckle.

"Take both," he insists.

Stuffing them into my backpack, I straighten and collect my coffee mug and the biscuits Mama wrapped up for me to take to everyone.

When I hear a car pull up, I feel a rush of excitement. "I'll call when we get there."

CHAPTER 25

VALI

Sitting across from Maggie, I can't keep my eyes off her. The way she's soaking in every moment of this trip is contagious. Shit, even I was excited when we crossed over the state line into Alabama.

There are so many things about her that make me smile, but this childlike wonder she has right now is maybe one of my favorite things.

I also love the way she argued a blue streak with Cage over paying for gas when we stopped earlier to fill up.

I love that she's going to meet her pen pal she's had since she was a kid. That was a little twist I didn't see coming, but I'm happy for her.

And I love the way she's scribbled in that damn blue journal off and on the entire trip.

Smiling, I wonder if she's writing down something that will end up in one of her articles. As promised, I've kept my word and her secret. It's been hard, actually. Every time I read the paper and there's something humorous or entertaining in *Trixie and Tess Tell All,* I want to brag about how witty she is or how smart she is.

"What?" she asks, looking over at me with a sly grin.

I hold her gaze until her cheeks tint pink.

Needing to kiss her something fiercely, I lean over and press my lips to hers. "Thank you for coming on this trip with me," I whisper, pressing another kiss to her forehead.

Everyone else is either sleeping, driving, or preoccupied. Tempest has been listening to audiobooks about babies the entire trip. Every once in a while, she'll pop an earbud out and give us some crazy fact about pregnancy or childbirth.

Did you guys know that in the second half of pregnancy, the baby will pee half a liter a day. Where does it go?

My uterus is going to stretch to the size of a medium watermelon.

The baby already has fingerprints.

That one had the entire van awing, even me.

She's now four months along, which means in just a few more weeks I'll know if I'm going to have a niece or a nephew. Honestly, I can't wait and I don't care if it's a boy or a girl. I'm just ready to spoil him or her. My parents are obviously hoping for a girl. Mom claims the Lord owes her since she birthed and raised all of us boys. I have to admit, having a niece scares the shit out of me. We Ericksons are good with manly things—fighting and sweating and running a gym. But we don't know the first thing about girls.

Occasionally, I have to sit back and soak it all in because it seems like just yesterday the five of us were fighting over video games and who got the last slice of pizza. Now, Cage is going to be a dad and my baby brother is getting ready to fight for a title belt.

Life just moves so fast and you don't even realize it.

"Hey, Vali," Maggie says a little later as she closes her journal and puts it in her backpack.

"Yeah, babe?"

She smiles every time I call her anything other than Maggie. I haven't decided on what I like calling her the most—Mags, babe, gorgeous. They're all so fitting.

Biting down on her lip, she looks out the side window and then to our fellow passengers before turning back to me. "I want to stay with you."

"You do?" I ask, trying to fight back a smile and losing.

Her gaze turns soft and she nods. "Yeah, I do."

Damn if I haven't been hoping she'd change her mind about getting her own room. I mean, if she hadn't, it would've been fine and I would've appreciated the extra time I get to spend with her this weekend. But I've been dying to have Maggie in my bed and I want her with me every second of every day.

Knowing that Maggie is going to be all mine and we're going to have hours of uninterrupted time together makes the last leg of the trip somewhat torturous. I feel like a kid asking their parents "Are we there yet?" But instead of being obvious, I just check Google Maps on my phone and count down the miles.

A few hours later, when we're exiting off I-10 toward downtown New Orleans, I'm amped up for more than one reason—the anticipation of being with Maggie, my other two brothers meeting us here, Gunnar's big fight, and a city I love. But it's Maggie's gushing that really has me beaming.

"Look how pretty!"

"Oh, look, a palm tree!"

And as we turn off the main thoroughfare and start hitting the French Quarter, she's even more enamored. "Everly sent me pictures over the years, but they didn't do it justice."

I still can't believe Maggie's never been further than Nashville before today. My brothers and I grew up traveling for fights. At first, they were our dad's fight, then people he trained, and eventually ours.

"When are you meeting up with her?" I ask, reaching over to lace my fingers through hers.

"Tomorrow morning at eight," she says, her eyes glued to the buildings we're passing by. Occasionally, she whips her head around to watch people. I must admit, I've never seen better people-watching than in New Orleans.

"Let's go out for a nice dinner tonight," Tempest suggests.

At that, Gunnar wakes up, noticing where we are. "Did someone say dinner?"

Frankie laughs, shaking her head as she glances up from her book she's been engrossed in for a few hours. "Of course you'd wake up for food."

"I'm a growing boy," he says, stretching and patting his stomach. "Besides, I'll need all my energy for tomorrow night."

"After weigh-in," Cage says from behind the wheel. "Then you can carb up."

Gunnar checks in at the Superdome in two hours. By that time, Viggo and Ozzi will be here and the party can officially start.

When we pull up to the valet, everyone gets out and grabs their luggage. As we're walking up to the front doors, Tempest hangs back and covertly asks about the room situation. I tell her Maggie is staying with me and she gives me a knowing smile.

"I knew it."

"You knew what?" I ask.

She shrugs, walking ahead and catching up with Cage. "Knew you'd take my advice."

I swear, she's getting as smug as my brother.

Once we're all checked in, we split off and head to our respective rooms to rest and freshen up. Gunnar and Cage will be heading over to the Superdome, but the rest of us have nowhere to be until dinner.

"We'll meet in the lobby at seven," Cage calls out.

With Maggie's bag on one shoulder and mine on the other, I slip the keycard in and open the door to our room. "After you," I say, stepping back and sweeping my arm out.

Maggie gives me a nervous smile before stepping inside.

"You okay?" I ask, dropping the bags on the bed. "If you've changed your mind about sharing a room, we can go downstairs and fix it."

Turning to face me, she shakes her head. "No, I want to stay with you... I do. It's just way, way out of my comfort zone." Her laugh is full of nerves and uncertainty and I want to put all of that to rest, but I'm not sure how.

"Tell me what to do to make it better."

Letting her backpack slip off her shoulders, she sets it down on the desk and makes a slow circle around the room. "This is a really nice hotel room."

"Are you avoiding the issue?"

"No," she says with a smile. "Just stating a fact. I've never been in a hotel this nice."

The room is beautiful, but not as beautiful as the woman standing in it.

"Want to rest?" I ask. She cocks an eyebrow at me and I laugh. "I mean that literally. Or if you're not tired, we can walk around the French Quarter, do a little sightseeing. There's also a great bar in the lobby. You can try a new drink."

Maggie's smile grows and I can feel the nerves dissipating as excitement takes over.

"I can't believe I'm here."

Closing the distance between us, I wrap my arms around her and pull her to me.

"Well, you are and I couldn't be happier," I tell her, kissing the top of her head. "And zero pressure for anything except having a good time while we're here, okay?"

"Okay," she murmurs against my chest.

An intense kiss turns into a little more, but I pull back, knowing we don't have enough time to take things further. To cool off, we end up taking a walk down Royal Street, checking out a few art galleries, and stopping in a coffee shop for a caffeine fix.

A couple of hours later, after we go back to the room and change clothes, we're in the elevator going down to the lobby to meet everyone for dinner.

"I'm nervous," Maggie says, fidgeting with the strap on her purse like she was the first night she walked into Genie's.

Taking her hand, I reassure her. "It's just Viggo and Ozzi. Once you've met them, you'll realize there was nothing to be nervous about. Besides, they're going to love you."

"I'm still nervous."

Chuckling, I bring her hand up and kiss her knuckles.

As we step out of the elevator, I scan the lobby, knowing it won't be hard to locate my brothers. We tend to stand out amongst a crowd, but it's not the brothers that catch my attention first, it's my parents.

"Vali," my mom says, coming over and wrapping me in a hug. "Surprise! Are you surprised?"

"So surprised," I admit, glancing over her shoulder at my brothers who are all grinning from ear to ear. When I feel Maggie tense at my side, I wish I could whisk her back upstairs and spare her from the unknown. But unfortunately, there's no turning back.

"And who is this?" my mother asks, stepping back and turning her attention to the woman at my side.

CHAPTER 26

MAGGIE

*M*eeting the other two Erickson brothers was one thing.

Meeting their parents is a whole other ball game and one I was not prepared for. Randy, their dad, is basically an older version of Cage and Gunnar. He's tall with broad shoulders, and even though his hair is graying, it's evident thirty years ago, he was just as blond and ruggedly handsome as they are. Well, he still is, but in a much more distinguished way. Their mother, Peggy, is beautiful. Her features are much more delicate, and her hair is darker, which is a lovely contrast to her hazel eyes. It's obvious Vali is a combination of the two.

A perfect combination. God was definitely showing off when he made him.

After a quick round of introductions, we exit the hotel and walk to the restaurant that's only a few blocks away. I'm thankful for the time and fresh air, it gives me a moment to get a grip and talk myself down from the panic attack I felt building moments earlier.

They're just people, I remind myself.

Vali's people.

But since we're not labeling our relationship, there's nothing to worry about. I'm just Maggie and he's just Vali. So, no pressure, right?

Then again, I'm sharing a hotel with him.

Does that make me seem easy? Like a girl who gets around.

Oh, God, why didn't I get my own room?

"I can practically hear your wheels turning," Vali says, leaning down to speak where only I can hear him. "Believe me, I had no clue my parents would be here and I'm sorry about that, but it's fine. They'll also love you, so don't worry."

"That's easy for you to say," I quip. I always feel a bit snarky when I'm on edge.

Vali chuckles, wrapping his arm around my shoulder and pulling me into him.

"I promise I won't leave your side," he says, kissing my temple.

Thankfully, when we arrive at the restaurant and the hostess seats us at our table, I end up with Vali on one side and Tempest on the other. They feel like warm security blankets as Vali's parents—Randy and Peggy—look my way.

"So, Maggie," Peggy says, offering me a smile, "tell us about yourself."

My heart begins to race as I try to think of what to say. It's not like I've ever been in this situation before. My limited dating history only allowed me two sets of parents to meet, but I'd known both of them since I was in diapers, so they don't count. If I'd known ahead of time I was meeting Vali's parents, I would've practiced what to say and prepared myself.

Maggie winging it never goes well.

"Well, uh…" I start, stuttering over my words a little until I feel Vali's hand on my thigh, giving it a gentle squeeze. Turning to him, I see his cool blue eyes, and I'm immediately calmed. Something about them makes me feel wanted, needed, and like I have a purpose for being here, more than just Vali's friend. So, I continue, "I'm from Green Valley."

That's a start. Probably super obvious, but it's better to start easy and work your way up to the harder stuff.

"Lived there my whole life," I add with a nervous chuckle. "My parents own a feed store and I help them—" I'm just getting ready to surge into my usual bout of oversharing when a waiter interrupts me, saving me from myself.

"What can I get everyone to drink?"

The table begins ordering and I exhale a breath of relief, leaning back in my seat. Vali kisses the side of my head and a low, seductive laugh warms my ear. "God, you're adorable when you're nervous. So delectable I could eat you up. I bet you taste better than this fifty-dollar steak I'm getting ready to order."

Now my pulse is racing for a different reason.

Long gone are the thoughts of parents and brothers. All I can think about as I select something from the menu and place my order is how it would feel to be consumed by Vali. The way he makes me feel, with just a few words, is something I've only read about, never experienced.

The other men—scratch that, *boys*—I dated seem like a joke compared to Vali. Sure, I thought they were cute, and when I kissed them, it wasn't a total turnoff, but I never felt the level of attraction for them that I feel for him. It's more than that, though, it's an undying need, one I know will only be sated by feeding the hunger.

A hunger that cannot be fulfilled at the dinner table with his family.

Clearing my throat, I try to shelve those thoughts for later as I take a sip of my water, letting it cool the heat burning in my belly.

Thankfully, conversation flows freely amongst everyone, Tempest and Frankie included. They reminisce about their time together over Christmas and Peggy insists they need another weekend together.

"Well, we know we'll be making a trip to Green Valley this fall," Peggy says, beaming at Tempest. "Maybe we can find a place to buy. Wouldn't that be ideal, Randy?"

He smiles, shaking his head at Cage. "The next thing you know, your mother will be moving in next door."

There are tentative plans made for the whole clan to descend on Green Valley for the birth of Cage and Tempest's baby. Everyone seems so genuinely excited about the new addition, but none more than Cage. He can't wipe the smile off his face as everyone talks about baby names and what the nursery will look like and how to babyproof an MMA studio.

"Well, you boys grew up in a gym and you all turned out just fine," Randy says, throwing an arm over Peggy's chair as she leans into his side.

She smiles and sighs. "I thought I'd go crazy keeping everything clean and safe." She and Randy share a knowing look and both laugh. "By the time Vali came along, we'd pretty much given up on babyproofing anything."

"So that's what's wrong with him," Ozzi says, earning him a wadded-up piece of bread to the middle of his head.

"Boys," Peggy admonishes, causing them both to retreat to their figurative corners.

This is the most entertainment I've had in a long time. Being an observer, I find myself sitting back and soaking in the banter and laughter, interjecting a few things here and there, but mostly watching. I've never been around a big family like this and I'm already addicted.

I want more.

More of the Ericksons.

More Vali.

And when I think the night can't get any better, right after the plates are cleared, Cage stands up, clearing his throat and turning to face his family.

"I've loved this woman since the first night I laid eyes on her as she danced on a bar," he starts, loving eyes turned to Tempest who blushes and swats at him, looking a little caught off guard by his speech. "She's given me new hope and purpose, showed me what true love feels and looks like. I can't believe I spent twenty-eight years without her, but one thing I know for sure, now that I have her, I'm never letting her go."

Glancing across the table, I see Frankie dabbing at the corners of her eyes and that's when I realize I'm crying too.

When Cage gets down on one knee next to Tempest's chair and pulls out a black box from his pocket, more than just our table reacts. It feels like the entire restaurant is waiting with bated breath as he slips the ring out and holds it up to Tempest who's covering her mouth with her hands as tears stream down her beautiful cheeks.

"Marry me," Cage croaks out, emotions taking over him too.

And that's when my tears pick up. Seeing women cry is one thing. Seeing a massive Viking drop to his knees, declare his love, and plead for his love's hand in marriage… that's next level and something I wish I could write about in my next column, but I won't. I've learned my lesson about dispelling Erickson family news before it's public knowledge.

"Oh my God, yes," Tempest says, first quietly, then loudly. "Yes, I'll marry you!"

Applause and well-wishes ring out around us. Everyone in the restaurant now feels like friends and family, like we all just shared a bonding moment that will hold us together. A few stop by the table and offer their congratulations in person. The management sends over a couple of bottles of champagne and Randy does the honors of pouring everyone a glass, except Tempest, who opts for some apple juice in a fancy glass. I've never had champagne before, so I take a tentative sip of the bubbly liquid. Surprisingly, it's not bad. I definitely like it better than the beer.

For a night I thought was going to be awkward and uncomfortable, it turned out to be amazing.

After we order dessert, Cage and Tempest are the first to make their exit. After all the travel and excitement, Tempest looks spent.

"Good night," everyone calls out.

Tempest flashes her new ring one last time before turning to leave.

"Well, that was exciting," Peggy says, her eyes growing wide.

"You knew that was happening," Vali says with a scoff. "And you'll never convince me otherwise."

"Mom knows everything and is always five steps ahead of everyone else," Viggo adds.

Their dad laughs, hugging the petite woman to him. "You can say that again. Try being married to her for thirty years."

"Thirty-two," she corrects.

The love and respect are evident between them and I'd love to know more about how they met and their life together. I've picked up on bits and pieces from listening to Vali and his brothers. I know their father was a professional boxer and opened Erickson MMA at a young age. He's obviously still very physically fit and active in the business.

Their mother is much smaller than I imagined. It's amazing to me someone so small made these giants. Vali and Viggo are probably the shortest, but they're still over six feet tall. And although they're not as ripped as Cage and Gunnar, the other three are still all muscles and good looks.

Good genes obviously run in the family.

"Vali," his mother says, getting his attention. "I thought you should know that Chloe has been dropping by the house asking about you—"

"Mom," Viggo warns, interrupting her.

She cuts her eyes at him, which shuts him up, but at just the mention of Chloe, Vali's whole demeanor shifts.

"He should know, Viggo," she says, raising her eyebrows and lowering her voice.

I watch as their father leans back in his seat and throws an arm over the back of their mother's chair. He's a quiet man, but his actions speak loudly. With one look, he basically tells them to let her talk.

"I'm not sure what happened between the two of you," she begins. "And I don't need to know. But there's obviously something unresolved between you and I think you should address it. She said you're not answering her calls."

"She doesn't have my new number," Vali grits out. "And I would appreciate it if you don't give it to her. It's over between the two of us. She's a liar and that's all you need to know."

And an adulterer, I think. And someone who made your son doubt himself and everyone else in the world. I don't even know her and she's my least favorite person. If Peggy knew what she did to her son, she'd feel the same way. I can tell that beyond anything, she loves her boys and wants them happy.

"Fine," she says. "I'll leave it alone."

"Thank you," Vali clips.

After a few minutes of awkward silence, the first of the evening, Ozzi starts telling us about this eighty-seven-year-old man who just signed up for kickboxing classes for the first time in his life. The funniest, and most heart-warming part of it, is that he mostly stands around motivating other people.

"I told him he can come do that for free any day he wants," Ozzi says, running a hand through his hair and reminding me of Vali when he does it. Except, Ozzi looks more like Cage and Gunnar, which I now know means he favors their father. "But he insists on paying for the class," he continues. "I guess it's more of a social outing for him. I love having him around. He even motivates me."

We all laugh and the tension from the Chloe talk finally eases from Vali. He reaches for my hand under the table and laces our fingers together—stroking my palm with his thumb—and setting my lingering nerves at ease while also reigniting the fire from earlier.

Why is that turning me on?

Maybe it's how relaxed I feel or this new city?

Maybe it's this new taste of absolute freedom?

Whatever it is, I'm ready to go back to the hotel room and cash in on Vali's promise from earlier.

Vali smiles knowingly at me and kisses my temple. "Ready?"

That question feels loaded, but I nod my response.

I am. I'm ready for whatever he's willing to give me.

Once we're out of the restaurant, Viggo and Ozzi try to convince us to go with them to Bourbon Street. As much as I want to fully experience New Orleans, I want alone time with Vali more. Thankfully, Vali reads my mind and declines. "We're beat from the drive and Maggie is meeting her friend for breakfast early in the morning."

"Maybe tomorrow night?" Ozzi asks, hopefully.

Vali nods. "Yeah, we'll celebrate after the fight."

"Yeah we will," Viggo adds.

"Don't get arrested," Randy warns. "And remember where you're staying. I don't want to have to come get your asses at three in the morning."

Something about his statement gives me the impression that's actually happened before.

"We'll be on our best behavior," Ozzi says with a mock salute and a smile that could easily get him arrested.

God bless their mother. I can't imagine all the trouble she's had to deal with over the years. With charm and charisma in abundance and the looks to back it all up, I know these boys have given her a run for her money from day one.

We enjoy the walk back to the hotel. It's a nice night, and even though we're off the main thoroughfare, the electricity of the city is still palpable.

"It feels alive," I say quietly, my eyes turned up as I take in the buildings and sights and sounds.

Vali squeezes my hand and pulls me closer. "I think that every time I'm here."

We say good night to Vali's parents at the elevator, since their room is on a different floor. Peggy hugs him and kisses his cheek, whispering something I can't hear, and he gets a hearty pat on the back from his dad. Then we're alone.

Like, alone, alone.

I have no place to be, no parents waiting up for me or expecting me home.

It's just me and Vali and I thought I'd be nervous. I was earlier. But not anymore. I just want to be with him, however that happens. I'm not setting any ridiculous expectations and I refuse to build it up in my head, because then I'll just overthink it and ruin everything.

Instead, I'm just going to let things unfold and trust Vali.

When he opens the door, he steps aside, allowing me to enter first, like always. Everything about Vali Erickson screams gentleman. He's been so kind and so patient, giving me what I need and desire but never pushing me too far.

It's funny, I never set out thinking I'm going to stay a virgin until xyz —I'm twenty-four, I meet the right person, I'm married... etc. There wasn't ever an agenda behind it. I just never felt like it was the right time or I was with the right person.

Until now.

"I'm just going to brush my teeth and get ready for bed," I say, going for my bag and digging out my pajamas and toiletries.

"Take your time," Vali says, those cool blue eyes warming me from the inside out.

I feel a buzz of anticipation, it's flowing like electricity under my skin. I wonder if Vali feels it too, or if it's just me, because I'm getting ready to do something I've never done before. Is everyone's first time like this? Would I feel the way I do with someone else?

My stomach squeezes and turns at the thought of being with anyone besides Vali.

When I'm finished in the bathroom, Vali gives me a searing kiss, something that feels like a promise, and then takes his turn.

A few minutes later, he steps out in nothing but a pair of soft gray jogging pants that hang on his hips, accentuating the deep v of his muscles and my eyes go straight to the trail of hair that disappears behind the waistband.

My mouth is watering so much I have to swallow.

I've seen Vali without a shirt on, but for some reason, this feels different. He's here and he's mine, for now. This isn't me sneaking a peek while he's working out at the gym. This is him offering himself to me, giving me anything and everything I want.

"We're on your watch, Maggie," he says, his voice turning gravelly. "You set the pace. Nothing happens tonight or this weekend without your approval."

Swallowing again, I nod. "Okay."

"So," he says, taking three slow steps toward me and making my body tingle at his proximity. "That means you're going to have to tell me what you want… communicate your desires… there's nothing I won't give you. I want you so fucking bad." His words sound as desperate and raw as I feel. "All insecurities and inhibitions are not welcome here."

This is Vali setting the rules, giving me safety in perimeters, but also giving me freedom to just be myself.

"I want you," I say, my breaths coming in short pants as he trails a finger down my cheek and to my collarbone. "I want… I want all of you, everything."

Shaking his head, he lets out a deep sigh. "Fuck," he mutters, pressing his forehead to mine. "I don't even know how to express how it makes me feel to know that you want to give me something like that, share it with me. I'm not sure…"

"Don't," I say, bringing a hand up between us and placing it over his mouth as my eyes lock with his. "Don't say you don't want me or that you don't want to take something like that from me. You're not taking it, I'm giving it to you and getting just as much, if not more, in return."

Sighing, I lean in and place a kiss on his bare chest. "I know we said no labels. I know you can't offer promises of tomorrow. I'm not asking for any of that. I'm just asking that you be with me while you can. Give me tonight and however many tomorrows you can. That's all I ask."

Something about my words flip a switch in Vali and his hands come back up to frame my face as he pulls me in for a kiss that I feel all the way down to my toes.

His slow hands trailing over my body, feeling every curve and appreciating them, makes my blood begin to heat up. Just like every time I'm with Vali, I feel alive and good and completely turned on by his touch alone.

As he continues to kiss his way across my collarbone and down my chest, pulling at the shoulder of my nightshirt to gain access to my breasts, a wave of wild abandon takes over. Reaching between us, I gather the hem of my shirt and remove it, tossing it to the floor behind me.

Vali's eyes go wide and then hooded as he takes in my breasts.

He's seen them, of course, and done things to them I never imagined, but it's always a peek here or a hint there.

Tonight, I'm ready for it all, with nothing between us but the fire and electricity that's become a constant whenever Vali is near.

"You're so fucking beautiful," he murmurs, reaching out and cupping my breasts, rubbing his thumbs over my sensitive nipples and sending shock waves to my core.

I never knew my boobs were so closely linked to my vagina until Vali.

After he's raked his eyes over my torso—up and down and back up—he leans in and begins making good on his promise from dinner. He devours me, starting at the top and working his way down.

When he kneels at my feet, I feel a sense of insecurity try to creep in —*what do I look like from that angle?* It can't be good. *What is he doing?*

Then, he looks up at me, his long lashes on full display against his blue eyes, silently asking me for permission to proceed as he loops his thumbs in the waistband of my shorts.

I nod and he pulls them down, panties and all, urging me to step out of them and tossing them to the pile with my shirt. And I'm fully naked with Vali kneeling before me, like I'm an altar and he's worshiping at my feet.

His hands caress my thighs and I close my eyes, getting lost in the sensation of being touched in a new place. That's when I feel his breath on my center and my body locks up, my hands going to his shoulders.

Oh, sweet, sweet Lord.

What is happening?

Glancing down, I see Vali's tongue dart out and lick between my folds and I'm done for. He barely touches my clit and my legs begin to tremble. When he eases a finger, then two inside me and continues to work his tongue in tandem, I lose all sense of control.

My insides are burning in the most delicious heat and then my muscles begin to shake. Just when I feel like I can't take it anymore, a wave of ecstasy crashes over me. It's not a slow, calm wave. It's a tsunami. If it weren't for Vali's hands bracing me, I would be on the floor.

Easing me onto the bed, he climbs over my body, a mischievous, sexy smile on his face.

"I love watching you come."

Letting out a laugh as I try to regain some composure, I tell him, "I love when you make me come."

"Good," he says, standing and removing his pants. "Because I plan on making it my job to see how many times we can accomplish that this weekend. By the time I get you back to Green Valley, you'll be thoroughly spent and in need of a vacation from your vacation."

Oh my God.

"Vali, baby… it's just Vali," he says and I realize I must've spoken out loud. But my eyes are fully trained on his large, hard penis… that doesn't sound right. Too clinical. But I have zero experience in this arena, so I don't know what I'm supposed to call it. And I have no clue if that's average or above average, but I'm leaning toward the latter and wondering how it's going to fit inside me.

"If you keep looking at my cock like that, I'm going to come before I even get inside you."

His boldness makes me bold and I sit up, wanting to feel his… *cock.*

Reaching out, I glance up at Vali and see him watching me intently. Just before my hand makes contact, it jumps and I squeal, making us both laugh. "Oh," I say, one hand covering my mouth and the other finally reaching its destination.

It's soft, like silk, but hard, and as I stroke it on instinct, I notice a drop of clear liquid on the tip. My curiosity is piqued, but before I can act on it, Vali stills my hand and reaches over to the nightstand for a condom.

With one hand on mine, he uses his teeth to open the package, then places the thin latex at his tip and uses both of my hands to roll it down his shaft.

Nudging my knees open, Vali lays me back on the bed and positions his body over mine as he begins stroking my center with his cock. *Cock, yeah.* I like that word. And *oh my God,* I like this.

This feels even better than Vali's fingers and possibly even better than his tongue.

Slipping two of those said fingers inside me, he pumps a few times, bringing me back to a state of bliss, but not taking me over the edge.

"This might hurt a little," he mutters, his voice ragged. "Tell me to stop and I'll stop."

"Okay," I reply, knowing he needs my words, but unable to make much coherent thought. With Vali rubbing my clit, it's hard for me to think of anything else but my next orgasm. It's not until I feel his hard cock nudging my opening that I begin to tense.

"Right here, baby," Vali says, his eyes locking with mine. "Stay with me."

Inch by inch, ever so slowly, Vali fills me up and I feel a pinch, followed by a burning sensation, but it's not horrible. When his lips crash down on mine, I begin to relax into it, letting my body stretch and adjust to this new level of intimacy.

After a few moments, Vali pulls back from the kiss and asks, "Are you okay?"

I nod, letting out a deep breath as my hands roam down his sides and then to his tight ass. Gripping him, I finally reply, "Yes, please move... I want to feel you."

CHAPTER 27

VALI

*F*uck.

Maggie wants me to move and my body needs me to move but I'm afraid that when I do, I'll lose control too soon. I knew it would feel amazing with her... knew it would be special but I had no idea, not one clue, it'd feel like *this*.

I shouldn't be surprised because it's Maggie for fuck's sake and she's completely rocked my world from the first day I saw her but still, I wasn't prepared.

I wasn't prepared for the sight of her, naked and vulnerable, to literally bring me to my knees.

I wasn't prepared for the taste of her to turn me into a ravenous wild man.

And, I definitely wasn't prepared for the feel of her to heal the remaining cracks of my heart.

"Vali, is something wrong?"

Cursing myself under my breath for not focusing on her like I should, I shake my head and kiss her gently. "No, baby, you're perfect. Everything is perfect. I just got a little too excited and had to calm down before this ended way too soon."

Even though her cheeks tinge pink with a blush, I can see the relief on her face at my admission. Damn me for ever making her doubt.

When I finally pull out of her a bit, then push back inside with a firmer thrust, she lets out a gasp that travels straight to my balls. I love how responsive she is and I can't wait to explore this new part of our relationship even more with her.

I continue to thrust, increasing my force and speed, until Maggie is panting, her nails clawing at my back.

"Am I hurting you?" I'm pretty certain I'm not but I can't help but ask. I want this moment to be worth the wait and everything she hoped it would be, and more.

"God, no." Her voice is deeper and raspy now. "It feels so good. I had no idea."

I chuckle while kissing down the column of her throat. "Just you wait."

Still increasing my movements, I reach my hand between us and find her clit, swollen and soaked, just the way I like it. I rub tight but firm circles around it, causing Maggie to buck up against me.

"Yes," she breathes out. "More of that. Please, Vali, I need…"

"Don't worry, love. I got you," I vow, speeding up my thrusts. I feel her hands clutching onto my biceps while her walls tighten around my dick, signaling that glorious and powerful tingle to travel down my back and into my groin, ready for release.

"Yes, yes, yes." Her words start out like a moan, changing into a whine as she gets closer to her orgasm, until finally, she cries out my name, her body spasming with pleasure beneath me. Her pussy pulses around me and I give in to the feeling, not wanting to hold back anymore, and come hard. Holding her body close to mine, I bury my face into the crook of her shoulder and pant her name.

Maggie, Maggie, Maggie.

This may have been a new experience for her, but I feel like I'm the one who's been forever changed.

Once my heart rate has slowed down some, I quickly discard my condom and slip back into the bed, wrapping my arms around Maggie and pulling her to my chest. She's quiet but I'm hoping she's just processing, like she's said she does, so I let her have her moment and simply relish the feel of her body against mine.

I can be patient.

After a few more minutes, she finally speaks. "I get it now."

Not really following, I ask, "Get what?"

"Why everyone is so obsessed with sex. I totally understand."

Laughter bubbles out of me and I hug her tighter, kissing the top of her head.

"I'm serious." She pushes herself up and looks at me. "What we just did totally lived up to the hype. But what I don't understand is why don't people do that all the time? I mean, I've only done it once and it's all I can think about doing for the rest of my life."

"Oh, really?"

"Well, yeah, if it was you I was doing it with, of course." She says this with enthusiasm but then her demeanor completely changes. "I'm sorry, I didn't really mean that. I don't think my brain has recovered from that incredible orgasm. Just forget I said anything."

"Whoa, whoa, whoa. What's all this about? Why would you take that back? I love that you love what we did that much. I'd like to take credit for some of that but, honestly, it's because of the chemistry we have. It's not like that for everyone."

"It's not?"

"Well, it hasn't been that good for me before," I tell her sincerely.

"Vali, that can't be true. I'm sure you've had many girlfriends. If sex wasn't good, why would you keep doing it?"

"I didn't say it wasn't good. Even bad sex is good, for the most part. I meant, it's never been as good—as amazing—as what we just shared." I reach out and tuck some of her hair behind her ear before cupping her jaw. "I mean it."

And I do. It's possible I'm still looking through orgasm-colored glasses, but that was the best sex of my life.

I want to do it again.

As if Maggie can read my mind, she asks, "So, when can we do it again?"

I take her hand and place it on top of my dick, which is already hard and ready for her. "I'm ready when you are."

Her eyes grow wide and her smile follows suit before she attacks my mouth, kissing me hungrily. It seems as though I might have created a monster—a beautiful, hot, sex-monster, and I have no regrets.

* * *

WHEN MY ALARM wakes me up, after some of the best sleep I've had in a long time, I'm relieved to find myself wrapped around Maggie's naked body. I was afraid last night was nothing but a dream but I'm so glad it wasn't.

Letting out a moan, Maggie stretches her body as she wakes up, causing my morning wood to make its presence known right against her back.

"Good morning to you too," she says with a giggle.

"Sorry," I say, but I'm really not. "This is how my body reacts to you. It always has."

She turns in my arms and looks at me. "I never thought you'd be interested in me. I assumed I wasn't your type and I could only have you in my dreams."

"I'm glad you didn't let that keep you from giving me a shot and going out with me."

"Me too." She snuggles back into my arms, kissing my chest as she lays her head on it. I can tell something is on her mind and I don't think it's about us, so I take a chance and ask her.

"Are you nervous about meeting your friend?"

"A little. No, a lot actually. I know we've written countless letters and emails to each other over the years, but I worry we won't hit it off in person. What if she doesn't like me?"

Her honesty and vulnerability hit me straight in my chest. Maggie is truly unlike any woman I've ever known and I feel obligated to help her realize just how special she is.

"Baby, that's not possible. She's gonna love you. She'd be crazy not to. But, if you meet her and things don't go as smoothly as you hoped, text me and I'll come get you."

"Okay," she acquiesces. "I know I'm overthinking this and being silly. I'm just feeling a little overwhelmed right now."

"I can help you feel better," I gladly offer.

"Oh, yeah? How so?" The side of her mouth quirks up as she asks.

"Take a shower with me."

"Umm, I don't know if I can do that."

"Of course, you can. It's perfect, really." I rub my thumb across her nipple, watching as it hardens. "I can get you dirty and clean all at the same time."

Maggie bites down on her lip, watching my thumb. "When you put it that way…"

CHAPTER 28

MAGGIE

*W*alking down to the lobby at about five minutes before eight, I feel much more relaxed than I thought I would and that's all thanks to Vali and his magic orgasms.

Also, praise be for shower benches.

If you'd asked me what I thought my first time having sex would be like, or *times* rather, I never would've been able to predict what happened between us over the last twelve hours. The emotions and feelings and sensations were so far out of my realm of thinking.

But now that I know, there's no going back.

It's only been an hour since I had sex with Vali in the shower and I already want him again. I missed him the second I stepped out of the hotel room. And the countdown to going home, back to Green Valley and not spending every night in his arms, is already looming over me, which is ridiculous because we still have two days left.

As I step out onto the sidewalk, Everly's sleek black hair is the first thing I see. She's impossible to miss—tall, put together, and absolutely gorgeous.

Like a scene from a movie, she turns toward me and we both break out into a chorus of giddy laughter as we embrace each other like two loons.

"Oh my God," I gush, hugging her tighter. "I can't believe I'm actually here." That's been the reoccurring thought the past twenty-four hours.

"I can't believe you're here," she says with a sigh, pulling back to look at me. "Maggie O'Neal, in the flesh. And you're absolutely gorgeous and glowing."

My cheeks flush with embarrassment, but it quickly fades, because this is Everly, *my Everly*. And in an instant, it's like we've done this a million times. In a sense, we have. Our thousands of emails over the years have taken many forms—laughter, hugs, tears, sympathy, understanding.

"Me?" I ask, grabbing her shoulders. "Look at you. A picture definitely doesn't do you justice."

She beams, becoming even more beautiful. "I need to figure out a way to keep you here."

Looping her arm through mine, she turns us in the opposite direction and we begin to walk.

"Let's go to my favorite coffee shop," she says, dodging a few people passing by. "They have great chocolate croissants, amazing locally roasted coffee, and a cozy spot for us to sit and dish. I don't know if you realize it, but you have a freshly fucked look about you and I need all the details."

Smoothing down my hair, my eyes go wide. "Really?" I ask, feeling a smidge self-conscious, but also a bit smug. Shit yeah, I've been freshly fucked... repeatedly. Part of me wants to yell it from the rooftops.

Everly throws her head back and laughs, squeezing my arm tighter. "Well, you just answered that burning question."

"Which one?"

"The one where I was going to ask if you came to your senses and ditched your room to stay with Vali."

Biting down on my lip, I fight back a smile so big it's painful.

"How much time do we have?" she asks, glancing at her watch. "Because I'm going to need a play-by-play."

"I have to be back no later than five to get ready for the fight."

Walking faster, she pulls my arm. "We've gotta hurry, then."

I can't help the laughter that erupts. It's carefree and only the kind you experience when you're with your best friend. I should've known there was nothing to worry about. After years of Everly showing up for me in all the ways that matter, I should've known she'd be just as great in person.

Once we're nestled in our cozy spot with our coffees and croissants in hand, the real fun begins.

"Tell me everything!" Everly demands.

So, I do.

I tell her about how sweet and thoughtful Vali is and how he makes me feel desired without putting any pressure or assumptions on me. I tell her how he most certainly knows his way around a woman's body and that I'm not intimidated by it. If anything, I'm thankful because I can reap the benefits of having such a skilled lover.

I also laugh at myself using the word "lover" because that's typically a word I roll my eyes at but, right now, it fits us. Since we're not using labels, it's the only way I know to describe him.

And, when Everly pushes for more details, I give in and admit how many orgasms he gave me in a span of twelve hours.

Yes, I'm gloating and no, I don't care.

I have to stop myself from oversharing and describing in full detail how beautiful his penis—*cock*—is because that's way too personal but, honestly, it could be award-winning. Are there awards for cocks? Probably not, but there should be. I'd gladly award him a blue ribbon for first place and score him tens in all categories: length, girth, beauty, strength, and stamina.

"Earth to Maggie! Hello!" Everly waves her hand in front of my face, effectively pulling me out of my daydream.

"Hmm? What? I'm sorry, did you say something?"

"Oh my God. You were dreaming about his dick, weren't you?"

"What? Me? No, no I'd never do that. I was, umm, thinking about the fight. You know, it's a big one for Gunnar. He has a lot riding on it," I lie, trying to change the subject without my cheeks burning off.

Everly laughs, shaking her head. "Girl, you're lying so hard your pants are practically on fire. Now, wipe that drool off your chin and tell me what's going to happen once you two are back in Green Valley."

My stomach flips at that thought. There are so many unknowns it makes me a bit queasy, to be honest.

"Well, that's the million-dollar question, isn't it?" I pick at the remaining crumbs on my plate, my mood deflating slightly. "This weekend is just getting started and it's already giving me lofty ideas and dreams about the future. How can I go back home and go back to how things were before we left? I'm not the same person anymore. At least, I don't feel the same."

Everly watches me intently, waiting as I talk things out like she knows I like to do.

"Do I tell my parents what happened between me and Vali? Do I ask their permission to sleep over at his house? Does Vali want me to sleep over? Can I just show up to the gym and rip his clothes off any time I want? Oh my God, what am I going to do?"

Chuckling, she places her hand on top of mine. "First of all, you're going to switch to decaf. Second, you're going to stop thinking so much. Live your life, sweetie. It'll all work out and you deserve all the happiness in the world."

I sigh and give her a relieved smile. "I'm so glad we did this. What would I do without you?"

"You'd live a sad, boring, and lonely life, that's what." She winks at me and I feel calmer already.

"Are you sure you can't move to Green Valley?" I ask, already missing her at just the thought of our time together being over. "Or at least Knoxville? Or Nashville? It's beautiful. You'd absolutely love it."

She gives me a sad smile, squeezing my hand. "I'll come visit sometime, but now that you've come here, you'll be hooked. New Orleans has a way of sinking its teeth into you and holding on tight."

I know she's right. Even after being here a little over a day, I feel it seeping into my bones. There's something about the people and the old buildings that you can't get enough of.

"Show me more of the French Quarter before I have to go back," I tell her, standing and gathering our cups and plates. "And maybe we can squeeze in another breakfast or lunch tomorrow?"

Everly stands, smoothing down her dress. "I'm at your beck and call. You just tell me when and where."

We spend the rest of the afternoon talking about anything and everything. Everly shows me her favorite artist in Jackson Square and I buy a small painting to take home with me. We walk through the French Market and grab a crepe for lunch. She walks me down Frenchmen and we peek our heads into a couple of jazz clubs.

It's perfect and amazing.

I couldn't have asked for a better day with my best friend.

When she walks me back to the hotel, I call Vali to see if he'll come down to meet her. Unfortunately, he's out with his brothers and parents and Everly has an appointment with a client, so we agree to make it happen tomorrow before we leave town early the next morning.

Just in case, I hug her so hard I'm afraid I'm going to squeeze the life out of her. She hugs me back just as fiercely. "You're as perfect as I thought you'd be, Maggie O'Neal. Thanks for being my friend all these years and finally coming to see me."

"This is the first of many," I promise.

"Have fun tonight," she calls out as she turns to leave. "In the bedroom!"

"Oh my God," I mutter, not even trying to fight back my smile. "Yep, that's my best friend."

Since I'm going to have the room and bathroom to myself for a little while, I plan on making good use of the alone time and do a little pampering before the big fight.

Just as I'm washing off a face mask, I hear the door open and close.

"Maggie?" Vali calls out and my heart leaps at his presence, like it's been days instead of hours since I saw him last. How is that possible?

Opening the bathroom door, I step out to find him standing there with a small bouquet of flowers. "A lady down the street was selling these and they made me think of you," he says, holding them out to me.

"First the most amazing sex and now flowers for no reason?" I ask, clutching them to my chest. "How will any other man ever live up to this?"

Vali's facial expression changes, growing more serious. "I don't like thinking about you with other men, so maybe that's my secret mission?"

No labels.

No promises.

"So when you leave me, I'll just become an old spinster?"

He smiles, reaching out and grabbing me by the waist and pulling me to him. "Let's not talk about that right now," he murmurs, his tone dropping to a low sexy growl.

"What do you want to talk about?" I ask, feeling breathless before his lips ever touch mine.

"How much I missed you today and how hard it was to not think about you naked... under me, on top of me... in positions I haven't even had the pleasure of having you in... yet."

Discarding the flowers on the bathroom counter behind me, I wrap my arms around Vali's neck and press my lips to his. "Tell me more," I insist between kisses.

Instead of telling me, he shows me.

He shows me twice before we're forced to take another shower and get dressed for the fights.

When we're ten minutes late to meet everyone in the lobby, Viggo and Ozzi give Vali a look that says they know exactly what we were doing. I feel my face start to heat but Tempest and Frankie come to my side and become the buffer I need.

"You look great," Tempest says. "I love those shoes."

Glancing down at my feet, I admire the kitten heels. "Thank you, I've had these forever but never had a chance to wear them. I thought if I couldn't wear them in New Orleans, where could I wear them?"

"Definitely," Frankie replies with a grin. "They're smoking hot."

"Ride's here," Randy announces, herding us all toward the door.

Cage sent a limo to pick us up. It sounds fancy and extreme, but according to Tempest, it was the most reasonable mode of transportation for a group the size of ours.

Look at me, marking things off my *One Day* list at lightning speed.

Travel outside the great state of Tennessee. *Check.*

Have the most amazing sex of my life. *Check.*

Meet my pen pal of thirteen years. *Check.*

Ride in a limo. *Check, check.*

"What has you smiling like that?" Vali whispers into my ear.

Turning toward him, I'm nearly rendered speechless by how gorgeous he is.

His dark hair is combed back and he's wearing a sexy button-down shirt with gray slacks that hug his hips and powerful thighs perfectly. Those blue eyes I love so much look extra blue tonight. Even in the dim light of the limo, they're stunning.

"We'd be here all night if I started making a list," I tell him, leaning forward and kissing his cheek. "In case I forget to tell you later, thank you for inviting me."

Vali's eyes soften and he looks like he wants to say something, but refrains.

Everyone else in the limo begins talking about the fight in great detail. Vali, Viggo, Ozzi, and Randy all know every stat for every fighter on tonight's ticket. Apparently, one of the guys fighting is the opponent Cage was in the ring with the night he injured his shoulder.

I glance over to Tempest and see her listening just as intently as I am.

How crazy to think that if Cage hadn't been injured, he might never have met Tempest. I won't say never, because I'm a hopeless romantic and I believe in fate and destiny. I believe if two people are meant to be together, the Universe will find a way to bring them together.

I hate to say I'm glad he got injured. I'd never wish pain on anyone, especially someone as good as Cage Erickson. But with that injury, the trajectory of his life shifted. If it hadn't, Vali would've never come to Green Valley and crossed my path.

My heart actually hurts to think about that.

A world without Vali would be a sad existence.

And that's enough of that... because if I let myself continue down that road, it'll end with me admitting exactly how I feel about a person who told me he can't promise me anything and isn't going to be around forever.

Get back in the moment, Maggie.

Just enjoy the moment.

Don't overthink, just be.

Taking a deep breath, I settle back into the plush leather seat and watch as the city passes by. The closer we get to the Superdome, the more crowded the sidewalks are. Thankfully, the limo pulls right up to the front and drops us off near the entrance.

Vali takes my hand as we step out of the limo. This place is enormous. I saw it as we drove in yesterday, but seeing it from a distance and seeing it up close and personal are two totally different things. And there are so many people.

Frankie and Tempest walk beside me and I glance over to see Frankie's eyes darting around like mine. Hoping she's not feeling overwhelmed or nervous, I reach out and touch her arm to get her attention. "Hey," I say, offering her a smile when she meets my eyes. "You okay?"

"Yeah," she says, taking a deep breath.

"Can you believe this place?" I ask, hoping I'm not the only one awestruck.

"No," Frankie says, letting out a laugh. "It's insane. I can't imagine how Gunnar must be feeling."

Viggo is walking behind us and overhears the conversation. "Don't worry about Gunnar," he assures her. "He's in the zone. By the time he gets out into the ring, he'll be so laser-focused this place could blow up and he wouldn't even notice."

Frankie laughs again, nodding. "You're probably right."

"He's going to kick ass," Ozzi adds. "I wouldn't be surprised if we get another TKO."

"That would be exciting," I say, my eyes growing wider as we walk through a tunnel and out into the bright lights of the arena.

"Where we're walking is normally the football field," Vali says, leaning down so I can hear him over the crowd. "Our seats are right up there." He points toward the front row and we follow his parents as they lead us to them.

The Erickson clan fills up almost an entire row of seats. Everyone around us seems to notice the brothers. A few are whispering and I wonder if they're really that well-known. Sure, they're a novelty in small-town Green Valley, but is that how it is everywhere they go? At least in the MMA world?

"People are staring," I whisper to Vali.

He laughs and shrugs. "We're used to it."

Viggo, Vali, and Ozzi go to get everyone refreshments, and while they're gone, the rest of us break into conversation about what everyone did during the day.

Since Gunnar had to weigh in early this morning, he and Cage have been at the Superdome since eight o'clock. Everyone else had lunch at the Palace Cafe and then took a streetcar tour around the Garden District.

"We missed you," Tempest says, reaching across to pat my arm. "Did you have fun with your friend?"

"I did," I tell her. "It was better than I hoped… perfect, actually."

"I can't believe you've been pen pals all these years," Peggy says. "People just don't stay in touch like that these days. I'm so glad you were able to finally meet in person."

Frankie sits forward. "Was she homeschooled too?"

"No, it was just a class project for her fifth-grade class," I reply, reminiscing. "She's two years older than me. In a way, I guess she's filled a few roles over the years—an older sister, friend, confidant."

Peggy sighs, reaching over to pat my hand. "That's so sweet."

"I'm an only child too," Frankie adds.

"Me too," Tempest says.

The three of us look at each other and smile. How crazy that we're all only children and now we've been brought together by a clan of brothers. One more thing that can be credited to Cage's change of direction. Even when Vali is gone, I hope I'm still friends with these two who are quickly becoming more like family than friends.

Kindred spirits, for sure.

"My boisterous brood must be a shock to y'all," Peggy says with a smile.

"I love it," I admit. "Being around your family is wonderful."

I can only imagine how proud she must be of all of them, each successful in their own right. Now that I've met Viggo and Ozzi, I can now confirm that all of the Ericksons are kind and caring and so very handsome. Many people probably judge them too quickly, see all the beef and brawn, and assume they're full of piss and vinegar.

Don't get me wrong, I know they're beasts in the ring. And I'm sure if provoked, they're all formidable adversaries, but as a whole, they're some of the nicest people I've ever met and the apples didn't fall far from the tree.

When the guys return, Randy is regaling us with tales from when the five of them were little. Tempest, Frankie, and I are laughing uncontrollably about when the boys turned the garage into a wrestling ring and put baby powder all over the mats so they could slip and slide on them... buck naked.

"Baby powder, huh?" I tease Vali as he reclaims his seat next to me.

He shakes his head, fighting back a smile. "It was Ozzi's idea."

Glancing down the row at the accused, I can imagine he was a handful growing up, probably still is. At the moment, he's giving Tempest a hard time about not bringing good luck muffins for the fight.

When the lights lower, signaling the fights are getting ready to start, my stomach flips in excitement. One of these days, I'd love to get a look behind the scenes and see what the fighters are going through right now.

Do they feel the energy?

Are they completely blocking everything out like Viggo said?

Maybe it's the writer in me, but I always want to know every perspective.

"I don't know what I'm going to enjoy more," Vali murmurs into my ear. "The fights or watching you." Heat floods my body and I bite down on my lip to keep from making any inappropriate sounds. "Keep doing that and I'll have to find a dark corner for us to occupy."

Vali has always been vocal about his desires, but now that I know what it means for him to fulfill those promises, a simple statement like the one he just made sends my body into a tailspin.

Fortunately, about that time, the announcer walks into the middle of the ring and the fights are on, giving me something appropriate to channel my energy into.

With the lights dimmed and the music pumping, my eyes are fixed on the fighters coming out of the tunnels. I don't even know who the men are, but as the introductions take place, I find myself gravitating toward one or the other and staking a claim on my favorites.

Vali, his brothers, and father are so animated throughout the fights, all offering praises and criticism. Listening to them is so entertaining and educational. They talk amongst themselves about strategy and it's obvious how much they love the sport.

Peggy chimes in from time to time, but she's a much quieter spectator. Her motherly instincts make her cringe when a fighter takes a hard hit and I wonder how she'll react when it's Gunnar in the ring. Glancing down the row at Frankie, she seems to be zoned into the fight, but if I had to guess, she's not as engaged as she appears. After talking to her, I know this is something she's worked up to. From the outside, she's another spectator in the crowd, but on closer observation—eyes fluttering closed, counted breaths—she's using all the tools in her shed tonight.

But she's here and she's doing this—for herself and for the man she loves.

When it's time for the title fight, I watch as Frankie shifts in her seat and the entire Erickson clan grows quiet. Tempest reaches over and takes Frankie's hand. On my other side, Peggy's beautiful face is a picture of calm, but the worry for her son is evident in her posture—spine straight, chin dipped, hands clasped. The brothers are pensive and Randy scoots forward, as if he's ready to leap to his feet at any moment.

Gunnar, on the other hand, somehow looks relaxed and zoned in on his opponent.

When the bell dings signaling the beginning of the first round, the crowd grows quiet as they wait for the first blow.

Unlike the first fight I watched, where Gunnar and his opponent danced around the ring for over three rounds, this one ends before it ever gets started.

Tyson "The Freight Train" Ferguson jabs at Gunnar only a few minutes into the round and Gunnar unleashes on him, like a caged animal on the loose. His blows land so fast I can't keep track, and before the buzzer can sound, Tyson is on the mat and the ref is lying down beside him, pounding out the count.

Vali, Viggo, and Ozzi are on their feet before he ever gets to ten.

Chaos erupts around us as the crowd goes wild.

Cage leaps over the ring and lifts Gunnar off his feet.

The rest of it is a blur of celebration.

After Gunnar is announced the winner and they present him with his belt, the entire family goes up into the ring, even Tempest and Frankie, but I stay back and watch from the sidelines. It's such an important moment for them and I'm more than happy to be an observer. Taking a few candid pictures with the camera on my phone, I send them in a group text to Tempest and Vali.

"Maggie," Vali calls out, his eyes searching the crowd for me. When he sees where I'm standing, he frowns, motioning for me to join them in the middle.

Reluctantly, I do as he asks and he pulls me to him, kissing the side of my head and squeezing me tight. "God, baby, was that amazing or what?"

"So amazing," I agree, leaning into him.

"We're going to take a family picture," he says.

I'm getting ready to argue that I'm not family, but Vali situates me in front of him, next to Tempest, and the next thing I know, a professional photographer is calling out for us to all look his way.

My heart both expands and squeezes at the thought of being included as part of Vali's family.

I want that, so bad.

But I know better than to want it.

Which is why I spend the half hour it takes for us to vacate the arena and find our way back out to the limo berating myself for allowing those thoughts to enter my mind.

Thankfully, by the time we make it back to the hotel, the only thoughts are of how we're going to celebrate Gunnar's win. It's late and even though we should all be beat, everyone has too much adrenaline pumping through their veins to think about going to bed.

The city of New Orleans seems to agree.

An hour later, everyone except Tempest is taking shots of whiskey at a bar called Le Booze on Bourbon Street.

"Oh my God," I cry. "It burns so bad."

Ozzi pats my back, giving me a sympathetic smile. "Only the first few will burn," he offers as encouragement. "After that, they'll go down smooth."

Shaking my head, I laugh. "No way," I tell him. "That's my first *and* last."

"We'll find something sweet for you," he says, pulling me back out onto the sidewalk. "This is like the buffet of booze. If you don't find what you like on Bourbon Street, it doesn't exist."

As we make our way down Bourbon Street, the music gets louder and the people get rowdier. After we pop into a few bars, only stopping for the guys to get refills on beer or shots of whiskey, which I politely decline, we start to lose people from our group. The first to retire back to the hotel are Randy and Peggy, claiming they're not as young as they once were and are leaving the wild and crazy antics to their children.

My one shot of whiskey has me laughing at that. This whole scene seems a bit surreal and I wonder what my parents would think if they were here. Trying to imagine my mother on Bourbon Street makes my head spin... or maybe that's the lingering effects from the whiskey.

I know it was just one shot, but for someone who's only had a few sips of beer and champagne, it felt like four.

"I think we're going to bow out too," Cage says, holding Tempest tightly to his side. His protective nature in full force with the wild crowd. "We'll make sure Mom and Dad get back safely."

"Have fun," Tempest says, giving us a wave as they head in the same direction as Peggy and Randy.

"And then there were six," Ozzi says, holding his arms out wide. "Who's ready for some fun?"

"We can go back whenever you want," Vali says in my ear, kissing my neck and making chills run down my spine. "Just say the word."

I smile up at him, feeling blissfully happy and free. "Let's hang out a while longer."

"Whatever you want," he murmurs, leaning down to capture my lips.

"Get a room," Viggo calls back over his shoulder, to which Vali pays no mind and keeps kissing me in the middle of the street as if we're the only people in the world.

He kisses me so thoroughly that when we finally come up for air, I'm more drunk on Vali than I am the whiskey.

A wide smile pulls on my lips as my heart beats wildly in my chest.

I'm not sure I've ever felt this alive in my life.

Vali's eyes are twinkling as he locks them with mine, his thumb brushing my lips. "You're so fucking beautiful and I'm the luckiest bastard in the world."

His words catch me off guard but also fill my heart. I want to tell him that he's also beautiful, inside and out, and I'm the lucky one, but I don't get the chance because a second later, he's lacing our fingers together and pulling us through the crowd to catch up with everyone else as they walk into a bar.

Glancing up at the sign, I see the words *Cat's Meow* in neon lights. Inside, a group of girls are on a stage singing their hearts out to "Tainted Love" and I'm enraptured by their off-key singing and passionate performance.

Our group finds a spot to the side of the stage with perfect access to the bar.

Vali and Viggo go to order drinks while the rest of us search for a song to sing.

When in New Orleans, right?

An hour later, I've found my new favorite drink—a lemon drop—and my new favorite pastime—karaoke on Bourbon Street. The six of us kill "Eye of the Tiger," dedicating it to Gunnar. We have the entire bar singing along and I feel ten feet tall by the time we walk off the stage.

When another rendition of "Baby Got Back" starts up, we decide that's our cue to make our exit.

As we all file back out onto Bourbon, it's like the time we lost while singing our hearts out inside the confines of Cat's Meow catches up with us and we all begin to drag. My arm is looped through Vali's as he basically carries me down the street.

"I think I'm calling it," Gunnar says, pulling Frankie into his side. "Frankie and I have some post-fight—"

"We don't need to hear about your sexcapades," Viggo says, holding up a hand to stop him. "Good fight tonight, though. Super proud of you." Reaching his arm around Gunnar, he traps him in a hug, and I can't help smiling at the affection these badass Vikings are capable of showing each other. It's heartwarming.

And that could also be the booze talking.

Thankfully, Gunnar doesn't have anything to ice down, due to his impressive knockout, but he's still exhausted from the past two days. With tomorrow being our last day in New Orleans, we agree to sleep in and meet for brunch before everyone heading back to Dallas has to catch their flight.

When we reach the hotel, we send him and Frankie off to their room with one last chorus of "Eye of the Tiger."

Moments later, as Vali closes our hotel room door behind him, I free-fall onto the bed. "What a night."

"How about a nightcap?" Vali asks, walking over to the bed and hovering over me.

"I can't drink anymore," I tell him with a laugh. "That last lemon drop was enough for me."

His smirk grows. "I was thinking of a different kind of nightcap."

"And what kind would that be?" I ask, running a hand over his taut abs and up to his chest.

"The naked kind," he says, leaning down to nip my neck.

Closing my eyes and relishing the feel of his mouth on my skin, I moan.

Moments later, when Vali and I are naked with nothing between us, I have thoughts of never wanting this weekend to end.

I know I said I was okay with no labels and no promises.

But I want them.

I want everything with Vali.

CHAPTER 29

VALI

*T*he sound of my feet pounding the pavement is the only thing I can hear.

Seven months ago, when I came to Green Valley, that actually drove me crazy. It was too quiet, too slow, too small, too boring. But now, it feels pretty damn perfect. The longer I'm here, the deeper this place burrows under my skin.

The deeper Maggie burrows under my skin.

She's so far under there at this point, she feels like a permanent appendage. She's part of me and I can't imagine my life without her. Thankfully, I have the luxury of sticking around and exploring the possibilities of us. Even though I had planned on being back in Dallas by now, it's okay that I'm not.

According to Viggo and Ozzi, everything is going great at Ericksons.

They're bringing in a new trainer next week to help with the large increase of clients. Viggo and Ozzi are both teaching classes, on top of doing the bookwork, and often accompanying fighters to matches. It's a busy life, similar to the one here in Green Valley with Viking MMA, but on a bigger scale. Thankfully, it's a well-oiled machine, but it's also a delicate balance, one I was afraid I would disturb by not being there. Seeing them thrive without me is comforting.

For the first time in my life, I feel like I have options. And it feels good.

Since we've been back from New Orleans, I've thought a lot about what my life would look like if I decided to move to Green Valley permanently. It's a crazy idea, but one that's felt more and more right as each day passes.

Of course, I haven't spoken a word of it to anyone, especially not Maggie. We agreed on no labels or promises and I'm upholding that decision until I know for sure what I'm going to do. Deep down I know we've crossed the point of no return. If this thing between us ends, there will be damage. On both sides.

When I arrive at my destination, a familiar face is walking out the door just as I wipe the sweat off my face and lower my shirt.

Miss Faye is standing there with a smile. "I came for muffins and got an entire meal."

"Good morning, Miss Faye," I say, switching positions with her to hold the door. "And how are you this morning?"

"Better now, thank you," she says with a wink as she walks out onto the sidewalk.

"Glad to hear it," I tell her, holding back a chuckle. If I'm ever feeling down about myself, I'm going to find Miss Faye so she can boost my confidence. "Have a great day."

She waves as she slides into the front seat of her Lincoln Town Car. "Same to you, Vali."

Shaking my head, I turn to find Maggie standing there, waiting for me with a newspaper, box of muffins, and two coffees. Have I mentioned she's the perfect woman?

"Well, good morning," I say, leaning forward and kissing her gorgeous lips right in the middle of Donner Bakery and her eyes grow wide, but she eventually gives in to the kiss.

When I take a step back, a nervous laugh escapes as she brushes a stray piece of hair behind her ear. I love that after kissing her so many times, she still blushes. It's fucking adorable and I'll never grow tired of it— or her, for that matter.

"Hope I got your order right," she says, her eyes darting down to the muffins and coffee. "But Tempest said these are your favorite and I went with black coffee because that's what you ordered while we were in New Orleans."

She's rambling and that's another one of my favorite things.

Kissing her nose, I slip a hand around her waist and pull her to me. "It's perfect."

"Want to walk to the park and have breakfast while we read the paper?" she asks.

It sounds like such an old people thing to do, but we've had to get creative on ways to spend time together since we got back from our trip. The occasional meetups and weekend dates just don't cut it anymore. I need more and so does Maggie.

"Sounds great," I tell her, glancing over her head at Tempest who's watching us from behind the counter with a knowing grin. Nodding my head in her direction, she gives me a smile and waves me off.

As Maggie and I start off down the sidewalk, I take the two coffees from her. "Thanks for coming to have breakfast with me."

"Well," she says, sighing. "I thought about sneaking through your window last night but wasn't sure how good I'd be at scaling brick walls. So, I decided to wait until at least daybreak."

Leaning over, I kiss her cheek, then nip at her ear. "You should've called me. I would've met you for a midnight rendezvous."

"What have you done to me?" she asks, stopping in the middle of the empty, quiet sidewalk. Her voice is growing more serious, and with it, a level of honesty I've come to appreciate with Maggie. "You're all I think about. Just when I think I've had my fill, I crave you more. It's like a sickness."

For a moment, we just stand there and stare at each other. There are words clawing their way up my throat that feel a lot like promises and staking claims—*you're mine and I'm yours and this is what it feels like when you're falling*...

Unable to go there, scared of what admitting that might mean, I decide to lighten the mood instead. "You're falling right into my evil plan," I say, my tone taking on a sinister undertone as I duck my head and go straight for her neck where I know she's ticklish.

Spinning away, her dark hair flies up behind her as she begins walking faster down the sidewalk until I'm practically chasing her. Her laughter filling the air is the best sound.

"Don't drop the muffins," I warn.

She turns to look at me, still running. "Worry about yourself, mister!"

I could catch her if I wanted to, but I'm enjoying the sway of her hips and the delicious curves of her ass way too much.

Settling on a bench that faces a beautiful tree, Maggie and I share the muffins Tempest boxed up—Folsom Prison Blues and Sugar Daddy, my favorites—and sip our coffees. The sun has risen but it's still low in the sky, casting a beautiful glow over everything it touches, including the woman at my side.

"Damn, you're gorgeous," I tell her before taking another sip of my coffee.

She fights back a smile, biting down on her lip. "Keep drinking your coffee, Casanova."

"I'm serious and it wouldn't matter how much coffee I do or don't drink... or how many days pass or what you're wearing or not wearing, you'll always be gorgeous."

Her smile falters and she clears her throat, turning her gaze back to the tree. "You're sweet," she says quietly. "And if we're going to talk about gorgeous people, then you're at the top of the list. No one is as gorgeous as you are... inside and out."

When her eyes turn back to me, they're serious, and like so many times lately, it feels like we're on the precipice of something more. But like always, the atmosphere shifts and we fall back into what's comfortable —lightheartedness, banter, teasing... whatever keeps us from discussing the fact we're both falling for each other.

"I wonder what Trixie and Tess have for us today?" Maggie asks, reaching for the paper beside her. "They've been on a roll lately, huh?"

She already knows what the article says and she also knows it's my favorite part of the weekly paper and highlight of my week. So, I don't even feel bad for snatching it out of her hands.

"Greetings, Good People of Green Valley," I start out, clearing my throat. "In case you haven't heard, we have a champion in our midst. Gunnar 'The Show' Erickson won his title fight in New Orleans against Tyson 'The Freight Train' Ferguson in a first-round TKO! Those Vikings are on fire. First, with the new ring, and now bringing a new notoriety to our town. It's safe to say this invasion is a welcomed one."

I stop and look over at Maggie who's blushing. "I couldn't *not* mention it," she says with a shrug.

"I love the way you love the sport and support my family," I tell her, nudging her shoulder with mine, hoping she knows there's nothing to be embarrassed about.

She goes on to talk about his next big fight, which isn't until later this year, in Las Vegas, and finishes up the article with a response to a person looking for advice. For someone who hasn't experienced a lot when it comes to relationships, Maggie is really good at giving a thoughtful response to people who come to her looking for help.

"Another great article," I tell her, scanning over the other articles in the paper. "You know what I'd love?"

"What?" she asks.

"To see your name here," I say, pointing to Trixie and Tess. "People should know you're behind this insightful, fun article. If not this one, because I understand the need for anonymity, then another one, where you can be yourself."

Squinting against the sun that's now above the buildings and shining brightly on the park, she nods. "I'd like that too… one of these days."

CHAPTER 30

MAGGIE

"Cheers to Frankie teaching her first self-defense class!" Tempest leads the gang in a toast and we all raise our various glasses and mugs, much to the embarrassment of Frankie.

"Y'all really will drink to just about anything, won't you?" Frankie asks with a laugh. "I only stepped in because Tempest wouldn't stop tossing her… muffins in the toilet. It was gross and I had to do something to distract the class." She gives Tempest a wink before finishing her beer.

Tempest groans, leaning her head back. "I don't think I've ever thrown up so much in my life. Whoever coined the phrase *morning sickness* needs to have their head examined. It's so much more than that."

"Look, I'm happy you and Cage are having a baby, but can we not talk about disgusting shit during our fun time at Genie's?" Gunnar asks, earning him a swat in the back of the head from Frankie and a large wad of napkins thrown at his face from Cage.

I take the opportunity to look across the table at Vali and catch him watching me. He can't seem to keep his eyes—or his hands—off me these days and I'm not complaining. No, sir, he can touch me anytime, anywhere. In fact, the only complaint I have since our *whatever you want to call it* became more physical is that we don't get enough alone time.

We see each other almost every evening and we sometimes sneak quickies during the day but it doesn't stop the ravenous feeling I get every time I'm around him. I don't even know if that's normal. Vali certainly has no complaints and has the stamina to keep up with my newly discovered sexual appetite, so if it is an oddity, he has it too.

Again, it's not a bad thing.

I quite like the soreness I feel in the morning after I've been with Vali. I also like finding the secret hickies and love bites he leaves on my body. And then there was that time, last week, when I happened to notice the rosy shade left on my backside after a particularly rowdy romp. I nearly attacked him the next time I saw him and demanded he smack the other side to even things out.

Now that I think about it, it's not the actual alone time we need, it's the *extended* alone time, the kind we had in New Orleans. I need hours with Vali, not just moments. But that hasn't happened and probably won't anytime soon, because I still haven't worked up the nerve to come clean to my parents.

How can I just tell them I'm spending the night with Vali?

And bless his heart, he's had more patience than Job. I know it must drive him crazy and he probably feels like he's reverted back to his high school days and is sneaking around with his girlfriend, if we were labeling our relationship, which we're not. And sometimes, he even seems hurt when I turn him down for his overnight proposals. But every time I kiss him good night, he returns it, fervently, and tells me he'll take whatever he can get.

I'm not sure how I got so lucky...

When I feel someone touch the top of my hand, I look up to see Vali still watching me but, this time, more intently. "What's wrong?" he mouths.

Shaking my head, I smile at him. "I'm fine. Just thinking."

"Want to get out of here?" he murmurs, leaning closer as he nods over his shoulder.

Normally, I'd say no because we've only been here less than an hour and we haven't even danced yet, but instead, I say yes.

I will always say yes to Vali Erickson.

As soon as we're inside Vali's apartment, my back is pushed up against the wall as he attacks my mouth. He lifts me up effortlessly so I can wrap my legs around his waist and feel his erection right where I want it.

"You and this fucking dress have been driving me crazy all night. I might have to fuck you in it right here against the wall. Would you like that?" His voice is clear but I hear the restraint in it, the desire, and it lights my entire body up.

"God, yes. That's what I want," I breathe out, not nearly as controlled as Vali is.

He surprises me when he unwraps my legs and puts me down. "I have to get a condom. Don't move."

I nod my agreement and watch him as he walks into his bedroom, straight to his nightstand. When he sees me watching him, he places the still wrapped condom between his teeth and slowly undresses for me, giving me a little show.

Sexy bastard.

Vali sheaths himself in the latex as he walks closer to me and my mouth waters.

Why is it so hot to watch a guy touch himself?

When he's standing in front of me again, he reaches under the skirt of my dress and grabs ahold of my panties. "Are you particularly attached to these?"

Not really seeing where this is going, I tell him no because I'm not. They're just panties—or they *were*—but then Vali rips them off my body and tosses them to the floor.

"Now, where was I?" he murmurs before lifting me back up and pushing inside me in one swift move. My eyes go wide at the sensation and I grip Vali's shoulders as he begins to move. It's equal parts punishment and pardon as he relentlessly thrusts into me, taking me to the edge of ecstasy faster than I can whimper his name.

A few hours later, I awake with a start, disoriented because the room is dark and there's a warm body wrapped around me.

Why am I waking up in someone else's bed?

And not just *someone's* bed, why am I in Vali's bed?

Panic floods my body as realization starts to sink in. Oh my God, I'm in Vali's bed and we fell asleep. For how long? Blindly, I begin searching for my phone and find it on the nightstand. Swiping my finger across the screen, it lights up and the answer is staring me in the face.

Two o'clock.

In the morning.

"Shit," I mutter, scrambling out of bed and running around the dark space like a chicken with my head cut off. I never even texted my mom and dad to let them know I was coming back to Vali's apartment. The last thing I told them was I'd be home after Genie's, which is usually around eleven, three hours ago. They're probably worried or pissed. Either option makes me feel terrible. If I call them and by some stroke of luck they're asleep, then I'll wake them up and have to face their wrath, so I decide to take my chances and just hurry home.

I'm not afraid, per se.

It's not like they can ground me or anything, we're so far past that phase, but we're also long overdue for a talk. The one where I tell them I'm an adult and I'd like to have the freedoms that go along with that, like sleeping over at Vali's. I just hate feeling like I've disrespected them.

"Vali," I whisper, trying not to startle him. He stirs awake, and when he sees me, he looks around the room and then back at me. Realization dawns on him a little faster than it did me and he sits up in bed with a start. "Oh, shit, baby. We fell asleep."

"Yeah, it's two o'clock," I say, still trying to fully wake up.

"I'm sorry… I didn't mean for us to fall asleep. Want me to drive you home?"

"No," I tell him, my heart still racing. "Go back to sleep. This was bound to happen at some point. I guess it's time for me to pull up my big-girl panties and confront my parents." Going over to the pile of clothes, I grab my dress and slip it over my head. As I look around the floor where I'm standing, I remember what Vali did to my panties earlier.

So, not only will I possibly have to face the wrath of my parents when I get home, but I'll be doing it commando.

Super.

I can tell Vali has noticed my predicament when he lets out a loud snort, trying to hold back his laughter.

"It's not funny," I tell him, my hands on my hips for emphasis.

"You're right, it's not. Well, only a little funny and, I swear, I'll buy you more panties to make up for it." He has the nerve to wipe under his eyes like he's crying from laughing too hard.

"Yes, you will," I say with an air of indignance before leaning down and kissing him quickly before grabbing my purse. When I get to the stairs, I hear him call out, "Call me and let me know how it goes!"

Ten minutes later, after driving as quickly as possible, I'm placing my car in park in the driveway. Glancing around the house, I try to see if any of the house lights are still on. From what I can see, it appears dark, which means my parents are in bed and I mentally cross my fingers, toes, eyes, and anything else I can think of, hoping it's true.

Quietly, I open and close the front door, relocking it behind me, before tiptoeing to the stairs. When my foot lands on the first step, the kitchen light comes on and a throat clears and I nearly piss my missing pants.

"Holy crap," I gasp, clutching my chest as I turn to see both of my parents waiting on me at the kitchen table. Dropping my purse onto the stairs, I walk into the kitchen to face them.

Kill me now, Lord.

Clasping my hands in front of me, I take a deep breath and start, "I know I'm home late and I didn't call and I'm sorry. I fell asleep at Vali's and just woke up about ten minutes ago. I drove home as soon as I realized what happened." I spit my words out in a rush, hoping things will be better if I rip the Band-Aid off myself and come clean.

The truth will set you free, right?

"Also, Vali and I are sleeping together. Not that it's really your business because I am an adult and adults have sex, but I just want to be honest with you. And before you ask, we care a lot about each other and we're being responsible."

Okay, maybe that was a little too much truth, but it's out there now.

Way to go with that TMI syndrome, Margaret.

Is there a hole around here I can crawl in?

When I'm finally brave enough to look up and make eye contact with my parents, I notice my mother covering her mouth with her hand. It's impossible to tell if she's crying, but I really hope not. But then again, her baby just admitted to having sex for the first time and that might be an emotional thing for a mother to hear. She's typically strong and in control, but everyone has their breaking point.

Shifting my eyes from hers to my dad's, I swallow. His expression is clearer—firm, unwavering, and pensive.

"Sit," my father commands and I obey, taking the chair closest to where I'm standing. "We were very worried about you, young lady," he says, cementing the guilty feelings I was already having. "All you had to do was call us."

"I know, Dad," I admit, another wave of regret washing over me. "I didn't plan on falling asleep, it just happened."

I can count the times I've been reprimanded by my dad on one hand, and at twenty-four, I can honestly say it never gets easier. I hate disappointing people, especially my parents.

"And while we know you're a very responsible... *woman*." He says that last word with some difficulty, I notice but quickly forgive because I know how hard this must be for him. "And you know how much we value honesty," he adds, clearing his throat before continuing. "You don't have to be quite that honest. A little communication would've worked just fine."

Right, communication. I might be a good writer, some might say a great writer, but I do struggle to communicate my needs and wants. It's one of my flaws and I'm not afraid to admit that.

Nodding, I glance over at my mom who gives me a quick wink.

Wait, what?

It's a surprising move but it makes me feel better.

"I'm going to bed," my dad announces abruptly. And just like that, he walks over to me and kisses the top of my head. "Don't be late for work."

Mama and I sit in silence until we hear the door to my parents' bedroom close. Then, we both start talking at the same time.

"Mom, I'm so sorry. Are you mad at me—"

"Why on earth did you admit that to your father? You're lucky he didn't have a heart attack right then and there—"

We both stop, look at each other, and fall into a fit of hushed giggles.

"Come here, child," she whispers, opening her arms wide. Of course, I run into them like I've always done. I don't care how old I am, I'll never refuse my mama's hugs.

"I can't believe I blurted that out," I admit against her shoulder.

She rubs my back soothingly. "Maggie, you must know by now your father and I aren't stupid."

Popping my head up and looking at her, I say, "Of course, I know that. I've never thought that of you."

"Then why do you assume we don't know what young couples in love do? Old couples in love do it too you know?" She quirks an eyebrow at me and I feel my face flush red. I'm going to pretend I didn't hear her last statement but her first one has me pulling out of her embrace.

"It's not like that," I sadly admit. "Vali and I aren't in love. We can't be."

"And, why is that?"

If I'm going to tell her part of it, I might as well tell her all of it. "When we started seeing each other, Vali was very upfront about what he could and couldn't give me. It's always been understood that he wouldn't be in Green Valley long and we agreed to not label our relationship. So, we're just enjoying being with each other for as long as time allows, knowing it can't last forever."

Damn, those words hurt now that I say them out loud.

How will I ever let Vali go?

"Well, that makes about as much sense as boobs on a bull, Margaret Hope. Anyone with eyes in their head can see that man is crazy about you and I know you feel the same. It might've started off casual, but I have a feeling that changed while you two were in New Orleans," she says, giving me a knowing look. "I've seen it on your face ever since you got back. There's been something different about you."

I'm ashamed at how shocked I am regarding my mother's astuteness. Moms really do see and know all, I guess. And, as warm as her words make me feel inside, I can't help the tears that well up in my eyes.

"I do love him, Mama," I admit, feeling a small tear in my chest. "So much. What am I going to do?" Pressing my hand to my mouth, I try not to full-on sob at the realization of my feelings and what that means for the condition of my heart.

She pulls me back into her embrace and hugs me tightly. "Tell him, sweet girl. I'd bet the store, he feels the same. Once you both know you're on the same page, then you can face whatever struggles you come against together."

I give her a squeeze before pulling away and wiping my eyes. "Thank you, Mama. I didn't realize how much I needed to hear that and to have this talk with you. I don't know why I thought you wouldn't understand. I'm sorry."

"Don't apologize. Sometimes it's hard for children to accept their parents are *people* too," she chuckles. "Your daddy and I love you more than anything, sometimes I worry we've loved you too much in the way we've sheltered you and have been overprotective. We waited so long for you, once we got you, we couldn't bear the idea of letting you go."

She shrugs and I feel my heart ache for a different reason.

"So," she says, letting out a deep sigh. "I apologize if we've held you back in any way. You're a remarkable woman, Maggie, and I couldn't be prouder. Just remember, we're not trying to squash your dreams or keep you from doing anything you want to do. More than anything, we want to prepare you the best we can so we can watch you fly."

CHAPTER 31

VALI

*W*hen I hear something outside the bedroom, I lift my head off my pillow. Maggie is still sound asleep at my side, so I know it's not her. Since she finally had *the talk* with her parents, she's been staying over a few nights a week and I love having her in my bed.

Rubbing my eyes, I try to see into the main room and catch the hulking form of my brother coming up the stairs.

"Vali," he whispers into the darkness, flipping on the light over the sink in the kitchen. "Hey, man. Wake up."

Shifting, I replace my arm under Maggie's head with a pillow and hold still for a minute to make sure she doesn't wake up. When I see she's going to stay asleep, I slip out of bed and pull on my boxers and T-shirt that are on the floor.

"Oh, shit," Cage mutters when he catches a glimpse of the sleeping form in my bed. "I didn't realize Maggie stayed over. Sorry."

"What's up?" I ask, walking toward the middle of the room.

Cage inhales and exhales deeply and I'm suddenly very awake and on full alert.

"Is Tempest okay?" I ask, my thoughts immediately turning to her and the baby. Why else would my brother be waking me up at this ungodly hour? The clock on the microwave says five thirty-two. I guess it's not that ungodly, except for the fact Maggie and I went a few rounds before we finally crashed around two o'clock. So, I've only been asleep for a few hours.

"Tempest is fine," Cage says, shaking his head. "But we need to have an emergency family meeting. Gunnar is on his way over."

My heart slows down and speeds back up. "If Tempest is fine, then what's so important we need to have a family meeting before daybreak?"

"Downstairs," he orders, already heading in that direction.

Glancing back over my shoulder, I see Maggie sleeping soundly and hope she stays that way until I can get whatever this is over with and climb back in bed with her. I've never slept as fucking good as I do when she's next to me.

And I need more of it.

More of her.

As I walk down the stairs and make my way into the main part of the studio, I notice Cage has the overhead light on and is sitting at the desk. I guess we're having the meeting down here. About that time, Gunnar walks through the front door looking as disheveled as I feel.

"Dude," he groans, scratching his head and then running a hand through his hair until it's smoothed down a bit. "If this is some fucking torture tactic that is supposed to make me a better fighter, I don't want it. You can have my belt... I need sleep." Slipping a rubber band off his wrist, he ties his hair back at the nape of his neck and plops down on a mat.

"Sorry," Cage says, sounding remorseful, which puts me on guard.

A second ago, I was tracking with Gunnar, thinking this was some stupid wild hair Cage got up his ass, but now I'm not so sure.

Deciding to stand, I cross my arms over my chest and face him. "What's all this about?"

"Viggo and Ozzi were in a car accident," Cage says, his voice gritty, like he's fighting back emotions and my stomach drops to my feet.

Gunnar jumps up off the mat like it's on fire. "What the fuck?"

"Calm down," Cage says, shaking his head as it drops between his shoulders. "They're going to be okay... I talked to Dad... he said they're going to be okay."

"What the fuck?" I ask, repeating Gunnar's words, because WHAT. THE. FUCK?

Cage sighs, pinching the bridge of his nose. "All Dad could tell me is that they're at Mercy and the doctor said Ozzi's left arm is broken and he has a concussion. They think he threw an arm out to protect Viggo and the airbag got him."

"And Viggo?" I ask, trying to imagine our oldest brother in less than tip-top shape. He's always been the epitome of a firstborn—in charge, goal-oriented, always on his game. Thinking about him being anything less than that is disturbing and gut-wrenching.

"Broken leg, fractured rib, and a punctured lung," Cage says, finally looking up and I see the bloodshot eyes and worry on his face. "He needed a few stitches above his eyebrow, but he's lucky. They were on their way to the gym for an early session. Ozzi's car is in the shop, so Viggo swung by to pick him up. Dad said a car ran a red light and side-swiped them on the driver's side. It could've been way worse..."

He drifts off and the three of us just stare at each other for a minute, maybe more.

If they're anything like me, which I know they are, they're thinking we could've lost them. Thank God we didn't, but just the close possibility is enough to make me want to hurl.

"What do we do?" Gunnar asks. "Do we need to fly to Dallas?"

Cage stands and walks over to the mats where Gunnar and I are standing. "Dad said there's nothing we can do. Viggo will be in the hospital for a while, and as soon as they set Ozzi's arm, they'll cast it and send him home. Mom's going to stay with him until he's out of the woods."

"And the gym?" I ask, hating we have to think about business at a time like this, but it is *our* business and with all of them out of commission, even Mom and Dad, who does that leave?

There's a long pause before Cage continues. "One of us will need to go."

My heart drops again, but for an entirely different reason. I always knew my days in Green Valley were numbered, but I felt like I was on my own timeline for once, calling my own shots. But I guess not, because out of the three of us standing here, I'm the only one with nothing holding me here.

Except for Maggie.

Maggie, who I haven't even had a chance to tell how I feel.

Maggie, who I agreed to not have any labels with… or promises.

Maggie, who I now can't imagine living my life without.

But what happens when that life is no longer in Green Valley?

"I'll go," I tell them, my eyes trained on the floor because if I look at them, I'm afraid they'll see right through me. At the moment, I feel stripped down and bare, my emotions are raw and frayed and I'm being forced back to the one place I no longer want to be.

"Vali," Cage starts, but I hold up a hand.

"No, I've overstayed my welcome anyway, right?" I ask, trying to lighten the mood, but failing miserably. "Besides, I'm ready to get back to the city. I can't stay here forever."

Gunnar's meaty paw comes down on my shoulder and he squeezes. I return the gesture and pat his back, thinking he probably needs a little brotherly love at the moment. Cage walks over and pulls me into a hug, then Gunnar. The next thing I know, the three of us are hugging it out right there in the middle of the gym. Thankfully, there aren't any onlookers, but fuck it if there were.

"I'll call Dad and let him know you're coming," Cage says, giving me one last slap on the back and then pulling away. "And I can book you a flight, if you want."

"That's okay," I tell him, wanting to go upstairs and talk to Maggie first before I do anything else. "I have some miles to cash in on, so I'll book it."

He nods, glancing over at Gunnar. "Go home and get some sleep. We'll take the day off."

Gunnar nods, his face still full of emotion. "Call me if you hear anything," he says, taking some tentative steps toward the front door.

"I will," Cage assures him, crossing over to lock the door behind him. "If anything changes, I'll call you. But they're going to be fine, just some bumps and bruises… nothing we haven't dealt with in the ring."

He's right. We've all experienced broken bones, stitches, concussions… you name it. But somehow this is different. It's like a fucking wake-up call from life, yelling at us about how fragile it is and how we can't take anything for granted.

After Cage heads back up to his apartment, I turn and go to mine, taking the steps two at a time. Seconds later, I'm walking into the bedroom and shedding my clothes before I climb back into bed beside Maggie.

"Where'd you go?" she asks, her voice raspy from sleep.

I think about lying and saying *nowhere* or *the bathroom,* just to prolong the inevitable. But I can't, because this is Maggie, and I promised to always tell her the truth. "Downstairs to talk to Cage and Gunnar."

"What time is it?" she asks, sitting up in bed and bringing the blanket with her to cover her gorgeous breasts. "Is everything okay?"

"Viggo and Ozzi were in an accident on their way to the gym this morning."

Her gasp echoes around the dark bedroom. "Oh my God. Are they okay?"

Sighing, I give her the same speech Cage just gave me and Gunnar. "They're going to be okay. Some broken bones, stitches, concussions... but they're going to be okay."

"Thank God," she says, exhaling a deep breath.

Without saying a word, like always, I can hear Maggie's wheels turning.

"I have to go back," I finally say, answering her unspoken question. "There isn't anyone else who can run the gym except for me. Mom and Dad are with Viggo and Ozzi. Cage is needed here and so is Gunnar."

She sniffles and I reach out to wrap my arms around her shoulders, pulling her to me.

"I know you said no promises... and no labels," she croaks out, her chin resting on my shoulder as her arms drop the blanket and come up to wrap around my neck. "I know all of that... and I know you said you'd eventually go back to Dallas."

Her words get more strained as she tries to hold back her tears, but it's not necessary, because I feel it too.

"But that didn't stop me from falling for you," she admits, making my heart squeeze in my chest.

Oh, Maggie.

"Come with me," I plead, holding on to her like I can keep her with me. "Come with me to Dallas."

Her body goes still in my arms and she eventually releases her hold and sits back. The faint light of the rising sun allows me to see her face, and when those brown eyes come into focus and are full of fear and uncertainty, I know the answer before she says it.

"I can't." She shakes her head, but her body says something different. When she leans back into me, holding me even tighter than before, she continues, "My parents need me... I... I don't... I can't just leave."

"Can't or won't?" I ask, taking her shoulders and putting some distance between us.

We stare at each other for a moment and it's on the tip of my tongue to tell her I'm falling for her too... I'm beyond falling, I have fallen. But saying it would make it real, and if she's not willing to come with me to Dallas, I don't see how we can move forward. Her life is here. Mine is there.

Whether I like it or not.

When her eyes flood with tears and her chin begins to quiver, I can't sit there and watch her cry, so I pull her onto my lap and hold her. Her immediate dismissal hurts, I'm not going to lie.

"You just said you're falling for me," I challenge, stroking her hair. "I'm falling too, but I can't see this going beyond what we have here if I'm leaving and you're staying."

The words, albeit simple, hurt as they come out of my mouth, because in a roundabout way, I'm giving Maggie an ultimatum and I never intended on it sounding that way. But fuck, I want her with me. And if I can't stay here, then I want her in Dallas. It's that simple.

"I'm sorry," she whispers with a heart-wrenching level of finality.

After one final squeeze of her arms, she lets go and slips out of bed… and what feels like out of my life. With her head bowed so I can't see her face, which I'm guessing is streaked with tears, she dresses quickly and quietly. "I have to go to work," she mutters, slipping into her jeans and then her shoes. "My dad needs me there early for a shipment."

I'm getting ready to call her on the bullshit lie, assuming she's running away from me, but about that time the alarm on her phone goes off and she walks over to silence it.

Refusing to let her go without a proper goodbye, I stand and walk over to her, wrapping my arms around her until she gives in to my embrace and hugs me back. When she tilts her head back to look at me, I reach up and wipe away the lingering tears on her cheeks with my thumb, stroking her cheek, memorizing every minute detail of Margaret Hope O'Neal.

"I'll miss you," I tell her, hoping she can read between the lines—I love you, you're keeping a piece of me, and I'm taking a piece of you. "Thank you for being you and for making my life better by knowing you."

She bites down on her bottom lip as her brows furrow in sadness. "Somehow," she starts but stops, shaking her head as if to clear the emotions in her voice but it doesn't work. "Somehow, I'd convinced myself I could keep you. Or that when you had to leave, it wouldn't hurt that bad because I've known from the beginning it was a possibility. But I wasn't prepared for you to be so amazing or my heart to feel this way. I just… I'm sorry," she says, sniffling and then breaking out of our embrace. "Thank you for… everything."

When she practically runs down the stairs, I let her go.

A few hours later when my bags are packed and Cage and I are headed out of town to the airport in Maryville, I think about asking him to stop by the feed store so I can see her one last time but decide against it. I'm no masochist, nor a sadist, and I know there's nothing that could make this better for either of us. So, I take the thirty-minute drive to commit everything there is about Maggie and our time together to memory, hoping it'll be enough to tide me over for the rest of my life, because I can't imagine ever being with anyone else.

When Cage drops me off at the arrival gate, we exchange a hug and I can see the understanding in his eyes.

"Watch out for her," I say, swallowing down the emotions.

"Will do, brother," Cage says in return, not needing an explanation. "Take care of yourself."

And like that, I'm gone, and my time in Tennessee is over.

CHAPTER 32

MAGGIE

Hey, Ever,

It's been a week since Vali left and it still hurts. Why does it hurt so much and why didn't you warn me? I thought I knew what heartache felt like and I thought I could handle it but I was so wrong on both accounts.

I now understand why there are so many songs about heartbreak and I'm pretty sure I've listened to them all. It really is a universal feeling, I suppose, but it doesn't lessen the pain.

Anyway, enough about me and my sad self. How are you? Any stories of love and happiness you can share to get me out of this funk and give me hope?

Your sad, pathetic friend,

Maggie

I send the email before I think better of it and close my laptop. I hate being such a gloomy Gus but Everly is the only person I can vent and talk about these things to. She's had her fair share of boyfriends and breakups, so I'm depending on her sage advice to get me through this.

My mom has tried to talk to me and console me but it's just not the same. She and my dad have been together since high school and have never broken up, so she doesn't really know how I feel.

I suppose I could talk to Frankie or Tempest, but I think I'd feel too weird. They're part of Vali's family and I'm not, and I'd hate for them to think I'm just trying to get information about him. I would like to know how Ozzi and Viggo are doing, though. I even went so far as to look up the accident online. The pictures of the crash I found were horrifying and made me even more upset because I can only imagine how Vali feels, being there and seeing his brothers so banged up.

I've officially stopped going to Tempest's class too. I just can't go into the gym right now. The other day, I had to make a delivery to Mr. Jones next door and I barely survived. Being that close to the gym and where Vali lived... where we were together... Let's just say, I had to take a long lunch to recover from the breakdown I had in my car. It was so bad; I had to drive back home and wash my face so no one at the store would notice.

Of course, my mom could tell I'd been crying. Cold water can only do so much to swollen eyes. Thankfully, she let me spend the rest of the day in the office so I could take care of the paperwork and not scare the customers away.

I'm sure Vali has so much going on right now—taking care of the gym and helping his parents with his brothers—and yet, I still can't help but wonder if he's thinking of me as much as I'm thinking of him.

Does he miss me too?

I know it's incredibly selfish but I'd love to know if he's as miserable as I am. Part of me hopes he is, and then, another part of me hopes he's okay because that's what you do when you love someone. You want them to be happy.

And I love Vali, make no mistake.

I love him.

I knew it when I told him I was falling. God, I probably knew it when we were in New Orleans. And the distance and time apart have done nothing to minimize those feelings. If anything, they feel bigger and more pronounced with his absence.

Sometimes I wonder if I should've told him how I felt sooner. Would that have made our time together better? I can't imagine it being more incredible than it already was, to be honest. Would saying those three little words make our parting hurt less? More? I honestly don't know. All I know is I hurt and it sucks and I have to figure out a way to push through this and start living again.

At least I now know what being in love feels like. Another thing to mark off my *One Day* list.

I busy myself around my room, cleaning, organizing, and doing anything to keep my mind off my current situation before sitting down and writing a few articles for the Ledger. I'm not feeling particularly chatty and have probably lost touch with what's going on around town, so I've been focusing my articles more on the advice column than local gossip. Not that I feel qualified to be giving out advice but I certainly have a lot more empathy than I did a few weeks ago.

As I wrap up another article, I get a notification that Everly has replied to my email from earlier. So, I quickly shoot the most recent article off to Sarah and then quickly open Everly's email.

Aww, honey, I'm so sorry.

Breakups suck donkey dicks and I hate that you're going through this. I'm not sure what kind of advice I can give you because everyone handles these things differently. But I believe, whatever you are feeling, you need to allow yourself to feel it. I mean, really feel it. Don't let it consume you but cry if you need to cry. Scream and punch your pillow, if that's what you need. Everything you feel is valid but you need to let it out. Don't hold on to it. I know it's hard to believe, but things will eventually get better.

I like to channel my emotions through my hobbies and art, things that always make me happy. I'll work in my garden or redecorate my house. You'd be amazed how painting a room a new color and moving furniture around can not only improve the space but improve your mood too.

What about your writing? Are you still doing that? I don't mean for the paper. I'm talking about the short stories you used to send me. I loved reading those and always thought you'd write a book one of these days. You never know, it could be the outlet you need, and then, one day, you can publish it and become a best seller!

The sky's the limit with you, Maggie O'Neal. Or should I say, Margaret O'Neal? That has a nice author ring to it. ;)

Your biggest fan,

Everly

Closing down my laptop, I actually manage a small smile. I'd forgotten how I used to send her short stories. They weren't anything too deep, just silly stories I'd make up to entertain Everly, but they were fun and I enjoyed writing them. I do remember that much.

Maybe she's right. Maybe I could turn all these thoughts and feelings into something productive and feel better. Publishing a book has always been a secret dream of mine—on my *One Day* list—but I've never taken the time to actually do it.

Since it's Sunday and I have nothing else to do—no work, no Vali—I open my laptop back up and start a fresh document. With nothing left to lose, I start to write. No plotting or planning, just the familiar comfort of connecting letters to make words and words to make sentences. I allow the cadence of the keyboard to soothe my soul as I begin to pour my heart out in prose.

CHAPTER 33

VALI

"*V*ali," Greg, one of the trainers, says from the open doorway of the office. "Brant called in sick, so there's no one to teach the afternoon kickboxing class. I'd do it but I'm scheduled for a personal training session at the same time. It's just you and me this afternoon."

Sighing, I push away from the desk where I've been catching up on bills and paperwork. Ozzi has been coming in and doing some of it, but since he's still in a cast, it's a slow process. I didn't realize how much of a step back Dad had taken over the months I'd been gone until I came back. There's a different vibe here. It's still a successful gym and we're still training winners in the ring; those things won't ever change. But behind the scenes, something has definitely changed.

"I'll do it," I tell him, standing and walking toward the door.

"How's Viggo doing?" he asks.

It's obvious my brother is missed around here and the feeling is mutual. Every time I call him to give him an update on something or check on him, he asks the same thing.

"He's glad to be home," I tell him, slapping him on the shoulder as we walk out to the gym.

The day after I landed in Dallas, Viggo went into surgery to have a rod placed in his thigh to repair a fractured femur. After a stint in the hospital, he was moved to a rehabilitation center for four weeks and finally got to come home yesterday, so we're officially roommates again. Since I gave up my apartment before going to Green Valley, I opted to stay with him for now.

"When does he get to come back and at least hang out?" Greg asks.

Letting out a deep sigh, I shake my head. "I'm not sure, but it'll be at least another few weeks. He's doing PT, but it's a slow process." It's already been a long haul and he still has a couple more months to go. "Good news is Ozzi's cast comes off in a couple of weeks, so we'll have him back in action soon."

Greg gives me a reassuring pat on the back before going to find his client.

It's hard to believe I've already been back here for over a month, yet in ways, it feels like years. One thing's for sure, I miss Maggie more today than I did when I watched her walk out of my apartment.

I miss her so bad I have to constantly distract myself so I won't think about her every second of every day. But that doesn't work most of the time. Even when I don't realize I'm thinking about her, I'm still thinking about her.

When something good happens, I want to call her.

When something bad happens, I want to call her.

When I can't find joy in a newspaper, I want to call her.

When someone with brown hair passes by me, I want to call her.

When I hear a sappy love song or watch a movie or see the sunrise... I want to call her.

But I don't, because I'm not sure I can handle it.

Just thinking about her makes my chest ache so bad I can't stand it. What would hearing her voice do to me? Knowing she's there and I'm here and there's nothing I can fucking do about it? Fuck that. I'm man enough to admit I'm not that strong, not when it comes to her. So even when my thumb is hovering over her name on my phone, I resist the urge.

Thankfully, the kickboxing class starts to trickle in, giving me a reprieve from my torturous thoughts. As I greet students and start the instruction portion, Maggie is still there in the back of my mind, but I'm able to put her in a box for now, one I'll open later when I'm alone.

After the class is over, I spar with one of our fighters who's training for a fight next week. The physical exertion is exactly what I need to really clear my head. Bobbing and weaving, I dodge his jabs and hooks, working up a sweat.

"Fuck," he says with a laugh, backing up and shaking out his arms. "You're faster than Ozzi."

I chuckle, swiping a leg out and catching him in the calf. "Someone's gotta make you work for it and keep you on your toes."

"Do you think Gunnar's ever coming back to Dallas?" he asks, adjusting his gloves and then coming back for more. "I'd love to get in the ring with him one of these days."

"Fuck if I know, man," I tell him, panting through my words as we continue to spar. "He's pretty solid in Green Valley. Only way he'll probably be back is if there's a fight in town."

Connecting a left hook to my ribs, he chuckles when I wince. "What's so great about Tennessee? Bigger is always better and there's nothing bigger than Texas."

My knee-jerk response is: Maggie. That's what's so great about Tennessee, but I keep that to myself.

When he spreads his arms wide, guard down, I take that opportunity to land a sucker punch to his gut. As his face crumples in pain, his gloved hands go back up where they're supposed to be.

"If you ever get a chance to go see the new gym Cage is building down there, you should. It's coming together nicely."

We go for a few more rounds, keeping our conversation to smack talk, and by the time we're finished, the rest of the gym is cleared out. Even Greg has packed up and gone home for the day.

"Need me to help with anything?" he asks.

"Nah, man. I got it," I tell him, waving him off. "Get out of here and ice those muscles. Be ready to go hard again tomorrow."

As I'm putting away some extra mats and tidying up the place, I hear the door open and close. When no one says anything, I walk toward the front and stop dead in my tracks.

"Chloe?" I ask, praying my eyes are deceiving me but knowing they're not. "What are you doing here?"

Her shoulders rise and fall. "I've been trying to get in touch with you for months now," she says, taking a few steps toward me. "Your mom told me you were out of town, but she never said where. When I tried calling, I got a disconnect message. Your apartment was empty... it was like you were a figment of my imagination."

I could only wish that were the case. Unfortunately, my and Chloe's relationship had been very real and the worst mistake of my life.

"I'll ask you again," I say, trying to rein in the anger and resentment her presence brings. "What are you doing here?"

Her face pinches as she tries to hold back her emotions. "I want you to know I made a mistake."

"You don't fucking say?" I quip, balling up a couple of dirty towels and tossing them toward the laundry bin.

She searches my face, silently pleading for me to give her something, but she won't find what she's looking for because everything I ever felt for her is gone. When I don't break like she thinks I will at the sight of her tears, she huffs as her shoulders fall.

"Please, just hear me out."

When I nod, deciding this was bound to happen at some point and it might as well be tonight, she continues. "I'm sorry... for everything. I'm sorry for lying and for hiding the truth. I'm sorry for ruining the amazing thing we had before we ever got started. If I could go back and change it, I would. Most of all, I'm sorry for hurting you. Of all the people in the world, you didn't deserve that."

Her voice cracks and I inwardly cringe because I know Chloe and her tells, and tears are getting ready to spill. I fucking hate watching a woman cry, regardless of who they are. It's something ingrained in my DNA.

"I'm just fucking sorry, okay?" she says on a sob, the damn breaking. "I should've divorced him a long time ago. Our marriage was doomed from the start. He cheated on me. I cheated on him."

"So I was a fucking pawn in your sick game?" I ask, letting her words sink in. "You used me to get back at your cheating husband?"

"No," she cries, her voice rising. "No, it wasn't like that with you. It never was. I swear!"

When she reaches for me, her hand brushing my arm, I flinch back like I've been burned.

"Don't touch me," I seethe. "Don't fucking touch me."

That's when her face crumbles and she falls apart. Her body slumps to the floor and she wails. "He left me... After all the bullshit I put up with over the years—mistresses, one-night stands—HE. LEFT. ME.

And now the only thing I want," she says, eyes turning up to look at me. "The only thing I want is standing right in front of me."

My blood turns cold. Her tears no longer pierce my heart. "Leave," I demand.

"Vali!" she exclaims, clambering up from the floor as she switches gears and tactics. "You said we were good together. You said I was the best thing that had ever happened to you... and then you asked me to marry you!"

"That was before I found out you were a lying, cheating bitch!" I roar, my hands clenched in fists at my side, wanting to destroy something. Not Chloe, not physically, at least. But something.

Her face turns a bright shade of red. "I was going to tell you, after I left him. You just surprised me with the proposal... I wasn't ready."

"Too late," I tell her, shaking my head. "It was too late. The moment I found out you had lied to me, it would've been off anyway."

"How can you say that?" she asks, her voice cracking again. "How can you forget all the good times? It was one mistake, Vali. I'm human... you're human. We make mistakes!"

Biting back a chuckle, I let out a sigh. "You just don't get it, do you?"

"No, I guess not," she says.

"What we had was built on lies and betrayal. It never would've worked. Even if you had managed to fabricate a way around your marriage, the lies would have always been there, festering. And it would've eventually come to a head, better now than after we'd wasted years of our lives."

My life, I think.

God, I was so close to wasting years with this woman. The thought alone makes my stomach turn.

"It's over," I inform her, just in case she needs me to spell it out for her. This is the last conversation I want to have with Chloe for the rest of my life. "It was over when it started. It's over now."

I also want to tell her I know what true love feels like now. I know what it means to connect with someone on every level and share a bond so sincere and genuine that time and distance could never break it. But I don't want to taint what I have with Maggie. Chloe doesn't get the right to even speak her name.

"Please leave," I tell her, feeling much calmer than I did a few minutes ago. Maybe my mom was right? Maybe I needed this closure with her?

"So that's it?" she asks, her arms going wide and then falling back to her side. "Just like that..." Letting out a rueful laugh, she turns to the door, but then pauses. "Can you honestly say you don't love me anymore?"

When she sweeps her long, blonde hair over her shoulder to look at me with her baby blues, I vaguely remember the woman I thought I loved, but feel nothing in this moment but relief that I dodged that bullet.

"With one hundred percent certainty," I tell her, not wanting to leave any room for doubt.

Pushing the door open, she walks out. "Goodbye, Vali," she says, just as it closes behind her.

Walking over I flip the deadbolt and lean back against the glass.

I no longer need to punch something. Quite the opposite, I feel drained and the only thing I truly need is hundreds of miles away. Sighing, I push off the door, shut down the lights, and walk out the back exit. As I start up my truck, everything inside of me is screaming to just drive... get on the highway and don't stop until I hit the Green Valley city limits sign, if they even have one of those.

But I can't.

My family needs me.

So instead, I drive to pick up some late dinner and then head to Viggo's with thoughts of mountains and a brown-eyed girl filling my head.

CHAPTER 34

MAGGIE

I'm at the Piggly Wiggly buying a few groceries when I hear my name being yelled down the aisle.

Naturally, after practically jumping out of my skin, I turn around to try and figure out where it came from. When I see Frankie headed down toward me, I let out a squeal.

"Maggie, oh my God!" she exclaims, abandoning her basket to meet me in the middle of the aisle. "Where have you been hiding? I've missed you so much."

Frankie pulls me into a tight hug and I'm instantly filled with memories. Memories I've tried to forget no matter how great they were because they hurt to think about. Then the guilt comes because as soon as Vali left, I threw away my two closest friends here without a second thought.

When she releases me from her grip, her face falls as she looks at me. "Maggie, what's wrong?"

"I'm so sorry," I blurt out. "I've been a terrible friend these last two months or so."

Scoffing, she waves me off. "Stop it. I understand; we all do. But we really have missed you. How have you been?"

"Awful." My voice sounds like a cross between a laugh and a cry because that's exactly how I feel. "I've been miserable without Vali and all of you, really. So many times I wanted to call or stop by the gym but I just couldn't. It was too hard."

"Aww, sweetie, don't worry about it. We all could've handled this better. Can we forgive each other and be friends again?"

"Yes, of course!" This time I'm the one to grab Frankie in a hug and I don't let go until our tears turn to laughter.

We finally pull away, both of us wiping our eyes, when a little boy with dusty blond hair zooms past us dropping cookie crumbs like Hansel from the fairy tale. Soon after, we see a statuesque woman chasing after him while wearing heels, no less.

"Oh, I almost forgot! Come with me." Frankie grabs my arm and leads me out of our aisle into one that is two rows down, bringing me face to face with a very pregnant Tempest.

"Maggie!" she squeals. "Don't just stand there, come give me a hug!"

I immediately do what she says, but it feels awkward because I want to hug her but I don't want to squeeze the baby out of her. Tempest laughs and says, "Relax, you're not going to hurt me or the baby."

Pulling away, I look down at her adorable baby bump and marvel. "I can't believe how far along you are. Do you know the gender yet?"

"I do, but no one else knows. Oh, but Cage doesn't know I know, so keep that to yourself, please." Tempest's laughter practically fills the grocery store and I can't believe I've gone this long without talking to her.

My face must tell all, because she reaches out and places her hand on top of mine.

"Hey, now, none of that," she says in her motherly way. "I know the last couple of months have been hard and we've all dealt with it in different and imperfect ways. Let's just look forward, okay? You ready to be social again?"

I cringe a little at the thought. As much as I want to hang out with them and escape the hermit status I've adopted the past couple of months, I'm worried. "Won't it be weird?" I ask. "I mean, my…" I was going to say *ex* or *ex-boyfriend*, but that's not technically true because we never used labels. "Vali," I finally say with a pained smile, because it still hurts to speak his name, "is going to be your brother-in-law…"

"It's not an all-or-nothing kind of deal, Maggie. I want you in my life because of *you*, not Vali. I've missed you and it was very sad to lose both you and Vali at the same time cold turkey like that. I understand but it still hurt."

God, I've been so selfish in my grief, but Tempest is right. My heart may not be fully healed but I can't hide any longer. It's time to start living again, even if it's only one step at a time.

Before I can reply, Tempest holds her hand up, stopping me. "Don't apologize again," she says firmly. "I can see it on your face, but it's not necessary. Besides, you've already been forgiven, so save your breath."

I can't help but smile because it feels really good to clear the air between Tempest and Frankie. I've missed them. Maybe not as much as Vali, but a whole heck of a lot.

"Now," Tempest says, her tone making it obvious we're switching gears, "would you like to help us with my baby shower?"

My smile grows even wider. "Seriously? Of course!"

She exhales and leans against the shopping cart. "That's so great because we need all the help we can get."

Right about that time, the woman in heels from earlier walks up to us, sweaty and out of breath, with the blond toddler held firmly on her hip.

"This child can never have another cookie, y'all hear me? These shoes were not made for grocery store escapades."

Laughing, Tempest introduces us. "Maggie, this is Anna, she's married to my cousin Cole. And this precious angel right here is Matthew." Tempest rubs the boy's back while cooing, "It's not your fault your mama doesn't know how to dress casually, is it. And, you know I'll give you all the cookies you want."

Anna rolls her eyes. "Just you wait. Soon enough, you'll be in my shoes and I can't wait for you to beg for forgiveness." She then turns to me and smiles. "Hi, Maggie, it's nice to meet you. Sorry for all the... crazy."

"It's no problem at all. I've actually missed this kind of crazy." It's true. I've missed this more than I can say and it feels so good to be back with my friends.

"Well, that's good, Mags, because things are only going to get crazier. Why don't we get together tomorrow at the bakery to go over the baby shower?" Frankie asks, looking between me and Tempest, checking to see if we're in agreement. Her use of Vali's nickname for me catches me off guard and I feel my smile falter just a bit before I push through and nod my head at her.

"Sounds great to me. I have to finish my shopping anyway. I'll see y'all tomorrow, though," I promise.

* * *

THE NEXT DAY, we have so much fun at the bakery, catching up and finalizing plans for the baby shower, we decide to continue the party at Genie's.

I admit it's hard being here without Vali, but my friends are making sure I stay distracted and it helps.

"Is it weird I still like coming here even while being pregnant?" Tempest asks, swirling her straw through her Shirley Temple. "I know some people are giving me major judgy eyes but I'm used to that. I just really like this place and I know I won't be able to come once the baby is here, so I'm trying to soak it up as much as I can before that happens."

"It's fine," Frankie assures her. "You're not drinking and no one can smoke in here, so ignore everyone else and have fun while you can."

"You're right," Tempest beams. "And now that the guys are here, I can get my dance on!"

When I look over my shoulder and see Gunnar and Cage walking toward us, my blood runs cold. Seeing them without Vali is a lot harder than I expected and I can't help but glance around on the off chance he's still here. My brain knows he's not but it's as though my heart refuses to catch up.

"Maggie, it's great to see you here. How's... everything?" Cage asks, obviously unsure how to proceed.

"It's fine, Cage. I'm fine. It's good to be back." One of these days, conversations won't be so awkward, I hope.

"Hey, Maggie. You mind if we hit the dance floor?" Gunnar asks while reaching for Frankie's hand and helping her out of the booth.

"Of course not," I say, waving them off. "Y'all go have fun. I'll be alright, I swear."

All four of them stand like they're still unsure if they should really go, so I say it a little more forcefully this time. "Go! I mean it."

Finally, they head to the dance floor and, to my surprise, it's not so bad sitting here and people watching. It used to be one of my favorite things to do... before Vali, of course. There's a comfort in blending in and observing rather than participating.

After a thoroughly entertaining and rambunctious performance of the Cotton Eyed Joe, I feel winded and I only watched. The music slows down and, as people pair up to dance, I decide to go to the bar for a refill on my water. As I wait to grab the bartender's attention, I feel a hand touch the middle of my back and work its way down to my hip.

"Excuse me, darlin', can I buy you a drink?"

I immediately pull out of his grasp and spin around. The man smirking down at me is one I've seen here before but I don't know his name. He's not bad looking but I'm not interested, so I decline his offer. "No, thank you," I say, trying to be polite and hoping he'll walk away.

"Aww, come on. You don't expect me to allow a pretty lady like yourself to buy her own drink now do you?" he asks, stepping too close into my personal space for my liking. "I'm a gentleman, after all. You can trust me."

Backing up to the bar, I put a hand out between us. "Listen, I don't know you, so I certainly can't trust you. You should save your offer for someone who wants it."

"Whoa, whoa, whoa," he says with a chuckle, glancing around the bar. "There's no need to get testy, sweetheart. I don't see that guy you used to dance with anywhere, so you must be in need of a good time. I can do that for you."

His hand reaches for me again but never makes contact. There's a flurry of commotion and then the man is crying out, and as he bows his back in pain, I see Cage Erickson twisting the offending hand behind the guy's back.

"Do not touch her, do you understand?" Cage growls.

"Yeah, man, my mistake. No harm, no foul, right?" he grunts out.

Cage lets go and shoves him a few feet. "Get out of here right the fuck now and don't come back until you've learned how to treat others with respect."

"Hey, now—" The man tries to argue but a bouncer shows up and officially shuts him down before leading him to the front door.

My mouth is still agape, wondering what the heck just happened. "You didn't have to do that, but thank you," I tell Cage.

"Like hell, I didn't," he practically growls, reminding me so much of Vali it hurts. "You're still family, Maggie, and I'll always look out for you. We all will."

His words warm my heart and I really don't want to cry in Genie's, so I deflect. "You didn't even give me a chance to use the moves Tempest taught me. I think I deserve a do-over."

Cage barks out a laugh. "Come on, I think we're all ready to go. We'll walk you to your car, unless you want to stay and practice your moves?"

"Nah, I'm good, but I'll take you up on your escorting services." When Cage gives me a funny look before shaking his head and walking toward the door with Tempest, I realize what I've just said... or what it sounded like I said, but decide to just keep my mouth shut so I don't make it any worse.

My gosh, will I ever act normally around these people?

Later, once I'm home and in my room, I wash my face and change into a nightshirt before settling into bed with a book. It doesn't take long for my eyes to start drooping and I must doze off for a few minutes, maybe longer, because when my phone starts ringing, I almost fall out of my bed.

Scrambling to pick it up, I almost drop it twice, and when I finally manage to bring the screen into view, my heart drops.

Vali.

Oh my God, it's Vali.

Should I answer it?

Maybe it's just a butt dial and he doesn't really want to talk to me.

That would be awkward.

What am I going to say?

But what if he needs to tell me something? Or needs something?

Allowing my curiosity to get the better of me, I swipe my finger across the screen and place the phone to my ear. "Hello?"

"Ahh, there it is."

"There what is?" I ask, confused.

This is definitely a butt dial.

"The voice I've been missing so much."

Oh, God. My hand goes to my heart as it stutters at his words. The feeling is so mutual—I've missed his voice terribly. And now that I've had this taste, I need more of it. But before I can respond, Vali continues.

"Is it okay that I called you?"

Sitting up in bed, I breathe out, "Of course it is."

"Johnnie told me it would be okay, but I wanted to hear it from you."

Umm, what?

"Johnnie? Is he a friend of yours?"

Vali chuckles and it's like warm water is being poured over my body.

"I guess you could say that," he says, and it's then I notice a slight slur. "Jose is for sure but, tonight, I'm with Johnnie… *Johnnie Walker.*"

"Are you drunk? Is everything okay?" My heart lurches at the thought of him drinking alone by himself or thinking he needs to before trying to contact me. Part of me wishes we were FaceTiming instead so I can see him and know he's okay.

For now, I'll relish the sound of his voice and pretend he's here with me.

CHAPTER 35

VALI

"*J*wish we were having this call face-to-face," I tell her, falling back on my bed and exhaling the pent-up stress and frustration. Last week, after a particularly rough day, I went home to Viggo's apartment and opened a bottle of Johnnie Walker. The next thing I knew, my thumb wasn't just hovering over Maggie's name in my contacts, like it had for the past couple of months, it was dialing.

And now that the ice has been broken, or the dam or whateverthefuck, I can't go back.

"Me too," Maggie says, sounding just as sweet and perfect as I remember. "But I'm glad you called."

"You are?" I ask, wondering if it was a bad move. All this time, I've been telling myself a complete disconnect was what was best for both of us. But now I realize that was never going to work.

She sighs and I can hear the smile in her voice. "Of course." Her words come out soft and low, and if I close my eyes, I can almost feel her lying beside me. "I'd almost called you a hundred times since you left," she admits, pausing and I give her time to say what she needs to say because I just want to hear her voice. "I was just scared and sad and I didn't know what the protocol was for something like this... no labels, no promises..."

"Maggie," I say, stopping her. "You know it wasn't like that in the end. We might not have put labels on our relationship, but you and I both know we were falling for each other. I was falling for you... you were falling for me."

"Was?" she asks with an edge of sadness in her question.

I swallow, staring at the ceiling. The last time I laid my heart out on the line for a woman, she stomped all over it, but this is different—Maggie is different—and I'm no longer scared to take the leap. "Was falling... have fallen."

There's a barely audible gasp and I smile, wishing I could see her beautiful face. I refuse to tell her how I really feel over the phone, those words will only come the next time I'm in her presence and can look her in the eyes when I say them. But for now, I want to erase any doubt she might have.

"I have fallen for you, Maggie O'Neal."

It's the truth and there's no going back.

"What are we going to do?" she asks, her voice cracking, causing my heart to break.

That is the question of the hour... of the day... of the fucking year.

What are we going to do?

"I'll be back in Green Valley when Tempest has the baby," I tell her, having thought this through quite a bit lately. "Ozzi will be back full-time and Viggo will be almost finished with physical therapy. I'm not sure what the exact plan will be, but I can promise you we'll have time to talk everything through and figure things out."

"So, two more months?" I can hear the hope seeping into her tone and it fills the cracks in my heart.

"Two months."

"We can do this," she says, almost like she's convincing herself.

"Two months," I repeat, packing as much promise into those two words as I possibly can.

* * *

ME: Good morning, beautiful.

Since Maggie and I started talking, every morning has started with the same sentiment. Some days, we just exchange a quick text in the morning and another at night before bed. But others, we have an open line of communication all day long. Either way, I love it.

I've missed her so much over the past few months. This way, even though I can't physically be with her, I can talk to her and know what's going on in her life instead of worrying about her and driving myself crazy with errant thoughts.

Did she find someone else?

Did she move on?

Did she forget about me?

Does she miss me as much as I miss her?

No, no, no, and yes.

And somehow knowing the answers to all of those questions has settled my mind, allowing me to focus on my task at hand and find a way to get back to Maggie, because now more than ever, I know that's what I want.

My family may always need me, but I'm ready to put Maggie first, above everyone and everything else. As soon as I can shake free from here and figure out a way to have a solid job in Tennessee, I'm gone.

Just as I enter the gym, my phone vibrates in my pocket and I smile, knowing it's the exact person I want to talk to. The same person I want to talk to every day for the rest of my life.

Maggie: Good morning, handsome.

Why do I smile so hard my cheeks hurt every time she types those three words? It's not like I haven't had people tell me how good looking I am. Not to be conceited or anything, but when people tell you something over and over, you start to believe it. Women, from the time I was a preteen, have told me how they feel about my appearance, even when I didn't ask for it.

Sexy.

Hot.

Fuckable.

I've heard it all, but hearing—or reading—Maggie O'Neal calling me handsome does something to me. After a few weeks of seeing those words every morning, I've come to the conclusion it's because there's a different connotation when it comes from her. I know her impression of me isn't just skin deep. She knows everything there is to know about me and she still thinks I'm *handsome*.

Thanks to being locationally challenged, which is how we've started describing our relationship status, we've been able to get to know each other on an even deeper level.

I've become Maggie's newest pen pal, of sorts.

Except unlike her and Everly's communication, which takes place mostly through emails, ours takes place through mile-long text messages and late-night phone calls.

One of which got a little R-rated.

I'm hoping to go full-on Mature Content, adults only soon, because fuck, I miss her body. I miss the way I feel when I'm with her and the connection between us. I miss that level of completeness that washes over me when I'm buried deep inside her.

And fuck, I need to think about something else.

Me: Talk to me about dead puppies or the population of Green Valley...

Maggie: What?

Me: Distract me.

Maggie: LOL

Me: I'm serious. I just walked into the gym, it's already packed and I started thinking about how much I missed being inside you and now my dick is hard. DISTRACT ME.

There're a few torturous moments that pass before I get another text notification and open my screen to find one of our famous long-ass text messages full of random facts about Green Valley... population, who founded the city, general census statistics, etc. The crazy thing is I bet she didn't even have to search for the information.

Chuckling to myself, I ignore a couple of people watching me from the bench presses and quickly type my response as I walk down the hall.

Me: Thank you from the bottom of my... Well, I was going to say heart, but we both know what organ is most thankful for you and your big brain.

Maggie replies with three laughing-face emojis and I smile, digging deep to remember the exact way she looks when she laughs, like really laughs—her head tilted back, delectable neck on display, dark waves flowing down her back...

Fuck.

This is going to be a long, hard day.

All puns intended.

Stepping into the office, I shut the door behind me and pull up the number I have stored in my phone. It rings a few times before someone finally picks up.

"O'Neal Feed and Fodder," Mr. O'Neal says in his gruff, yet somehow cordial tone. "How can I help you?"

God, please don't let this blow up in my face.

"Mr. O'Neal, this is Vali Erickson," I start, not missing the way his end of the conversation goes completely silent. For a moment, I wonder if he hung up on me, but when I pull my phone away from my ear, it's still connected, so I continue. "Sir, I know this phone call is probably unexpected."

He huffs and I can see his stern face in my mind's eye. If I had to guess, he's giving me the same look as the day he caught me fondling the horse harness.

"I have a proposition for you."

* * *

TODAY, before I even had a chance to put a pot of coffee on, my dad called and asked if Viggo and I could swing by my parents' house on the way to the gym. The last week or so, Viggo has been riding in with me and doing some office work as he slowly eases back into work. With his physical therapy still going strong, he's a few weeks away from being cleared by his doctor for anything more, but it's a start.

So, it's not even six o'clock in the morning and we're headed across town.

"Dude," Viggo says from the passenger seat, sipping his coffee. "What the fuck is so important that we have to do this before breakfast?"

Keeping my eyes on the road, I chuckle. "Maybe Cage's stupid-ass family meetings have made it to Dallas? I know he and Dad talk practically every morning, so who the fuck knows."

"There better be bacon," he murmurs, shifting in his seat to get comfortable. "That's all I'm saying."

Fifteen minutes later, we're pulling into the driveway of our childhood home. My parents bought this place the year Viggo was born, so all of us grew up here, and no matter what, it always feels like home.

Tapping on the front door to announce our arrival, I push it open and check to make sure Viggo is doing okay up the steps. The frustration on his face is always so evident these days, but I can't blame him. He's used to being at full speed and optimal shape, so this injury and recovery has really taken its toll.

"In the kitchen," Mom calls out and I hear Viggo groan behind me, but this time it's because the smell of bacon and eggs hits us like a brick wall as we walk through the foyer.

Dad is already set up at the big table, coffee in hand and his laptop open in front of him. When I hear Cage's voice coming through the speakers, I realize this is an all-hands-on-deck meeting. My curiosity is piqued, but I distract myself with a slice of bacon and plant a kiss on my mom's cheek.

"Ozzi will be here any minute," Dad says as Viggo gingerly takes a seat at the opposite end of the table. "We'll get started as soon as he shows up."

Mom serves us up some breakfast. Eventually, Ozzi shows up. Even though he's not the baby, he still has a lot of the same qualities of one being second to last—easygoing, fun-loving, and never gets too concerned about anything.

Throughout this recovery process, which granted, his injuries weren't as severe as Viggo's, he's kept a positive attitude and not really let it affect him much.

"I'll show up for a family meeting every morning as long as Mom makes us breakfast," Ozzi says as Mom puts a plate in front of him.

She smiles down at him lovingly and he tilts his head back to give her a kiss on her cheek.

"You'd probably move back in if Mom didn't frown at your poor choices in female companionship," Viggo grumbles. He and Ozzi work closely together, but that doesn't mean they get along all the time.

It's a very love-hate relationship. Neither of them would ever let anyone talk shit about the other, but they love giving each other a hard time.

"Shut up, gimpy," Ozzi shoots back, which earns him a look from Mom.

Viggo doesn't say anything, just lets it roll off his back, probably because he knew it was coming. Like I said, Ozzi doesn't let much get to him, so he's taken to making light of Viggo's injuries as well.

"Cage, is Gunnar there?" Dad asks, obviously ready to get this party started.

I'm using the term party very loosely.

If Dad has called us all here and even had Cage and Gunnar Skype in, something is up and it's either really good or really bad.

"He's here," Cage says matter-of-factly.

Dad clears his throat and clasps his hands and my stomach does a weird thing causing me to push my plate back as I wait for whatever news he has for us.

"We've had an offer to buy Erickson MMA."

CHAPTER 36

MAGGIE

"*M*aggie," my dad calls out as he walks to the front of the store where I'm manning the register. "Will you be around for a couple of hours?"

I check my watch and see it's only two o'clock. "Yeah," I reply, confused why he's asking. "I plan on being here until six, as usual. Unless you need me to stay later."

"No, I just need you here at three," he says, putting the inventory sheet back under the counter. "I have a meeting and your mama has her quilting class."

When he passes me by and heads to the office, I follow. "A meeting? With who?"

Straightening up, he adjusts his pants and fixes his shirt. "I'm meeting with someone about marketing."

"Marketing?" I ask, still confused. I've been trying to get my dad to consider investing some money in marketing and advertising for a few years now, but he's always turned me down, saying *the best advertisement is word of mouth.*

Sighing, he picks up the sales reports I ran him earlier today and adds them to a stack of papers. "Yeah, I decided you're right, and after all these years, we could use a little advertisement. After all, we have expanded our inventory and there are probably people in the outlying communities that don't know everything O'Neal Feed and Fodder has to offer."

My eyes grow wide. "Are you really my dad or is this a case of alien body snatchers?" I ask, only half-teasing. "I've always thought those shows were made-up conspiracy theories."

He chuckles, patting my shoulder as he breezes back through the office door and walks back to the counter. "Who says you can't teach an old dog new tricks?"

"Miracles never cease to exist," I mutter.

Just as I'm getting ready to ask for more details on who he's meeting, a slew of customers filter in and I spend the next hour ringing up sales, checking the stock room for inventory, and helping customers to their cars with purchases. So when the bell rings, signaling a new customer, I don't even look up from my task. "Good afternoon," I call out.

Before I can get the *how can I help you* out, my eyes land on the person who just walked in the door and I lose my ability to speak.

Vali.

Vali?

"Vali?" I finally manage to breathe out the same time my dad says the same thing, walking around the counter to shake his hand.

"I'm a little early," Vali says, offering my dad an apologetic smile, but his eyes are glued to me. "Hope that's okay?"

My dad's hearty laugh is startling and makes me jump. "Of course it is," he says. "The early bird catches the worm, right?"

"That's my understanding," Vali says, accepting my dad's outstretched hand and giving it a firm shake.

"Ready for that meeting?"

Wait. Vali is who my dad is meeting with?

Stepping toward the breakroom in the back, my dad tells Vali to follow him and I watch with wild abandon as he gets closer. "Hey, Maggie," he says in that low timbre that makes my whole body tingle.

"What are you doing here?" I ask, still shocked, and wondering if I'm on an episode of *The Twilight Zone*. A really great episode, one where the love of my life walks back into my store with no warning.

Maybe I'm dreaming?

I could've fallen asleep at the counter. I was up late last night talking to a certain someone until two o'clock in the morning.

The same certain someone who's still standing there looking at me like I'm the freaking Mona Lisa or something.

"God, you're a sight for sore eyes," he says, glancing back to where my dad is. "I have to go, but I was hoping we could talk when I'm finished with this meeting."

Nodding, I search for the right words. "Ye—yeah, of course. Definitely."

"Great," he says with a wink, leaning forward and kissing my cheek before walking away.

Closing my eyes, I try to get my mind to catch up with my body… or maybe it's the other way around. All I know is that simple kiss on my cheek keeps me reeling the entire time Vali and my dad are in their meeting.

Thankfully, the few customers who come in next are regulars who don't need much assistance and I run on autopilot for the next hour, until I hear the door open and my dad's voice.

"I look forward to working with you," he says.

"Same here, sir."

Turning, I see them shake hands, like old business partners and then my dad gives me a wink. "I think you have more important matters at hand," he says, giving Vali a pat on the back. "Maggie, I'll cover the store and lock up."

"O—okay," I stutter, my eyes shifting to Vali who's smiling like he just won the lotto.

Once we're out of the store, I pivot on my heels and press my hands to his chest. Unable to stop myself, my lips crash to his and I devour his mouth, much like he's done to mine in the past. We don't stop until an approaching customer clears their throat and brings us back to the moment.

"You have a lot of explaining to do," I tell Vali, pulling him with me as I walk backward to my car, refusing to take my eyes off of him for fear he'll disappear. When my back hits the door, Vali's arms come up, caging me in, a lot like that first night we kissed in Genie's parking lot.

So much has happened between now and then, but somehow, when his lips find mine again it feels like no time has passed.

"We should take this somewhere more private," he whispers against my lips. "As badly as I want you, I also want us to talk first."

"Where to?" I ask, fumbling behind me for the door handle.

Vali reaches around and opens the door for me. "I would say the apartment, but that's too close to a bed and I don't think I'm strong enough to resist that temptation."

"The park?" I offer, figuring it's public enough and private enough. Plus, it's where we started spending mornings together before he left, and occasionally over the past month, I've gone and sat there to feel close to him.

On the short drive over, I can hardly pay attention to the road for looking at Vali.

Has he always been this handsome?

Has he always looked at me that way?

Have I died and gone to heaven?

"What?" Vali asks, giving me a sexy smirk as his hand grips my thigh sending shivers up my spine.

I focus back on the road and clear my throat. "Nothing, except for I can't believe you're here and I don't understand what's happening right now… and I'm trying to remember if you were this handsome before you left. I mean, I know you were but I think our time apart amplified your attractiveness. They do say absence makes the heart grow fonder and I guess they're right."

When I pause to breathe, inhaling deeply to catch my breath, Vali chuckles and it's low and deep and goes straight to my core.

"God, I've missed you," he says, leaning over the center console and taking my hand to his mouth to kiss my knuckles. "I've missed looking at your gorgeous face. I've missed your openness and the way you'll tell me exactly what you're thinking. I missed everything about you."

As I pull up to the curb and put my car in park, I turn to Vali. "I didn't realize I could miss someone as much as I missed you," I admit. "But I guess that's because I'd never been in love before I met you."

Vali's eyes soften and he leans in even further and brushes his lips against mine.

"You love me?"

I nod, still so close our noses touch. "I do. I've known it for a while now, but I was too afraid to say it before you left." I don't know how long he's here for and in case it's not for good, I lay all my cards on the table. "I was scared of a lot of things… giving my heart away, chasing my dreams, doing new things, but I'm not anymore. Losing you, even though it was for only a short time, it put things into perspective for me —made me think about what I want and what I'm willing to do to get it."

"Tell me more," Vali encourages, pulling me as close as he can get me in the confines of my car. "I want to hear everything."

"I wrote a book," I tell him with a chuckle. It still sounds crazy when I say it out loud, although I've only told a few people. Everly read it a few weeks ago and sent it to a friend of hers who's a freelance editor. Since then, it's really started to sink in and become more real.

Vali pulls back, sheer excitement on his face. And pride. That's my favorite reaction.

"You wrote a book?" he asks. "Just since I've been gone?"

"Yeah, once I got started, it just flowed out of me, like it had been pent up inside all this time," I gush. "It was like I'd been stuck underwater and came up for my first breath of air. It felt good... alive."

His smile is so bright it's blinding. "Can I read it?"

My laughter fills the car and it feels so good. To be here with Vali, telling him all the things I've wanted to over the past few months, it's all I've wanted.

"Sure," I finally say, biting down on my lip as I think about the book and Vali's reaction to it.

"What's that look about?"

Shaking my head, I try to hide my blush but it's too late. His fingers brush my chin, urging me to meet his gaze. "Well," I start, wanting to hide, but remembering this is Vali and he knows all my secrets and fantasies. "It's a historical romance... about Vikings."

"Really?" Vali asks, already enjoying this way too much. "Naked Vikings?"

I quirk an eyebrow. "Maybe."

Vali attacks me, kissing my lips and then down my jaw to my neck, making me moan. When we're both panting, he pulls back, putting a little space between us and exhibiting more restraint than I'm feeling at the moment.

"I have something to share with you too," he says, rubbing a hand through his gorgeous hair.

I've missed that too.

"About your meeting?" I prompt.

"About so many things," he says, pausing as he collects his thoughts. "The meeting today was something I set in motion weeks ago. I've been working on setting up my own marketing business, something I can do from anywhere, but I've been focusing on small businesses around this area. Your dad was my first meeting of several. I'm planning on doing some pro bono work to build up my portfolio, and of course, I'll continue to do the marketing and PR stuff for Viking MMA."

He can work from anywhere, meaning he could work from *here*.

"I was going to tell you that if you want me to move to Dallas, I will," I blurt out, needing him to know. "I've thought a lot about it and it's a sacrifice I'm willing to make. I mean, it's not like we'd have to live there forever and I'd never want you to give up on your dreams or not be there for your family—"

Vali brings a finger up to silence my ramble. "We sold the gym."

My eyes go wide, unsure I heard him correctly. "You what?"

"We sold Erickson MMA," he says with a smile that's not completely happy, but also not sad. "My dad called a family meeting a few weeks ago and told us about a buyer who came to him out of the blue wanting to buy the gym—equipment, clientele, the whole nine yards—for a solid amount of money."

"How much?" I ask, not that it matters, but my inquisitive mind can't help but ask.

"Enough that my parents can retire wherever they want and the five of us got enough of a cut to open our own gyms or other businesses without having to worry about startup costs," he says, taking my hand in his. "Enough that I can live wherever I want... and I want to live with you."

With me.

WITH me!

That's what he said, right?

"I love you, Maggie O'Neal," he continues, bringing my hand up to kiss it, holding it to his mouth. "I'm sorry it took me so long to tell you, but I couldn't say it without seeing this beautiful face when I did." Reaching out with his other hand, he strokes my cheek. "I'm hoping we can stick around here and figure things out. If you still want to move to Dallas, we can go. If you want to move to Timbuktu, we can go there too. I'll go anywhere, do anything, whatever it takes to help you make all your dreams come true."

EPILOGUE

THREE MONTHS LATER

Vali

"Are you nervous?" I ask Maggie as the plane taxies down the runway.

This is her first flight and most people are at least a little apprehensive at first.

"No," she says matter-of-factly, her nose practically pressed to the small window next to her seat. "I'm so excited I might pee my pants."

Leaning over, I kiss her neck, making her squeak.

"Vali," she admonishes, but it carries no weight. She knows she likes it when I kiss her there. She told me once it makes her *clench*, so of course, I do it every time I get a chance. Plus, I love kissing her neck, it's so soft and she always smells amazing, like coconut and sunshine.

"If we're joining the Mile-High Club, we need to warm up," I tease.

"We're not joining the Mile-High Club," she says, still watching out the window as the captain announces we've been cleared for takeoff. "I already peeked inside that bathroom and it's tiny. You're a giant Viking and I'm not small. It would never work. But I would like to have lots of hotel sex."

God, I love this woman.

I've been to Vegas so many times I've lost count, but I'm excited about this trip because doing things with Maggie brings a new level of excitement. I'll never get tired of seeing the world through her eyes.

As the plane increases speed and eventually lifts off the ground, Maggie reaches over and laces her fingers through mine.

"Wow," she says, letting out a deep breath. "What a rush."

"Did you mark this off your One Day list?"

She shakes her head, finally turning to look at me. "Not yet," she says. "I can't mark it off until it's done. That's the rule."

"Oh, there are rules? I had no idea."

Smirking, she swats at me and I catch her arm, pulling it to me. Thankfully, we're flying first class so it's just the two of us on this row. Cage and Tempest are two rows ahead of us and Gunnar and Frankie are across from them. Baby Freya—who is now three months old and the object of all of our affections, especially her grandparents—is having her first sleepover with Tempest's mom and dad. The rest of the family will be flying to Vegas tomorrow. Since we sold Erickson MMA, a lot has changed, but a lot has remained the same. We might all be venturing out on our own—doing new things and exploring new options—but we're all still a team.

When one of us needs the others, we're there.

"What do you want to do first when we get there?" I ask Maggie, leaning my head against the plush seat and admiring her profile. It's a gorgeous profile—long dark lashes, perfect nose, full lips. And my favorite thing about it is I've been waking up to it every morning. After I came back to Green Valley, unannounced, Maggie moved most of her things to the apartment the next week.

Typically, when two people move in together, there's an adjustment period, but so far, it's been perfect. Sure, I've been yelled at for leaving the toilet seat up. And Maggie has this weird habit of washing her bras out in the sink and hanging them everywhere in the bathroom. But all in all, it's been the best three months of my life.

"I was thinking we could find the secret pizza place at The Cosmopolitan," she says, turning to face me with an excited grin. "Then, maybe we could ride that huge Ferris wheel thing."

"Sex, Ferris wheel, and then secret pizza place," I challenge. "Just in case the Ferris wheel thing doesn't work out so well, we've at least had amazing hotel sex. If it does work out, and we survive, we'll celebrate with pizza."

Her smile grows and she chuckles. "Sounds like a plan."

Through the rest of the flight, Maggie chatters about every little thing she sees out the window—clouds, mountains, another plane. It's adorable and so endearing. She also pulls out her blue journal and writes for a while. So, while she's doing that, I get out my phone and open up my Kindle app. Last week, I got an advanced reader copy of The Viking Invasion by Margaret O'Neal.

Not going to lie, it's probably the coolest thing I've ever read.

I'm not a romance reader, but the fact my amazing, smart, talented girlfriend wrote this book is enough for me to be its biggest fan. At twelve chapters in, I'm totally hooked.

"Oh, God," Maggie groans. "Are you reading it again?"

Smirking, I don't look up from the page as I continue to read about Odin pillaging a village. I have my suspicions that later, he'll be pillaging Estrid. And that's the shit I've been waiting on for the last twelve chapters. "Hush, woman," I mutter. "I'm getting to the good stuff."

"I told you not to read it in front of me," she whines, but it's so cute and goes in one ear and out the other.

"Worry about yourself," I tell her, waving my hand toward her journal. "Get busy on the follow-up. I'm expecting you to hit a best-seller list and become my sugar mama."

Laughing, she shakes her head and buries her nose in her journal.

A couple of hours later, as the plane comes in for a landing, Maggie squeezes my hand for reassurance. "I think I like takeoff better," she says, eeking out a nervous smile. "That was a little bumpy."

"You did great, baby," I tell her, bringing her hand up to kiss the soft skin of her knuckles. "Flying into Vegas is always a little bumpy. It's the mountains, but nothing to worry about."

After we deboard and make it out to the van Cage scheduled to pick us up, we all agree to take some time to explore the city and then reconvene tonight for dinner at a sushi place Tempest picked out. Since that was one of the things she couldn't eat while pregnant, she eats it as much as she can now.

"I'm living it up this weekend," she exclaims. "This mama needs some adult time."

Cage growls, pulling her closer. "This daddy needs some mama time."

"This brother needs a puke bucket," Gunnar quips, earning him a swat to the chest from Frankie.

"What?" he asks. "Would you want to hear about your brother boning your sister-in-law?"

We all laugh, even Cage, but everyone understands their need for some alone time. We've watched them become amazing parents. But between a newborn, a gym to run, and Tempest still working at the bakery, there's no way they have much time to themselves. I'm with Gunnar, I don't want to think about them *boning*, but one of these days, we'll all be in their shoes. So, no judgment.

"Well, there won't be any boning for me," Frankie mutters under her breath, causing another round of laughter to fill the van.

"Babe, you know I can't have sex before a big fight," Gunnar reasons. "But you also know that I'll make it up to you—"

"Wait," Tempest says, throwing up a hand. "Let me get this straight. So, you can sit there and tell Frankie all the ways you're going to make it up to her, but your brother can't talk about getting a little loving from me? I don't get it."

Gunnar chuckles. "Touché."

"I think we all know what we're really here for," Maggie says from my side, her insinuation coming on strong, causing me to squeeze her thigh.

Fuck, if she starts talking about sex, I'll be walking into the hotel with a tent in my pants.

"Sex," Tempest says. "No offense, Gunnar. I really want you to win your fight tomorrow night, but more than anything, I want to spend as many uninterrupted hours with my soon-to-be husband... naked."

"Amen, sister," Maggie says, leaning over to offer Tempest a high five.

Tempest, Frankie, and Maggie have become quite the girl gang and are often a united front. I can see now that whatever they want is what they'll get, for many years to come.

After we check into the hotel, it's like the Amazing Race as we all pair off to our rooms. Maggie is stripped naked before I can even get the luggage stowed. Breathless, with her hair falling loose from the bun she's been wearing today, she smiles and I realize in that split second, I want this for the rest of my life.

Her.

Me.

Wherever the road takes us, whatever obstacles come our way. I want the good, the bad, the mediocre, and I want it all with Maggie.

She squeals in delight when I close the distance between us in one long stride, gripping her hips and pushing her down on the bed. Hovering over her, I take a second to just look at her, this woman... the unexpected, unplanned, unassuming woman. I didn't see her coming. I wasn't expecting to find her. But, dear God, I'm glad I did.

Bracing myself above her, I slowly lower my body to hers, pressing my growing erection against her wet heat. Maggie groans, closing her eyes and lacing her arms around my neck as she lifts her hips and eagerly tries to get herself off. It's hot, and if we keep it up, I'll be coming in my pants.

Pushing off the bed, I strip, unceremoniously tossing my clothes behind me while Maggie's eyes roam my body. She bites down on her lip when her attention lands on my dick and it twitches in anticipation.

When she bends her knees and scoots her luscious ass to the edge of the bed, I smile. Over the months, Maggie's sexual appetite hasn't wavered, if anything it gets stronger by the day, and she's not afraid to ask for what she wants or try new things.

"Hold on tight, baby," I instruct, grabbing her thighs as I line my cock up to her entrance.

In one swift thrust, I fill her, and like every time with Maggie, I feel complete and whole.

* * *

Maggie

We're on the High Roller, at the tip-top, with all of Las Vegas at our feet and the mountains in the distance. It's one of the prettiest sights I've seen, outside of Tennessee.

Excluding the gorgeous man at my side.

As if on cue, Vali slips a hand around my waist and positions himself behind me. We're not the only people in the car or pod or whatever you want to call it. But the rest of the people in here with us are visiting on their own, so it feels like we're in a bubble at the top of the world.

"So beautiful," I tell Vali, leaning into him.

His lips find my cheek and then my neck. "I think the same thing every time I look at you," he murmurs against my skin.

"Thank you for bringing me here."

His arms squeeze tighter around me, hugging me to him. "You never have to thank me for taking you places. I'll always want you by my side."

"Always?" I ask, kind of teasing, but also loving the way that sounds and making sure he knows the kind of hope he gives me when he says things like that. "You might get tired of me one of these days."

"Never," he says with so much conviction I believe it.

Sighing contentedly, I turn in his arms and wrap mine around his neck. "I love you, Vali Erickson."

"More than anything in the world," he says, brushing his lips against mine and pausing, our mouths merely touching. "We should get married."

My stomach flips and I'm not sure if it's the motion of the Ferris wheel or Vali's statement, but I pull back so I can see his eyes. "What?" I ask, needing to hear him again to make sure my ears aren't playing tricks on me.

"I know this isn't the proposal you deserve, or even what I had planned, but if finding you taught me anything, it's that the best things in life aren't planned." His eyes search my face and, for a split second,

I see a wave of nerves wash over him. Then, he drops down on one knee and my heart goes with him.

"Margaret Hope O'Neal," he says, taking a deep fortifying breath. "I don't have a ring, but I'll buy you anything you want. There's no way I can go another second without knowing you'll be mine forever. I want every new experience with you. I want to figure out our lives together, have babies together, grow old together."

With each passing word, my heart beats faster and faster as tears spring into my eyes.

"Will you do me the honor of a lifetime and marry me?"

There are murmurs around us, people prompting me to say yes… sighs and exclamations… but none of it matters. The only thing I see, the only person I see, is Vali. I knew my answer to this question months ago, so when I bend down and press my lips to his, I tell him, "Yes.

"A million times over, in any scenario you can dream of, my answer will always be yes."

"I already asked your dad," Vali murmurs against my lips. "I know it's kind of old-fashioned, but I wanted his blessing. And I know our families might be pissed, but I'd love nothing more than to make you my wife tonight."

Pulling back so I can see him clearly, I try to wrap my mind around the turn of events.

Vali Erickson asked me to marry him.

I said yes.

And he wants to do it tonight.

Here, in Las Vegas.

It's so crazy and unplanned and out-of-character. And he's right, our families won't be happy, but we can make it up to them when we get home. We'll have a big celebration with everyone, but tonight, in this moment, I want nothing more than what Vali is offering—to be his, to be one… forever.

"Okay," I tell him, my voice confident even though there's a tremor as tears start to fill my eyes.

When he swipes a thumb across my cheek, his brows furrow. "If you want to wait, we can. I know this seems impulsive, but—"

"No," I tell him, unable to hold back the sob that's followed with a laugh. "I want this. I want everything with you. And we'll figure out how to tell everyone later… we're good at figuring things out."

We are good at that. Over the past few months, Vali and I have learned how to compromise and work together to realize our dreams. Getting married on a whim is nothing.

After our Ferris wheel ride ends, he takes my hand and flags down the first taxi we see, asking the driver to take us to the nearest jewelry store.

A few hours later, I'm carrying a bouquet of white roses down an aisle where Vali is waiting for me. The minister is in a light blue velvet suit that coincidentally matches the flowers in the dress I'm wearing. It's nothing like I've dreamed my wedding to be, but it's everything I ever wanted and more.

The next thing I know, we're walking out of the Little White Chapel as husband and wife.

We celebrate by finding the secret pizza place at The Cosmopolitan and end the night having the most amazing hotel sex as newlyweds.

Vali is my husband and I am his wife.

Once our families know, I can't wait to tell the entire world.

Trixie and Tess will have a lot to talk about in the coming months.

One of these days, I can't wait to tell our children the story of how I went from being Margaret Hope O'Neal, a girl who was happy to stand on the sidelines of life, merely observing, to Maggie Erickson, a woman who knew what she wanted and chased her dreams.

ACKNOWLEDGMENTS

First and foremost, we'd like to thank our families. They're the ones who have to put up with our lack of domesticity while writing words. Thank you for being so understanding and supporting our dreams. We love you more than our luggage!

We'd also like to thank Pamela, our bestie/pre-reader/and cheerleader! We're so thankful for your continuing support and encouragement. Thank you for always being our fresh set of eyes when we needed it.

And God bless our editor, Nichole. She's always willing to work us into her schedule and help make our words the best they can be! We appreciate her insight and the way she pushes us to be better writers.

To Staci, Penny, and whoever else is responsible for this AMAZING cover, THANK YOU!! We're so in love with the new covers and we hope everyone reading this is too!

We'd also like to send out a blanket thank you to the entire Smarty-pants Romance team... Fiona, Brooke, pre-readers, readers... We love this world so much and we feel so blessed to be a part of it. Thank you, each and everyone of you, for all you do!

If you've made it this far, bless you. We're so thankful for you. Writing is what we love to do and like most writers, we'd still do it even if we were just writing for ourselves, but having readers is what makes it so wonderful and worthwhile. If you loved this book or even liked it a little… if it brightened your day or gave you a new perspective, we've accomplished our goal.

Until next time, Jiff and Jenny Kate

ABOUT THE AUTHOR

Jiffy Kate is the joint pen name for Jiff Simpson and Jenny Kate Altman. They're co-writing besties who share a brain. They also share a love of cute boys, stiff drinks, and fun times.

Together, they've written over twenty stories. Their first published book, Finding Focus, was released in November 2015. Since then, they've continued to write what they know--southern settings full of swoony heroes and strong heroines.

* * *

Website: http://www.jiffykate.com
Facebook: https://www.facebook.com/jiffykate
Goodreads: https://www.goodreads.com/author/show/
7352135.Jiffy_Kate
Twitter: @jiffykatewrites
Instagram: @jiffykatewrites

Find Smartypants Romance online:
Website: www.smartypantsromance.com
Facebook: www.facebook.com/smartypantsromance/
Goodreads: www.goodreads.com/smartypantsromance
Twitter: @smartypantsrom
Instagram: @smartypantsromance

Read on for:

1. Jiffy Kate's Booklist
2. Smartypants Romance's Booklist

OTHER BOOKS BY JIFFY KATE

Finding Focus Series:

Finding Focus

Chasing Castles

Fighting Fire

Taming Trouble

French Quarter Collection:

Turn of Fate

Blue Bayou

Come Again

Neutral Grounds

Good Times

Table 10 Novella Series:

Table 10 part 1

Table 10 part 2

Table 10 part 3

New Orleans Revelers:

The Rookie and The Rockstar

The Ace and The Assistant

Smartypants Romance:

Stud Muffin (Fighting For Love, book 1)

Standalones:

ALSO BY SMARTYPANTS ROMANCE

Green Valley Chronicles

The Love at First Sight Series

Baking Me Crazy by Karla Sorensen (#1)

Batter of Wits by Karla Sorensen (#2)

Steal My Magnolia by Karla Sorensen(#3)

Fighting For Love Series

Stud Muffin by Jiffy Kate (#1)

Beef Cake by Jiffy Kate (#2)

Eye Candy by Jiffy Kate (#3)

The Donner Bakery Series

No Whisk, No Reward by Ellie Kay (#1)

The Green Valley Library Series

Love in Due Time by L.B. Dunbar (#1)

Crime and Periodicals by Nora Everly (#2)

Prose Before Bros by Cathy Yardley (#3)

Shelf Awareness by Katie Ashley (#4)

Carpentry and Cocktails by Nora Everly (#5)

Love in Deed by L.B. Dunbar (#6)

Scorned Women's Society Series

My Bare Lady by Piper Sheldon (#1)

The Treble with Men by Piper Sheldon (#2)

The One That I Want by Piper Sheldon (#3)

Park Ranger Series

Happy Trail by Daisy Prescott (#1)

Stranger Ranger by Daisy Prescott (#2)

The Leffersbee Series

Been There Done That by Hope Ellis (#1)

The Higher Learning Series

Upsy Daisy by Chelsie Edwards (#1)

Seduction in the City

Cipher Security Series

Code of Conduct by April White (#1)

Code of Honor by April White (#2)

Cipher Office Series

Weight Expectations by M.E. Carter (#1)

Sticking to the Script by Stella Weaver (#2)

Cutie and the Beast by M.E. Carter (#3)

Weights of Wrath by M.E. Carter (#4)

Common Threads Series

Mad About Ewe by Susannah Nix (#1)

Give Love a Chai by Nanxi Wen (#2)

Educated Romance

Work For It Series

Street Smart by Aly Stiles (#1)

Heart Smart by Emma Lee Jayne (#2)

Lessons Learned Series

Under Pressure by Allie Winters (#1)